DARK ESCAPES

EFFIE CAMPBELL

Copyright © 2023 by Effie Campbell

All rights reserved.

No part of this book may be reproduced in any form or by any electronic or mechanical means, including information storage and retrieval systems, without written permission from the author, except for the use of brief quotations in a book review.

To all the people who crave someone to see who you really are.

Especially if you're looking forward to a heavy dose of needy loving.

WARNINGS

This book contains spicy content, depictions of death and sexual assault (not full, and not with the main male character).

It is also written in the UK, and I use British English for spelling. If you are from elsewhere - forgive me! Just imagine smouldering Scots saying the words and it'll all be fine, promise.

ONE
ESTHER

'I don't care what you say, there isn't a chance in hell that I'm marrying him!' My voice shook with anger as I squared up to my father for the first time in my life. I'd be lying if I said my knees hadn't quaked beneath my false bravado.

'Calm down,' my father, Malcolm, said, my anger nothing but an annoying mosquito for him to brush off. 'You don't have a choice.'

My brothers loitered around the edge of the room, all finding ways to avoid my eyes. 'None of you are going to stand up for me? Logan? Ewen? Not even you, Mac?'

Fear rattled my chest as they continued to ignore my pleas for help. Shit, my dad must have briefed them long before he broke the news to me.

'He killed Mum. His guys killed Malcolm Jr. How can you expect me to become his wife? It's fucking sick.' Mac flinched, yet still, none of them came to my aid. 'It's sick!'

'I will not lose any more children to his bullets. You've always known you'd marry for the good of the family.' Dad ran a hand over his stubbled chin and looked as rotten as I felt. He didn't want this either.

'I thought you meant some rich mafia kid my age. Harold is older than you. You'd lose me to save them?' It hurt. Pain gripped my stomach and set my intestines roiling like a pit of snakes.

'I'm trying to save you all. Would you prefer it to be Maeve?'

Tears pricked my eyes as I stared my father down. What a fucking question. Me or my younger sister? I didn't want either of us to end up beneath that sick bastard. 'No.'

'I haven't got a choice. We need his ties. We've fought long enough and someone has to bury the hatchet to stop the killing.' My father sighed as he leaned back heavily on his ornate mahogany desk.

'Why does it have to be me? What about what I want?' I'd never truly fit in my mafia princess mould. Sure, I enjoyed the trappings of our wealth, the indoor pool, the holidays, and being able to have whatever I wanted, but the pressure of the lifestyle had never suited me. I didn't know if others felt the same or mostly just ignored it, but I hated it. If it hadn't been for my family, I would have started fresh somewhere a million miles from gloomy old Glasgow and our crime-ridden lifestyle. We lived in a gilded cage atop a steaming pile of dung as far as I was concerned. What about love? Freedom? Happiness? I was to have none of it and I'd swap every penny, every designer dress, and even our family mansion to be happy. no one cared.

'You are my eldest daughter, and it's you he wants.' Dad's voice snagged in his throat, decades-old hatred still there despite the so-called agreement.

'And what if I say no?'

'You don't have that choice.'

'You can't force me to sign a marriage certificate or to say vows.'

'I'm sure that won't be a problem for Harold. He knows enough people in the system to have anything he wants approved. It's not all bad Esther. With the wedding will come a new era of peace between us and the Thompsons. And you will be the wife of the most powerful man in Scotland. Think of the opportunities it will open up to you. You'll want for nothing.'

'If I survive that long. You know what happened to his wife, not to mention the string of women he's abused over the years. You can't paint this like some fairytale to smooth over your guilt. He will hurt me, he will rape me, he might kill me. And what then? Will Maeve be next?'

Dad shuddered at my words while my brothers shifted uncomfortably. no one denied it, as we all knew it was the truth. He'd beaten his wife and torn her apart mentally for years. She'd run and left her two children with him. They were grown now, similar ages to us, but had spent the last decade or so without her. She had loved them with her entire soul, yet even that wasn't enough to stop her fleeing Harold's wrath.

And I'd be next.

Dad steeled himself, pulling up to his full height and glaring at me. Getting angry was his usual response to not having a good answer. 'The deal is done, Esther. You'll marry him, and that's the end of it.'

Just like that. He left the room in a storm of rage as I crumpled on one of the dark green Chesterfield sofas. The tears flowed fully as hope scattered around me. My whole life was fucked. Torn apart before I'd even done anything. Twenty-eight years old and I'd loved no one, never had a job, never gone out on my own without someone trailing behind me for protection. A little bird going from one cage to another, much more terrible, cage.

Logan slipped down beside me and pulled me gruffly into his arms as Mac and Ewen joined us. They thrust tissues into one fist as a cup of water filled the other.

'Why didn't you help me?' I accused, my vision blurry beneath the sea of tears.

'We tried Esther. We've been trying for days. He's not moving on it.' Logan wiped away one of my tears as he pulled back to meet my eyes.

Mac's whole body thrummed with anger, ever the hot-headed sibling. 'I should find him and put a bullet in his head.'

'You should,' I said.

'No. You can't.' Logan had become far more serious since our eldest brother had gone down in a blaze of bullets. He'd had to step up as the one who'd take over the McGowan syndicate. The responsibility weighed heavy on him, having to shoulder a role that was never meant for him. 'It would only result in your death or an even greater war between us. Things are too unstable. I don't like it, but we need to try to make peace before the entire of Scotland's crime scene implodes. This is only the very tip of the card tower. Beneath it lays a finely balanced series of deals and agreements that limit the bloodshed. If we go in swinging, everything will fall.'

'Why me?'

'Harold always wanted Mum, but she chose Dad. You look a lot like Mum did at your age, and he's a sick bastard. This way punishes Dad in a way that will hurt him the most.'

'I think it will hurt me more.'

I LAY IN MY BED, my heavy curtains not quite blocking out the light that taunted me. Groaning, I pulled the duvet over my head and tunnelled under. There was no room in my world for light at that moment. The air under the duvet became hot and stifling as the minutes passed, yet I remained buried. Maybe I could suffocate myself. At least I wouldn't have to marry Harold.

My door clicked open and shut, but I remained unmoved, ignoring it entirely. A weight at my side made the bed shift beneath me before a set of light fingers found my hair, stroking softly.

'You can't stay in here forever,' Maeve said, muffled as she was through the duvet.

'I can.'

'Your room stinks. It's gross.'

'What's the point?' I said as she pulled the covers back enough to reveal my face, her expression soft as she swept my greasy hair from my eyes.

'You can't let them win. Come on, I've never seen you like this. Everyone is worried about you. It's been days, Esther.'

'Good. They should be worried. There is absolutely no way I'm marrying him.'

Maeve lay down beside me and rested her arm over my waist, pulling me in close, taking on my big sister role rather than her usual one as the baby of the family.

'I wish I could help,' she whispered against the duvet.

'What can I do?'

'Could you run away?'

'He'd find me. I'd have to disappear forever. I'm not even sure that's possible these days. Harold wouldn't quit until he dragged me back here.' The idea of disappearing sent a small flicker of hope in my chest. Could I do it? What about Maeve? Would he try to take her instead? That doused any hope with a cold dose of reality. But she was so much younger than me, Dad would never give up the baby, would he?

'I know a guy who can get you a false name. Wee Dave from school. Do you remember him?'

'Kind of...'

'Remember how he'd always get us fake IDs to get into clubs? Well, he's gone legit. Well, not like legally legit, but he does the big stuff now. New names, passports, national insurance numbers, the lot.'

Rolling towards my sister, I searched her face. Did she really think I could just go? Everyone who meant anything to me was under our roof. Sure, I'd miss my friends, but I'd give them up to avoid Harold. My family? That was different.

'I don't think I could live without you all.'

'He'd move on after a while. We'd find a way to get in touch and see each other.' Maeve pulled me tighter to her. 'God, he's such a cockwomble.'

'I think that's putting it lightly,' I said.

'You're right. He's a grade-A fuck bucket. A downright piece of shit-ridden bollocks. I'd kill him if I could.'

A giggle escaped me. I kissed Maeve's cheek. 'I love you so much.'

'I love you too, but fuck, your breath doesn't half reek. We need to get you in the shower and within twenty feet of your toothbrush.'

'Oi!' I laughed and whacked her with a pillow.

A sharp knock on the door had us both jumping.

'Who is it?'

Alec popped his head around the door and I dived back

under the duvet. *Fuck*. I did not need him to see the absolute mess I was. Damn, he was a tall glass of deliciousness. Terribly wrong for me. I half wondered if I held a bit of a flame for him because he was entirely wrong for me. I'd always known I'd marry into another wealthy family, likely the son of a crime boss. But Alec wasn't from a wealthy family. No, he'd come in from the bottom of the business and worked his way up. Largely, he did so by hunting down people on the run or torturing details out of others. Half bounty hunter, half intimidator. One hundred percent a tall, tattooed, dishy motherfucker. Big hands, crystal blue eyes, and a body to die for.

He'd been around increasingly often for the past year or two, and I'd long considered him for a sneaky benefits-on-the-side sort of deal, but he'd shown no signs of being interested when I'd subtly tested the waters. He probably had a tonne of girls throwing themselves at him.

'Just me. Sorry to interrupt, but your dad wants you at dinner tonight.'

Maeve shifted next to me as I remained steadfastly secured under the duvet, barely daring to breathe in case it drew attention to me. 'No worries, Esther's just going for a shower and then we'll be right down.'

As the door shut, I pulled the blankets back and took a breath, finished stifling myself for now.

'Damn, I did not need him to be in my room when it's like this.' Cold coffees and uneaten plates of food littered the bedside tables and the room was dark, dank, and musty. Not at all how I usually kept the place, well the maid did, but I'd banished her since I'd gone into despair.

'Still hoping for a bit of rough, hmm?' Maeve laughed as she pulled the duvet fully off of me and tossed it to the floor before shoving me out of the bed.

'He'd make a fine last supper, that's for sure. Why's he here?'

'I think he's here to make sure you don't go missing before the wedding. It's set for next week.'

My mouth dried out as I stared at Maeve. One week? No, it couldn't be that quick.

Tears pricked anew as Maeve came around the bed and wrapped her arms about my shoulders, soothing my hair as I gave into the sobs. 'You'll be okay. We'll fix it even if you have to go old school and start poisoning his food.'

Like a zombie, I let her get me into the shower, my brain going into protective mode.

I needed a way out.

Fast.

TWO
ALEC

It was none of my business.

None of my damn business.

So why couldn't I get Esther's state out of my head? Usually, she was smiley and feisty, but since Malcolm had announced her engagement to Harold, it was like it had drained the life right out of her. Who could blame her? I'd been around the McGowan's long enough to see how he'd terrorised them. Murders happened often in the Scottish crime scene, but it was rare for it to be amongst the elite. Far more often it was the people down the tiers in the organisations who got bunked off.

People like me.

Pulling my car into my driveway, I waved as Gladys. My elderly next-door neighbour, opened her door and shuffled out. As sad as it was, she was the only person I had outside of the crime scene who cared about me. I didn't have grannies or grandpas, parents, or siblings. No aunts, uncles, or cousins. Just me. Barring my work, Gladys was the only person who would notice if I disappeared.

It was a sad state of affairs.

'Hello,' she said as I closed my car door. 'Could you help me a minute?'

She was as alone as I. Long widowed and with her only son dying young and child-free. I liked to tell myself I was just being helpful, but whenever she invited me in, her warmth filled that gaping chasm in me for a little while. She wasn't my granny, but it felt like she was while I was with her. The tiny snippet of what normality could be was something I held dear.

'No problem, Gladys, what's giving you jip today?' I followed her into her house, the mirror image of mine in layout, but a million miles away in decor. Her home was busy, clean, and tidy, but stuffed to the gunnels with brick-a-brac. Photos from her younger years filled the walls, faded with time. Happy smiley faces of her family life. Happier times. A pang in my chest reminded me how I lacked any images from my childhood. If any existed, they weren't in my possession. When the system shifted you from house to house with a bin bag of meagre belongings, photos weren't a priority. Her son's face beamed out from behind the glass. If any photos of me existed, I doubted they would look in any way happy. The closest I'd ever come to happiness was when I finally bought my home, in this leafy little corner of Glasgow, miles from work and the criminal underbelly that stretched through the city.

My commute was horrendous, but I hadn't wanted a townhouse or city centre flat like most bachelors. No, I bought a family home in a suburb, surrounded by the elderly and young families. I'd dreamed of filling the house with a family of my very own. Instead, it remained as lonely as the rest of my life, the view from my windows a daily reminder that families were for others. Happy children riding bikes up and down the pavement, parents scooping them up and kissing away grazed knees. Each one another is arrow to my soul. The closest I got was the occasional one-night stand where I indulged in physical closeness, but was yet to find someone that could break through the emotional wall.

Gladys fixed me with a soft smile as I looked at her pictures, her fingers trembling as she reached up and stroked her son's smiling face.

'Come, I made biscuits.'

Sweat started forming as soon as I entered her kitchen. It was always a balmy temperature. She said it helped her aches. I'd hate to see her heating bill. 'Shall I put on the tea?'

I'd already flicked the kettle to boil. Asking was a mere formality. The routine was always the same: loose tea from the clipper attached to the side of the cupboard, the overly large maroon teapot that must have made a million cups of tea over the years. Milk in the striped jug, never from the plastic bottle. Sugar in lumps, never loose.

'What did you need help with today?' I asked as we waited for the tea to steep.

'The light in the sitting room has gone. I need help to get the step stool out of the shed so I can change it.'

I levelled her with a look. She was in her late seventies. She shouldn't be up any step ladders at her age. 'I'll change the lamp for you. No step stool needed.'

She smiled at me and placed a cool hand on top of mine. 'You're such a helpful boy. Thank you.'

How her hand could be cold in the positively tropical heat of the kitchen perplexed me. But I savoured the brief touch, my heart aching at the moment of tenderness. Another glimpse into a life I didn't have.

'It's not a problem. You know I'm happy to help.' I had

nothing else to be doing outside of work, anyway. Sure, I could go into the city and trail a bar for a hot body to warm me for a night, but come morning, it always left me feeling more empty than I had before. When the women left, it highlighted how devoid of life my home was.

'How is work?' Gladys asked as I poured the tea and sat back, helping myself to the outrageous amount of biscuits she'd piled onto a plate. The buttery, crumbly biscuit melted in my mouth. Damn, she made a mean shortbread.

'It's the same as always, really. Nothing ever changes.' Gladys didn't know what I did, thinking I worked in some mundane office job. Would she let me in her home and feed me biscuits if she knew I tracked, mutilated, and often killed people for a living? Probably not.

'What about your co-workers? No weddings or babies to fill an old lady's heart with some joy?' She loved to hear about life. Other than going to the local shop for food, she spent most of her time sequestered in the four walls of her home. I couldn't imagine my life reduced to seeing no one, my only proper company being the telly.

'There was an engagement, actually.'

'Oh, lovely!' Gladys looked positively thrilled, and I hadn't the heart to tell her that the bride was terrified of her future husband. For good reason.

'Do you think you need to be in love to have a good marriage?' Political and economic marriages were nothing new. Maybe Esther could find some happiness with Harold. Somehow.

'You need love to have a happy marriage. Life will limp along whether you are happy or sad, but love makes everything better. Fills all the cracks that will swallow you up if you are miserable.'

I helped myself to another little golden square of deliciousness as I mulled over her words. The dark cracks in Esther's marriage would be great soul-swallowing chasms. A pain gripped me at the thought of her with Harold, in his home, surrounded by fear instead of happiness. For the years I'd been involved with her brothers, I'd watched her from afar. Petite, curvy, and with a glint in her eye that flared whenever she got an idea into her head. A spoiled mafia princess, for sure. I'd often dreamed of taking charge of Esther when she let her mouth run away with her, imagined her looking up at me from her knees, imagined...

I cleared my throat. Sitting in Gladys' kitchen wasn't the place for that train of thought. Esther had always been way, way above my station. Not the sort of woman that would even dream of being with someone like me. No, she had her pick of men at her level of society, the rich, undamaged children of even richer men and women. The others who had never known struggle, never felt gnawing hunger or the despair of being unwanted. Or if they were unwanted, had the money to drown their sorrows in champagne while sunning themselves on a beach somewhere. A million miles from my life.

Gladys filled me in with everything going on in her soap operas as I supped my tea, my head filled with a picture of Esther's pale face, eyes red-rimmed and despondent. So far from her usual vivacious demeanour. It wasn't my place to get involved. It was never my place.

An hour or so later, after fixing the light, and a few other bits and bobs in Gladys' home, I let myself into my house. The door clicked shut behind me as I leaned back against it.

Another night alone.

I wasn't ready to face the cold bed that awaited me. With a sigh, I grabbed my gym bag. Exhaustion usually made sleep swallow me up faster.

THREE
ESTHER

Maeve stayed in sight of my dad's men, ensuring they remained near the clothing shop that they believed we were both in. A quick change of clothes and a blonde wig pulled snugly over my dark hair later, I'd slipped out of the shop, walking right past them with my stomach in my mouth.

I needed it to work.

My nerves only settled as I made my way through the streets, slipping into the alleyway where Wee Dave operated. The stink of piss hit my nostrils as I picked my way down the lane, trying to avoid litter, cigarette ends, and lord knew what else. My knuckles burned as I rapped loudly on the door, feeling very much like I didn't belong.

After a few moments, the door pulled open a crack, and a dishevelled bearded face appeared.

'Well, well. If it isn't Esther McGowan. I'd have thought you were well out of needing my services. Old enough not to have to sneak into bars with a fake ID.'

'Can I come in?' Not that I really wanted to. If his house was anything like the alleyway.

An eyebrow raised sceptically as he looked me up and

down, the wig already stuffed in my bag as soon as I'd gotten out of the henchmen's sight. 'I suppose you should.'

The door swung open, and I took one last look at the bustling street at the far end of the alleyway. My whole life I'd gone without being in a dangerous situation. There was always someone nearby armed and ready to jump to my defence at my father's bidding. I twisted my fingers in my necklace as I walked in through the door, hoping he wasn't a scumbag. My mother's wedding band slid around the chain as I fingered it, eyes widening as I looked about Wee Dave's place. It was in stark contrast to the urine-soaked alley outside. Cool blue lights emanated behind the many screens he had along the back wall, which he flicked to a screensaver with a touch of one keyboard, hiding whatever nefarious thing he was working on.

I licked my lips as my mouth took on a similar water level to the Sahara, taking in the neat office with the dark leather couches along one side. He even had a water cooler.

'You look like you expected to walk into a crack den,' Dave said, his eyes crinkling in the corners in amusement. 'I'm not selling hokey little fake IDs anymore.'

'Sorry,' I said, heat flushing my cheeks. 'I've just never...'

'Never had to be the one dealing with the real world?'

'Yeah.' His words stung, but he wasn't wrong.

'So what can I do you for?' Dave leant casually against the edge of his desk and indicated to the couch beside me. I sat gingerly on the edge as I dropped my necklace back against my chest and smoothed my skirt over my knees.

Coming here was dangerous. For both me and him.

'I need documents. A new name, a passport. I need to disappear without being traced.' The words flew out in one breath, reality hitting as I said the words aloud. *Disappear.* I swallowed hard as he ran a hand through his shaggy, red beard.

'I'm guessing this has something to do with your soon to be husband?' My eyes widened almost painfully as I inhaled. He knew.

'Please don't tell him. It's fine, I'll go. Just pretend I was never here.' I stood on shaky legs. He could extort a lot if he wanted to get on Harold's good side.

'Hey,' Dave said, coming over and pressing gently on my shoulders until I sat back down. 'I'm no rat. Especially for that fucker. I can help. Give me a few days, and I'll have a whole new identity ready.'

'I don't have a few days. I'm supposed to get married on Saturday.'

Dave inhaled sharply before pressing his lips together in a solid line. 'It'll cost you.'

'Whatever you want, I've got plenty of funds. I'll pay double if you can keep anyone from finding out the new name too. I'll tell Maeve to get the cash to you if I'm still gone after six months.'

'I never share details of my client's business.' He looked almost offended.

'Not willingly, perhaps, but Harold doesn't play fair.'

Dave shifted from foot to foot as he mulled it over. 'Triple, and you have a deal.'

Tension fled from my tight shoulders as I flopped back against the back of the couch.

'Thank you. Thank you so much.'

'Let's get your pictures now. It will make everything quicker. I'll have them to you in twenty-four hours. Discretely, of course.' Dave pulled a camera out of a drawer and grinned at me. 'Hope you're passport photo ready.'

AS THE SUN dipped below the horizon outside, I sat surrounded by clothes and knick-knacks, struggling to figure out what to take with me. Taking sizeable sums of money out of my account would have looked suspicious, so I'd taken what I could out while shopping and then raided my emergency stash. It was only a few thousand, but would be enough for accommodation and food for a while, if I was careful.

I'd decided on Spain. I'd search for somewhere rural where no one would look for me. Somewhere small and quaint. Then I'd find a job. Lord knew what, though. I had no particular talents. I'd never even learned to cook or clean. But if it would keep me from Harold's clutches, I'd take whatever work I could get. Cash in hand, under the radar. Thankfully, Dave had suggested a forged work visa along with my new identity, so I wouldn't have to worry about deportation.

Once I'd packed a small collection of my things, I went to Maeve's room and snuggled in beside her as she watched some bubblegum TV.

'I'm going to miss this,' I said as I snuggled in beside my baby sister.

'Don't be silly.' Maeve rolled her eyes at me. 'I'll still see you all the time. Harold won't keep you locked up.'

The need to tell her burned at the back of my throat. I didn't want to disappear without letting her know where I was going. She may have suggested disappearing, but she didn't for a moment suspect that that was exactly what I intended to do. It was safest if she didn't know. However hurt she'd be when she discovered I was gone.

'I want you to have this,' I said, taking off my mother's necklace and slipping it into her hand.

'Esther, you are acting like you are dying. I know it's bad, but it's going to be okay. Dad won't let Harold ban you from seeing us. It's supposed to bury the hatchet.'

Yeah, bury it right in my back.

'Please, just look after it for me.'

'Fine, but can you stop being so weird?'

'I'll never stop being weird,' I said with a forced smile as I cuddled into her side.

We went back to watching the telly quietly for a bit as I soaked in the feeling of my sister by my side. Fuck, I'd miss her. All of them. I'd never known life on my own. There'd always been a whole gang of us McGowans wherever we went as kids, filling rooms with our play-fighting and noise.

A solo McGowan was basically unheard of.

'Did you see Alec tonight?' Maeve asked, mock fanning her face.

'Yeah, he's been hanging about to make sure I'm being a good little wife-to-be.' Much to my chagrin.

'When he rolled up his sleeves and leant back against the door frame, I thought I was going to need a cold shower,' Maeve said. It hadn't failed to catch my eye either. He'd been laughing along with my brothers when he'd stopped to slowly roll up his shirt sleeves, baring those muscled, tattooed forearms. He certainly made for some delightful eye candy.

'I wish I'd had a night with him before going off to be with Harold. I deserve a hen night. One last cock before having to deal with his for the rest of my life.' The sour taste of vomit tickled at the back of my throat at the thought of being anywhere near Harold's nether regions.

'You should. Hell, he looks like he could be done with a good ride.'

Alec had always been far more reserved with both myself and my sister than he was with my brothers. He looked at them almost as though he coveted their attention. Then again, when you looked like he did, he probably had women hanging off of him left, right, and centre.

I'd thought about it over the years that he'd been sporadically in and out of our home. He was attractive, well dressed, well groomed, and had those big hands you couldn't help but imagine being pinned beneath.

Ever the professional, he'd never risen to any of my flirting.

Maybe I hadn't been trying hard enough.

FOUR
ALEC

Laughter filled the small kitchen, where we often ended up late in the evenings. The McGowan mansion held multiple kitchens; the extensive chrome-filled one that the chefs used to cater to the household, a show kitchen in the main part of the mansion that I'd only seen used during events as a sort of go-between for the waiting staff, and this cosier kitchen that the siblings used for their own snacking. It was still bigger than my one and only kitchen, and definitely better stocked too. One thing I loved about the McGowan's place was that they fed me like a king, even if I wasn't one of them.

Ewen grabbed some beers from the fridge and passed them around. I declined. Unlike the brothers, I was on the clock. It was easy to forget for a few minutes here and there, to pretend like I was one of them, but soon enough someone would give me an order or a task, and my place in the organisation, and their home, would come screeching back.

'I'll just grab a water,' I said, helping myself before leaning back against the counter. My presence had been required more in the lead-up to the wedding. My task? To ensure things went smoothly. Both the McGowans and the Thompsons had a whole horde of enemies who would like the thwart their attempt at a union. All hands were on deck to ensure that the wedding went ahead without a hitch.

Logan was all business as usual. 'Everything is set for Saturday. The cars will arrive at twelve and have us to the chapel at half past. The route is being managed by our security firm and they'll also be on hand in the chapel itself.'

'Aye, I've briefed everyone, and they know their tails are on the line if they fuck up,' Mac said, launching a peanut up into the air before catching it.

'The suits have arrived, and you should have all done a last fitting by now.' Logan gave a pointed look at Mac, who gave him a sheepish grin. He forever skived anything he found boring. 'If you haven't, get to it.'

Mac groaned, downing his beer and heading for the door. 'She doesn't even want to marry him. Why would she care if my suit fits?'

'Dad will care. I'll care. Go get it done.' Logan flexed his eldest son privileges. They may all be siblings, but that didn't stop the hierarchy from being very succinct. Logan was the eldest after stepping in after his eldest brother's demise. Then Ewen. Esther was next in age order, but women come last in the crime families. Treasured often, but not given any real responsibility. They had most definitely not caught up with the new millennium. Mac was next in line. He was the youngest male, and his absolutely wicked level of 'don't give a flying fuck' showed it. Then Maeve, the baby of the family. It seemed insane to me they all lived in their father's house still, although they were in their twenties and thirties. But I guess if I had an enormous mansion surrounded by people who loved me, I'd be loath to leave too.

'Alec, you're on Esther patrol tonight and tomorrow night. She's been acting weird. I want you outside her room overnight, so get some shuteye before then. It's covered until ten pm and then you are on the clock.' Logan slathered butter over crisp toast as he spoke. Epic chefs at their beck and call, yet still a slice of hot buttered toast appealed. The rich are wild.

'Got it, Logan.' Even the water tasted better, ice cold out of their expensive fridge and in condensation-clad glass bottles.

'Right, Ewen, you're with me. We need to go over the marriage contract again to make sure Harold hasn't slipped in some wording that will fuck us over. The lawyer should be here by now.'

Silence surrounded me as they left, and I sighed. They treated me pretty well for a bunch of criminals, but I still always felt *other* around them. I hated that I wanted too desperately to be accepted. To be needed.

I pulled out the bread and got to making myself some toast. It was going to be a long night.

'I'll have some if you're making.' My shoulders bunched as Esther's sweet, lilting voice surrounded me.

'Sure.' The atmosphere in the room changed as she entered it, her perfume drifting over and mingling with the smell of the toast. She always wore just a bit too much. What would she smell like without it? The thought of my face pressed into her neck teased at me, and I shook it quickly out of my head.

Fucking hell, Alec. She's about to be married.

Soon enough, I passed her a plate of toast, and she leant against the counter beside me, flashing me the occasional look as we ate in awkward silence.

'I hear you're babysitting me tonight.'

'Yeah.'

'I'm a bit old for that, don't you think?' She blinked up at me through long eyelashes, green eyes duller since they announced her marriage.

'Just following orders.' I shrugged, taking another bite.

'I enjoy following orders,' she breathed. Toast clogged in my mouth and I nearly choked on it. My eyes flew to her face as her cheeks tinged pink.

'I'm going to pretend you didn't say that.' Because I'd end up hard as a rock if I kept thinking about her obeying. About her on her knees and following my directions. *Fuck*.

'I did though.' Esther turned her body toward me and reached out, drifting a finger gently down my chest as I froze. Everything in my brain flashed red with a huge fucking danger warning sign. What was happening? 'Have you never thought about it?'

I'd be lying if I denied having ever fantasised about her. How could I not? Her petite, curvy, soft lines just begged to be enveloped around hardness. The band of freckles over her nose was just a fucking delight. And those eyes. Those eyes blinking up at me? Man, I'd dreamed about those eyes.

I cleared my throat and tried to form words while fingers grazed over my thigh as she smiled. The evidence of how much I'd thought about her was quite obvious in the strain of my trousers. I gripped her wrist. She needed to stop.

A gasp left her mouth as I held her tight, turning her so her hips pressed against the counter, those fucking eyes facing away from me. Her arm twisted behind her back as I held her there, my groin pressed against her lower back.

'You're engaged,' I said against her ear, aiming for menacing but sounding far more salacious than I'd meant to.

The whimper that she let out before grinding herself back against me gripped me to the core. Holy shit. Did she enjoy this? I enjoyed sex that was a bit on the more risqué side, but never in a million years would I have suspected it of Esther. She was a pampered princess, living off of her daddy's coin.

'To a monster.' Her voice was breathy and dripping with want.

'How do you know I'm not a monster?'

'Better the devil you know.'

I glanced toward the door. Being caught with her pressed between my erection and the toast-crumb-dusted counter would be bad news for me. But she was intoxicating. I leaned my lips in close to her ear, inhaling her scent as she moaned ever so prettily.

'Don't test my loyalty to your family, Esther. I'm here to make sure you get married, not to be teased.'

I released her somewhat reluctantly and stepped back, my heart racing as she turned toward me. She narrowed her eyes and crossed her arms over her chest.

'You can't pretend you haven't thought about it. I've seen the way you look at me. Your dick was just hard against me. You want this too.'

'And what exactly is *this*?'

Her mouth opened, then closed as she looked for the words.

'Is it sex Esther? A mouth on your cunt? A last foray before you are tied down? What do you want from me?'

'Never mind,' she said, straightening out her shoulders and visibly pulling that princess mask back onto her face. 'You probably couldn't give me what I want, anyway.'

'Don't be a brat,' I said, already imagining taking her

over my knee. If I got any harder, my cock would fucking pop.

'What are you going to do about it?' The sparkle twinkled back into her eyes as she closed the space between us. 'You strike me as the type who's all talk.'

Within a breath, I had her hair gripped in my fist, holding her tight as I leant down, our mouths a hair's breadth apart. 'You keep telling yourself that, pretty girl.'

Her mouth opened, her pink tongue dashing against her lower lip as she looked from my mouth to my eyes.

Tasting her was not an option.

Reluctantly, I let her go, a pout settling over her face as I made space between us.

'You aren't mine to be touching like that.'

Disappointment made her frown as I shook my head, trying to clear my mind. Grabbing my water bottle, I left the room, needing air. Hoping no one would spy my erect cock on the way out.

I loved a brat.

My fingers itched to put her in her place.

But she belonged to another.

FIVE
ESTHER

I stuffed clothes willy-nilly into my large designer suitcases, not caring in the slightest what was in any of them. They were to be sent to Harold's house ahead of our wedding day. All going well, I'd be overseas under an alias long before then. Wee Dave had come through. I'd stashed my new documents in my rucksack under the bed. *Emily Reid.* The new me.

There was one tiny hitch in my plan. Alec had taken up residence outside of my door the previous night and had taken up his position once more. Staying wasn't an option. I had to find a way past him. If I tried to leave the room, he either escorted me or found someone else to.

Fuck.

I sat on the suitcase, trying to heave the zip closed as it strained beneath me. I had to make it look like I was all in. Like I'd accepted my fate. I'd never accept being married to Harold. I'd rather die.

Blowing my hair from my face, I tugged against the sharp edges of the zip, red indents marking fingers, before giving up with a groan.

The clock ticked up on my wall, each second lost making me itch. I needed to be on the bus by eleven at the latest. I'd arranged an intricate pattern of different stops that would ultimately end with me at the airport for my red-eye flight to southern Spain. An Uber would have been much more direct, but without the redirection, I'd be far too easy to trace. Which also meant leaving behind my phone, my smart watch, and anything else that contained location software. I'd already stashed them in my secret hiding place behind a loose board. Over the years, it had held plenty of my secrets. Diaries full of teen angst, money, anything I didn't want my sister to 'borrow'. The longer it took for anyone to find anything of mine, the longer I had to disappear.

First, I needed to deal with the tall, tattooed pile of trouble dogging up my door. One of Mac's dark hoodies waited in my wardrobe with some loose tracksuit bottoms and sturdy boots. I even acquired a cap to tuck my hair up into. With the hood pulled up, I should look a million miles from my usual quite feminine style. Alec couldn't see my disguise clothes, or it would utterly ruin the point of disguising myself. Standing in front of the mirror, I looked at myself. Our altercation had affected Alec the previous day. The hard dick in my back assured me so. He'd still turned me down, though. He needed to say yes, to give in to desire. It was imperative to my escape plan.

Trying to seduce him was only to aid my escape, I told myself. So why had his touch thrilled me so much? Yes, he was attractive, and I'd appreciated his form a few times over the years, but he was just another guy. I'd had plenty of liaisons previously, and while they were fun, none had filled me with wickedly delightful thrills like I'd experienced trapped between Alec's erection and the kitchen counter.

When he'd held me by the hair, I'd practically turned to jelly. An enormous pile of lusty mush. It had been quite extraordinary. Men often felt threatened by who I was. My family name always put me in a position with the upper hand. When Alec had treated me without the kid gloves, well, I'd be lying if I didn't get some *feels* right between my thighs.

I pulled off my lounge pants and changed them over for some scandalously short pyjama shorts, covered in the sweetest tiny red and pink hearts. My baby-pink laced bra peeked out behind the straps of the matching pyjama vest top, and I hoped he liked the cutesy look. Leaning forward, I wiggled my bra at the wired band, my tits perking up when I stood.

My lips shone as I dabbed on a touch of dark pink lip oil, not as thick as lipstick, but still giving them that sultry, just-kissed appearance. A dusting of blusher on my cheeks and a swipe of mascara, and I was ready. He'd better bloody fall for it. There was no plan B.

With a tremble in my breath, I counted to five before opening the door, not letting myself chicken out. It was now or never.

'Alec,' I said, honeying my voice and blinking out at him with my best doe-eyed look. 'Do you think I could borrow you for a moment?'

He looked up from his phone, and a tingle gathered at the base of my spine as his eyes swept up my bare legs, pausing at the hem of my tiny shorts before making their way up my body, over my chest, and at last to my face. His knuckles whitened as his fingers tensed against his phone.

'What is it?'

'Could you come in to help me zip up my case? I just can't get it closed.'

He didn't move, and I bit my lip as I foresaw my entire plan unravelling. Then he stood and slipped his phone into his pocket.

'Yeah, but quickly. Your brothers will kick my ass if they find me in your room.'

Relief crashed into me. Phase one, complete. Now to seduce him into phase two.

'Thanks, I've got so much to pack and not nearly enough suitcases. I just need a pair of strong hands.' I hoped my look was as sultry as I intended it to be. I pressed back against the doorframe and looked up into his face as he passed me. Nerves gripped at my belly. He was a loyal man to my family. I only hoped I could rock that loyalty long enough to get away.

It took barely two minutes for him to press down on the case and zip it up. Shit. I clearly hadn't stuffed it nearly enough. I knelt beside him and fit a tiny padlock onto the two zips. As he stood, I caught his hand with my own.

His breath hitched as I ran my fingers over his hand and onto his thigh beyond, my nerves mingling with lust as I grazed his well muscled-leg.

'What are you doing, Esther?' His voice was gravelly as he looked down at me. Remaining on my knees, I tried to find the courage to go through with it. The idea of seducing him wasn't repulsive, quite the opposite, but my motives were all wrong.

'I wanted to thank you.'

'You don't have to thank me.'

I slid my hands upward and to his belt, his whole body stiffening as I did. His eyes darkened as he gripped my chin and tipped my face upward, his thumb gently running over my bottom lip. There was hope. His face dripped with lust.

'Please?' I whispered, unbuckling him while he continued to hold my face, his eyes searching mine.

'Why are you doing this?'

'I...' Fuck, I didn't have an answer for that. 'I'm going to be tied to Harold for the rest of my life. I deserve to worship one last cock before then, don't you think?'

Purposefully licking my lips as I worked my fingers quickly to undo his trousers, I smiled up at him.

'Worship.' His voice trailed off as his cock sprung free from his boxers. I stifled a moan as I eyed his erect dick, thick and swelling more with each passing moment. A surprising wave of need flashed over me. 'Do you want to please me, Esther?'

Alec sounded different than I'd ever heard him, with a commanding edge to his voice that made me squirm. I hadn't intended to enjoy this, but fuck me, I was hungry to taste him.

'Yes.' He slipped his hand up over my hair, petting me softly. It should have been demeaning, him stroking me like a pet, but it sent a slickness right to my crotch. What was wrong with me?

'Then you'd best ask nicely. I don't let just anyone suck my cock.' It bobbed just inches from my lips, and I pressed my thighs together. The temptation to let it go further, to climb atop him and ride him into the night, stole over me. But I couldn't. I didn't have time.

'Please, can I suck your cock?' My cheeks reddened as the words spilled out of my mouth.

'Yes, pretty girl, you can suck my cock.' The words caught in his throat. I leant forward and spread my tongue flat, licking up his length, all the while keeping my eyes on his face.

'Fuck,' he groaned, reaching down to fist his cock and pressing the tip along my lips, spreading salt there. 'You are so beautiful there on your knees. Made to worship dick.'

I spread my fingers over his still clothed thighs and took him into my mouth, flicking my tongue over the hot, flared head of him.

'Such a good girl. Use that tongue to show me how much you want to please me.'

His words were sweet, so why did they feel so dirty? So delicious. Why did they make me want to feel him swell against my tongue and fill my mouth with his cum?

I took him deeper when his fingers traced my jaw, wishing I could take him right into my throat, but knowing well it wasn't a skill I possessed.

'That's it, baby, you swallow me down.' His breath quickened as I increased the pace and suction. As much as the idea of kneeling there with him in my mouth turned me on. I had a job to do. I needed him to cum, and fast.

I added a hand as the base of his cock, alternating between strong pumps of my fist and the slip of my mouth over the head of him.

'Fuck, Esther.' His muscles thrummed beneath my touch, and he tipped his head back as he wound his fingers into my hair. 'Just like that.'

My pyjama shorts were sodden, and I wanted so desperately to slip a hand between my legs. I hadn't expected him to be so damn hot. So commanding. I'd imagined a quick BJ like the ones I'd half-heartedly given in college. Being turned on to the point of grinding myself against my heel had been a total surprise.

Alec tensed, and I felt him try to retreat, but I reached around and clasped him firm about the hips.

'Esther, I'm going to cum if you keep that up.'

'Good,' I mumbled around a mouthful of cock.

'You want me to fill your mouth with my cum?'

'Please?'

He grunted, his eyes fixing on my face as he thrust against my tongue. 'You're so fucking hot. So needy. I'm going to come all over that pretty little tongue of yours.'

A whimper surprised me as I sucked him eagerly back into my mouth. His tattooed hands pulled at my hair as he pumped into my face. It made my head all spacey as I focused solely on his blue eyes.

'Get ready to swallow it down, baby.' The urge to do exactly that made me writhe at his feet. I wanted to see his satisfaction if I swallowed every drop. But I couldn't. I still had a plan, and in this, I couldn't deviate.

I coughed as he held my mouth firm over him, ropes of hot cum hitting the back of my tongue as I gagged. When he released me, I spat the lot out, right down the front of his trousers.

'Sorry,' I murmured as he looked down at the cum streaking the front of his black trousers.

'Shit,' he said, but when he saw my face, he smiled down at me and stroked my cheek. 'Don't worry, you did so well.'

The praise in his voice filled me with a warm feeling before guilt stole over and dashed it.

'Though I can't go out there like this.'

'Maybe you could say you spilled your drink?' It was undeniably cum. It had to be for my plan to work.

'Your dad will kill me if he thinks I've been wanking on the job, more so if he knew I'd had my cock in one of his daughters.'

'You can use my bathroom to clean up. There's a shower

in there too. I'll grab you some spare trousers from the laundry room. I think Logan's would fit you.'

He looked over to the bathroom door, and for a horrible moment, I thought he'd refuse. When he looked down at me with a soft smile, I saw him relent. He'd fallen for it hook, line, and sinker.

'Okay, but be quick. Harold will have me castrated if I'm found trouserless in his fiancee's room.'

His hand was warm as he pulled me to my feet and tipped my chin up to his face. My pulse quickened when I thought he'd kiss me, but at the last second, he pressed his lips to my ears. 'After I'm all cleaned up, I'd like to return the favour. I've dreamt about tasting you and, good girls get rewards.'

A shiver stole right down the length of my spine. A night on his tongue was tempting, but my new life, my chance at freedom, awaited.

'I'd better get those trousers quickly, then,' I said, reaching up and running my fingers over his jaw. Rewarded with an intense look from his icy blue eyes, I tried to capture it. I wanted to remember that lust-filled look, because within an hour he'd hate me.

As soon as the bathroom door closed, I ran to my closet, pulling on my baggy clothing and tucking my hair up into my hat. Working swiftly and with my heart thundering in my chest, I grabbed my bag and was out of the door within a minute. I stole through the house, checking my old analogue watch as I finally made it outside. The one good thing about having lived in the same house forever was that I knew the best ways to sneak out of it and evade detection. My teenage years proved ever so handy.

I made it to the bus with seconds to spare, tossing change into the fare meter before finding myself a seat near the back, my hat pulled low, and my hoody up around my ears.

Phase two complete.

Now to hope I made it out of the country before anyone figured out where I was.

SIX
ALEC

Esther's bathroom was almost as big as my bedroom, with a sprawling stone tub in one corner and a huge rain shower in the other. Never had I dreamt I'd be in her bathroom, or her room, and definitely not in her mouth.

It had been a stupid, stupid idea even stepping foot into her room after the moment that had passed between us the previous day. I went in expecting to close a suitcase and left with my head reeling and my balls empty. Fuck. I was playing with fire.

The way she'd looked up at me from her knees had been my undoing. Those cute frilly heart pyjamas had shown off her curvy thighs, and her tits were about bursting over the top. I'd always been an absolute sucker for cute, flirty clothes. I loved a submissive playmate, and while I wasn't sure she was actually that way inclined, she'd played the part ever so well.

When she'd gone gooey-eyed at my first good girl, I'd lost all reserve and given over to the stolen moment of pleasure.

I couldn't quite believe that it had happened. Never

mind another league, Esther McGowan was in a whole other stratosphere than me. Even worse, it had to be a one-off. But I'd make her scream into her pillow before I left, feel her come around my mouth with my name on her lips. I doubted Harold would be so giving in bed.

Before I knew what I had been doing, I'd found myself in her bathroom, desperately trying to clean jizz off of my trousers. I couldn't sit outside her room all night looking like I'd creamed my pants. Her brothers may like me, but I was pretty sure they had limitations on that. Not only was Esther their sister, but she was getting married in the morning. Thinking about Harold having her made my guts twist, filling my mouth with an acrid taste. He was an absolutely horrific man. He didn't deserve her sweet face in his life. Or his bed.

As the minutes ticked by, I got the worst of the stain out, waiting to hear the click of the door upon Esther's return. Hopefully, with clean trousers. The house was pretty big, but how long could it take to find some?

Stepping from foot to foot, I checked my watch again, eleven fifteen. It had to have been twenty minutes or more, was she fucking with me?

The damp patch sat right against my groin as I pulled on my trousers and fastened my belt. Silence enveloped her bedroom as I opened the door and looked around. Empty. Where on earth was she? There was a chance a family member had waylaid her, so I decided to give her another ten minutes.

Each minute ticked by tortuously slowly as I checked and rechecked my watch, my eyes, otherwise, fixed on the bedroom door. Sweat beaded at the back of my neck, and I wiped at it while feeling jittery. By eleven twenty-five, I was pacing the room.

By eleven thirty, I was tearing her door open and going in search of her.

By eleven forty-five, my stomach felt like it was full of lead.

By twelve, I realised how truly fucked I was.

By twelve-thirty, Malcolm had hauled me in front of him, the siblings, and a smattering of henchmen. I gulped down air, half expecting a bullet.

'How the fuck did she get past you?' Malcolm's face was beet red as his voice tore through the room.

'I had to use the bathroom.' It was the best excuse I had.

'You had scheduled breaks where someone else would take over. You couldn't hold it in?'

I tensed my fingers into a fist, furious at Esther. She'd used me and deceived me. For a moment, I had believed that there had been some sort of attraction on her side, too. Yet again, the desperate little boy inside of me had seen affection and lost himself to it. How had I still not learned that no matter the circumstance, it would always end up with me being fucking shat on by others?

'Sorry. It was a stupid mistake. I didn't think she would notice me gone for the few minutes, and figured that we were trying to keep her safe, not locked up.'

Malcolm slammed his hands down onto the table, the heavy wood juddering beneath his anger. 'Harold is going to rip you a fucking new one.'

'I'll find her,' I said, steeling my voice with more confidence than I had. Showing weakness was never an option in front of those guys. They'd have me strung up by my guts at the first sign of it.

'You'd better. Because if you don't, you'll be the one feeling Harold's ire. I won't hesitate to turn you over to him and his son. You'll be sent home in chunks.'

Malcolm stormed out, swiftly followed by Maeve. I'd have to grill her later. The way her eyes dove away from my face made me instantly suspicious. The sisters were close enough that she might know where Esther would have gone.

Her passport had been in her room, but her phone was gone. Her suitcases remained. I hoped that meant she'd just run off to a bar to drown her sorrows. I'd already sent out some guys to canvas the local area.

Logan breathed through his teeth in a low whistle. 'Didn't think she had it in her to run off. Let's hope she sees sense and is back by morning.'

Mac laughed and shook his head. 'She won't go far. She'd miss the family too much. But I respect her for trying. I'd flee if I had to marry that fucker too.'

'It's not funny,' I said. I couldn't explain the fact she must have planned it, that it wasn't a coincidence she'd left while I was in the bathroom. She'd put me there by spitting my cum all over my trousers. When I found her, I'd make her pay for that.

Ewen rubbed a hand over his face. 'Find her Alec. Dad might be furious, but I can pay you well to do what you best. We need her back. In one piece.'

Most of the targets they required me to get could lose a few pieces without it being a problem.

'How much?'

'It depends how far she's gone. If she's at the pub, I'll throw you a fifty. If she proves harder to track down, whatever you want to bring her back.'

I swallowed hard. It was my fault she was gone, but if she had planned this out, she might be hard to track down. They would need me.

'Ninety thousand.' The words left my lips before I could consider how outlandish a number it was.

'You bring her back, and it's yours,' Ewen said without a moment's hesitation.

Sometimes, I forgot how such a huge number to me was like pocket change to them. It would pay off what remained on my mortgage. The house would be all mine. I'd be able to be more selective about the jobs I wanted to take. Financial freedom.

Just the issue of finding Esther.

An image of her lips wrapped around my length thrust into my head, her perfectly freckled nose, and those big green eyes. Her lips flaring as she took more, as she licked and sucked like such a good girl.

But she wasn't a good girl.

And I'd drag her back to Harold's feet and leave her there gladly, for trying to fuck with me.

She could have cost me my job. Shit, she could have cost me my life if the McGowans didn't need me to locate her.

I'd bring her back kicking and screaming, if necessary.

SEVEN

ESTHER

Spanish sun warmed my body from head to toe as I luxuriated next to the small pool at the quaint little hotel I'd found. It had been almost a week since my escape from the wedding, and instead of being crushed by Harold's rule, I was free. For the first time in my life, I had no one tailing me, no one telling me where to be or how to behave. No expectations of me.

It was glorious.

Bubbles fizzled over my tongue as I took another sip of sweet Cava, closing my eyes and relaxing my muscles.

It had been a busy few days of trying to make my tracks the most difficult to follow. I hopped from bus to bus throughout the Scottish central belt until I reached the borders. From there, I took a train headed south at one of the tiny rural stations. I figured they would check the main Glasgow stations, but it would take weeks to check every backwater village one. The train took me to Manchester, where I picked up a last-minute flight to Spain. Then it had been a series of buses and cabs to dot me about the rural Spanish countryside, going from one tiny family-run hotel to another. Thankfully, they were a bit more cost-effective than the more touristy places by the sea or in the larger towns and cities.

Still, my funds wouldn't last forever, and there was no way I could access my bank accounts. I hadn't even taken my cards with me. Any transactions would pinpoint exactly where I was, and it wasn't a risk I was willing to take.

A whisper of guilt stole through me as I thought about home. My father would be apoplectically mad. My brothers would probably be a mixture of annoyed and finding it tummy-achingly hilarious. But Maeve, my poor baby sister, well, I feared it would hurt her. What if she suffered the same fate? What if Harold decided any McGowan sister would do? I shook the idea from my head. That thought pattern would bring nothing but pain. While I was too young for Harold, Maeve was almost five years younger than me. Dad wouldn't offer her up to him. The age gap would be sickening. Plus, the fallout of losing me would surely eradicate any truce between them. Another wash of guilt flitted over me. What if he took it out on my family in the way he had previously? I'd already lost a mother and a brother to Harold. I didn't want to lose anyone else.

No.

I scolded myself for letting the guilt sway me again. It was not my fault. None of it was. A life of misery and fear wasn't something I deserved because of being born a woman in a man's world. I deserved happiness. I deserved love.

The guilt kept coming, though, in great waves that made the bubbling wine taste bitter on my tongue. I had fucked over Alec. If they'd let him get away with my escape, he would be furious. I hoped they hadn't killed or maimed him for my running.

A flutter of excitement wriggled through me as I

remembered his tattooed arms near my face while his hands twisted in my hair. I wish I could have taken him up on his offer returning the pleasure. The way he'd looked down at me while I sucked his dick had made me positively giddy. I'd never enjoyed going down on a guy as much as I had him. Was it just the excitement of my ruse? Was it the long-seated attraction I'd had for him? Or was it just because he was absolutely not the kind of guy my dad would allow me to date?

Whatever it had been, it saddened me to not be able to follow it through. A night tangled in the sheets with him would have been a delight, I was sure of it. A tingle had me squeezing my thighs together. Maybe I just needed to find a one-night stand here to scrub Alec from my mind. All going well, I hoped to never see him again.

Seeing him would mean they had caught me.

And going back wasn't an option.

Rolling onto my stomach, I let the heat wash over my back. It would be time to move on soon. I couldn't stay in one place too long. Until funds ran out, at least. Then I'd have to use my falsified visa and pick up a job. I'd never had a job. There had never been a need for one. My life was a series of events, parties, shopping, and a lot of boredom. I'd been privileged, but my life had been a gilded cage. A little bird sat there waiting until the day I became useful to Dad and married off to the most useful second owner. The lifestyle wasn't worth the payoff. Not for me, at least.

I'd cling to my freedom with sharp claws.

ANOTHER BUS, another village.

I looked out of the window as the night sky replaced the

evening sun. I'd need to find a hotel soon. The bus slowed as it trundled to a stop.

'Your stop,' the driver said in broken English.

'Thank you.' I gathered up my bag and pulled my hoody tight around my body. It was getting pretty cold. 'Is there a hotel here?'

'Taverna. Top of the hill.'

'Gracias.' I shoved some euros into his hand before alighting from the bus and looking around. The village was cute, even in the dark. The streets were still warm beneath my shoes, the large flat stones warmed by the day's heat. Red-topped roofs glittered in the moonlight atop the muddy-coloured stone buildings, all entirely unique in construction. It was breathtaking. As was the hill, which made my thighs burn as I ascended it. The entire village had been built onto a hillside, and I definitely wasn't used to traversing hills like it.

By the time I'd almost reached the top, my calves were protesting against even one more step, and my lungs gulped down air like it was in short supply. At last, I could see the taverna peeking out over the crest of the hill. Warm light spilled out of the windows, with music lilting out into the night air. It was adorable. I really hoped there was an available room.

My breath whooshed out of my mouth as I finally reached the flat portion at the top of the hill, and I smiled when I saw all the greenery surrounding the outside of the stone-walled inn. I couldn't wait to collapse into bed.

A hand slapped over my mouth as I was wrenched back, my scream stifled. Hard stone cut into my hands and knees as I hit the ground. Before I could figure out what was happening, a series of kicks connected with my side, winding my already laboured breathing. I struggled to my knees as the dirty, beer-scented hand bruised at my lips. The man was much stronger than I, and the only weapon I had that wasn't proving ineffective was my teeth. I bit down hard on his hand, grinding my teeth until the salty taste of blood filled my mouth.

'Perra!' my assailant said as he pushed me to the ground and levelled a series of punches directly into my face. Tears blurred my vision as pain blossomed from every part of me. More salty blood in my mouth, mine this time. I cried out again as he stood, sending more blistering kicks into my side, stomach, and back.

Through bleary eyes, I saw him pick up my bag.

'No,' I tried to scream, the words barely a whisper as pain radiated through me. Everything I owned in the world was in that bag. Everything.

He spat at me, a wet globule running down my chest as I struggled to get up. I couldn't. It hurt too much.

Footsteps rang out as he left the alley he'd thrown me into. Blackness claimed me as I gave into the pain, welcoming the dark to block it all out.

EIGHT
ALEC

Seven days.

A whole seven days had passed since Esther fucked me over, and I still hadn't tracked her down.

How hard could it be to find a pampered mafia princess? Evidently, much harder than I at first expected.

She couldn't have just disappeared, but I was running into dead end after dead end.

We searched her friends' houses from top to bottom, whether or not they were willing to help. Ellis, my hacker friend and technical whizz, had been poring over hundreds of hours of CCTV footage. We'd found enough to know she caught a bus close to the mansion and had been in dark, baggy clothes with a baseball cap on. It was proving an absolute nightmare to trace her route to find where she had gone. If she had used the major stations, it would have been far easier, but she must have used smaller bus stops in rural areas which either lacked CCTV or had it on the blink. It was a fucking nightmare.

I stood in her bedroom, looking around at the carnage I'd wrought in the usually tidy place. I'd ripped the bed apart, in case she'd hidden anything inside the mattress. Every cupboard and drawer upended with their contents spilled in lumpy piles over the floor, every single item gone through by hand. Her passport and purse were there, but as yet, her phone hadn't been located. So she was either still in the country, or using false documents. Ellis had scoured local airport security footage, but nothing had shown up so far.

Running a hand through my hair, I groaned. Malcolm's veins popped more with each day that passed, and Harold was losing his already thin patience.

Where the fuck was she?

'Ellis,' I said, calling him up to check on his progress. I sent up a silent prayer that he had something, anything, to go on. 'Any news?'

'The phone is definitely in the house, mate. You need to find it. It's our best chance of seeing what she was up to before she left.' Ellis's Irish drawl sounded bored from the other end. Easy to be as cool as a cucumber when your ass wasn't on the line.

'I've torn the place apart. It's not here. Wouldn't she have deleted her messages and calls, anyway?'

'Deleting them doesn't mean I can't find them, but I need the device to do it. Find it Alec, and I can do the rest.'

My fingers tensed against my phone as I scanned the room. There wasn't a single part of it I hadn't checked. We'd searched the other rooms too, without success. 'How sure are you it's in the house?'

'One hundred percent. It never left the house after she did.'

With a deep sigh, I closed my eyes. 'Alright. I'll call you back.'

There was one person who might hide something. One person who had been cagey the entire week.

Maeve. She and Esther were close, and if anyone had helped her, or was covering for her, it would be her little sister. I'd tried pressing her for info, but never alone. I'd do whatever it took to get an answer, daughter of the boss or not.

Within minutes, my fist clashed with her door as a series of bangs echoed throughout the wide hallway. Her eyes bugged as she opened the door, swiftly trying to close it again. Using my foot to stop the door, I pushed it open and made my way into her room.

Her gaze darted to the door as it closed behind me, her usual protection failing to be outside as I had every able body out searching.

'No one's out there.'

I winced as she let out a high-pitched scream for help. Two steps toward her, and I put my hand over her mouth, grabbing her up against me and applying pressure to her mouth and chest. 'Cut that shit out. I'm not here to hurt you. I need your help.'

Maeve writhed against me, fighting against my hold. Despite her toned figure, she wasn't strong enough for it to have any actual effect. 'Quit it. I want to let you go, but you need to stop the screaming. Understood?'

Her chin bobbed against my hand, and slowly I lowered it from her mouth.

'Get off of me,' she said, her voice laced with anger. No one treated those spoiled mafia kids like that, but I was losing the ability to give a fuck.

I released her from my hold as she moved away, wrapping her arms around herself as she gave me a foul look.

'What did Esther say in the days leading up to leaving?

Where did she go? Did she do anything suspicious? I need the truth.'

'She said nothing.' Her face was sullen as she barked out her words at me.

'So nothing out of the ordinary happened at all?'

Maeve's eyes fell on the door again, but I stood between her and it. There was no chance she could reach it without me catching her. Her shoulders sagged as she gave in, slumping down on her bed and giving me a foul look.

'There was one thing. She asked me to distract the guys when we were shopping. To make it seem like we were just taking a really long time in one shop while they waited outside. I saw her leaving with a change of clothes and a wig.'

'Where was she going?'

'She didn't say.'

'How long was she gone?'

'Maybe an hour?'

Those guys were idiots. They stood outside a shop for an hour and didn't find it suspicious? I'd deal with them later. 'And you didn't think to ask where she went?'

'I asked, but she wouldn't tell me.'

'Which shop?'

Maeve fidgeted with the hem of her top as she bit her lip. She was still trying to find a way out of betraying her sister.

'I can ask the guys who escorted you. Either way, I'll have an answer. It will be much easier if you just tell me.' There were much quicker ways to get answers, but I was pretty sure Malcolm would draw the line at me torturing an answer out of his youngest kid.

'Avery's boutique.'

I fired off a text to Ellis with the info, hoping he'd be

able to access some of the CCTV on the high street around the store and follow where she'd gone.

'Good girl. Next, we need to find her phone.'

Her shoulders lifted in a shrug.

'Listen to me. What do you think is going to happen if she doesn't come home? Do you think there is a happy ever after? She left you without a word. Not only does she intend to disappear, but she left you here. And you are next in line.'

Her face paled as I spoke, her eyes widening as my words sunk in.

'If she isn't back soon, you'll be marrying Harold. And he'll take out this infraction of Esther's on you. Is that something you will endure for your sister? Are you willing to become Harold's wife? To marry him to save her? To submit to his dick so she doesn't have to? That is the position she's forcing you into.'

Maeve trembled, looking very close to vomiting as my words hit the mark. I hoped Malcolm wouldn't promise his youngest to Harold, but he must be pretty desperate to appease him. What's another daughter when you've already promised one?

'He wouldn't,' she whispered.

'Do you really believe that?'

The way her eyebrow furrowed told me she didn't.

'What do you want?'

'I need to find her phone. I know it's in the house, but I've ripped her room apart, and I can't find it. Did she give it to you?'

'No. She gave me Mum's necklace, but nothing else.'

'Is there anywhere she could have hidden it?'

Maeve sat up straighter as realisation crossed her face. Hope surged in my chest.

'She'll be furious with me.'

'Your father and Harold will be worse, trust me.'

With a resigned sigh, she gave in and stood. 'Come on. There's one spot it might be. She used to hide her diary, but I saw her put it away one night when she thought I'd fallen asleep.'

I followed her through to Esther's room as she gave a sad smile over her shoulder.

'I used to sneak in and read it. I think it might have been the least salacious diary in the world. Eventually, she binned it and stopped hiding anything. I haven't thought about it for years.' Stepping over the mess I'd left strewn on the floor, she picked her way to the far corner and crouched beside the wardrobe. I already knew it was empty, the hope I'd been clinging to shredded. But then she gripped at the skirting board next to the wardrobe and tugged hard. It groaned before giving way, revealing a small dark gap behind it.

Maeve's arm disappeared as she reached into the space, her hand searching to the left, then twisting to the right. A rustle sounded as she frowned. Then she pulled out a plastic bag, and when she tipped it out, I could have kissed her. Esther's phone fell out onto the floor with a clunk. The battery was long dead, but victory gripped me.

'Thank you, Maeve.' I scooped it up and helped her to her feet. She looked downright dejected.

'What if she hates me?' Her face almost pulled at my heartstrings. Almost.

'Is helping me any worse than her leaving you to live the life she was supposed to have?'

'I guess not.'

I left her there, surrounded by her sister's scattered belongings as I called Ellis, already heading for my car.

'I've got the phone. I'll be with you in twenty.'

For the first time since she'd swallowed my dick, I smiled.

'Game's on, Esther,' I said as I slid into the driver's seat.

I never lost.

THE STENCH of piss burned at my nostrils as I made my way to the door near the end of the alley. Rubbish flitted in the wind, a small tornado of old crisp packets and cigarette ends. Ellis had found the information we needed, a deleted WhatsApp message to Wee Dave himself, and after tracking where she went, we'd narrowed it to that alleyway.

Fingers crossed, we were right.

I had no idea how someone like Esther would know the forger. It's not like she was involved in the running of the crime empire, she merely profited from the family's involvement.

Minutes passed as I rapped at the door once, twice, three times. If he wasn't home, I'd find a way in and wait. Either way, I'd have an answer by the end of the evening.

The door opened a crack, and a scruffy face peeped through the gap. His eyes widened enough that I could tell he knew of me, knew the jobs the McGowans sent me on. Knew it was bad news for him.

I strong-armed my way in as he tried to push the door closed, and grappled with the smaller man. He slipped out of my grasp and ran toward a locked cabinet, fumbling to enter a code on the keypad.

With a sigh, I stormed him, dragging him back by his shaggy hair and slamming his body into a wall. The cabinet swung open to reveal a bevy of weapons just a second too late for him to grab any.

'What do you want?' Dave said, spitting venom. I pressed his face hard into the wall.

'Information. It would be a lot easier if you gave it up willingly.'

'Fuck off. No one hires a grass.'

'No one will hire you if you're dead either.'

His cheeks flushed as he continued his struggle.

'Let me go.'

'So you get another chance at your cabinet of toys? I don't think so.' I pulled him over to his desk, turning his computer chair around, and pushing him into it.

'Sit still,' I said through gritted teeth as he struggled against me, head-butting my lip. The coppery tang of blood wetted my tongue. I spat a glob of bloody spit onto his floor as I grabbed a handful of cable ties from my pocket, using them to secure his hands to the chair's armrests. Once I similarly secured his feet to the base, I sat back, my breathing heavy.

'You have no beef with me, there's no need for this.' Dave licked his dry lips and looked every bit the cornered animal.

I shucked off my jacket, placing it neatly over the edge of a sofa before slowly rolling up my shirt sleeves. 'I have beef with you alright. Do you know Esther McGowan?'

A wrinkle crossed his brow at her name.

'I know of her. But what would she have to do with me?'

'Are you denying that she came here?'

'Yeah.' My knuckles crunched against his jaw.

'Don't lie to me, Dave. My fists are the least of your worries.' I crouched down in front of him, my eyes level with his. 'My knife is still in my pocket, but if I'm tempted to take him out, you'll be losing body parts instead of gaining bruises.'

A dark bloom wetted his jeans as the telltale smell of urine invaded the space. I grinned as terror stole over his face. The wonderful thing about having a horrific reputation, as an enforcer who was willing to use torture to get answers, is that you rarely actually have to use it. The rumours were almost always worse than reality, and while I wouldn't hesitate to do whatever was necessary to complete my task, more often than not, a few punches and verbal threats did it.

'So,' I said, gripping Dave's hairy chin sharply in my fingers, digging them into the already purpling spot I'd punched, 'are you ready to talk?'

'I can't. Half my fee depends on her staying hidden.'

'All I need is a name. You helped her get a new ID, didn't you?'

Dave swallowed hard, but kept his mouth shut. Unfortunately.

Warm metal grazed my fingertips as I reached into my pocket and pulled out my trusty flick knife. I'd stolen it from one of my many foster fathers as a teen, and it was my baby. Sharp as sin, old as fuck. The wooden grip worn from years of use.

The satisfying click as I opened it brought a sob wrenching out of Dave's throat.

'What would you like to lose first? A toe? A finger? Your balls? I'd take your tongue, but you'll need that to give me the name.' I leaned in close and dragged the knife slowly down his cheek, not cutting, but letting him feel the sharp edge against his skin.

'Stop. Please?' Another sob strangled his words.

'Finger it is.' He tried to grip his fingers tight into a fist until I brought my fist down sharply on the back of his hand. There was a crunch as his hand compressed between the armrest and my fist. When he cried out, I prised a finger free and held it against the armrest, my knife digging into the flesh.

Whole body quakes shook him against the chair as I let the knife press into the skin enough for blood to bubble against the metallic blade.

'It's Emily,' Dave sobbed, his face as wet as his crotch. 'Emily Reid.'

'Good lad,' I said, removing my knife and cleaning it off against his jumper. 'That wasn't so hard now, was it?'

Dave trembled in the chair as I put back on my jacket, smoothing out the slight crumples from laying it down. 'And what did you give her?'

'Passport, driving licence and a work visa for most of continental Europe.' He sighed as I opened the door, the chilly breeze carrying a crisp packet into the room. 'You've just cost me two-thirds of my wage. I hope you never find her.'

'Better that than losing your dick.'

'Aren't you going to let me go?' His eyes widened as I opened the door fully.

I walked over to him and smiled down as I opened my knife back up, his flinch extra satisfactory. 'I'll give you a chance, one hand freed and one favour owed. Understood?'

He nodded reluctantly as I slid my knife through one of the cable ties, his hand clenching as the blood flowed back into it.

'And if anyone else comes looking, you don't tell them a thing. Otherwise you'll choke on your own dick.'

Halfway up the alley I stopped and took a breath, sliding my knife back into my pocket. It never got easier.

Being good at my job didn't mean I enjoyed it. Maiming people, killing people, terrorising people, it all took a chunk out of my soul. But it was all I offered. Without it, no one would need me at all.

Now, to track down the so-called Emily Reid.

'I'm coming for you,' I whispered into the wind.

NINE

ESTHER

The murmur of voices startled me awake, a sharp pain ringing between my ears as I tried to sit up. 'Where am I?'

'Ah, English. No, don't sit up fast,' a woman's voice said, heavily accented with the local dialect, but speaking English well.

'You'll pass out again if you rush it, lass.' Fear spiked in my chest as a Scottish lilt reached my ears. Had they found me?

The early morning light made my eyes ache as I forced them open to look at two people who were crouched next to me. Where was I?

Everything ached with bitter cold as I took in the cobbled street below me, my legs dirt-covered and streaked with dried blood.

'Don't worry, we'll call an ambulance. They'll get you patched up in no time,' the man said.

But my documents were gone. The previous night flooded back into my head, a tremble quaking my body at the memory. He could have molested me or killed me. I'd been lucky to get away mostly intact. Or I thought I was intact. It was hard to tell. My lips were thick and dry, one eye swollen almost shut. Were my ribs broken? It hurt when I inhaled too deeply. I probably needed an ambulance, but they'd want proof of who I was, and I no longer had that.

'No. No hospital, please.'

The strangers shared a look. 'Will you let us help clean you up? We own the taverna, and there is food and water there. You'll need it to get better.'

I didn't want to owe anyone anything, but what choice did I have? I had no money, no ID, no work visa. Nothing. I nodded and winced as they helped me to my feet. Pain shot through my knee as I bore my weight on it, and I whimpered with each step out of the alleyway and toward the taverna.

'We found a bag too, emptied on the road.'

A kernel of hope.

'It was mostly just clothes. I think whoever attacked you must have taken your money.'

Hope dashed. 'And my documents.'

We entered the sweet taverna, the smell of fresh herbs wrapping me in cosiness. They were everywhere, bringing an indoor garden vibe to the place. I loved it.

'Jock, can give you a ride to the embassy to fix your documents once you are feeling better.' The woman spoke softly as she sat me in a seat and retrieved a bowl of warm water and a cloth. I hissed between my teeth as she dabbed at my bruised face.

'I don't want to go to the embassy.'

'They will get you new documents.' Jock fixed a plate of crumbly, sugar-coated biscuits and a cup of tea and brought them over to me. A rumbling stole over my stomach at the sight of them.

'They won't be able to replace the kind I had,' I said in a

whisper. It was opening myself up to potentially being turned in, but I had no choice.

'Eva, a word?' Jock said. The sugary biscuit melted in my mouth as I took a bite, damn it was delicious. I'd eaten three by the time they came back across the room despite the crumbs making my tattered lips ache, and Eva took back up the cloth and continued washing my many cuts and bruises.

'We have a spare room. You can stay until your injuries heal.' The older woman smiled up at me as she spoke.

'I don't have any money.'

'That's okay. Most of our patrons are local, so we have the space going unused.' She patted my hand as tears pricked at the inner corners of my eyes.

'Thank you,' I whispered, their generosity more than I could have asked for.

'Are you running from an ex-boyfriend?' Jock asked, pouring a bowl of rich spiced soup out and placing it beside me with a spoon.

Hesitation gripped me as I looked at him. Would he know anyone back home? Would he try to turn me over?

'Don't worry, lass, I ran from Scotland myself thirty years ago. You're not the first waif and stray that Eva has taken in.'

'I ran from an arranged marriage with a terrible man. I can't go back.' I laid out my cards, so to speak, hoping pity might keep me safe.

'Aye, well, you can stay here until you figure out what to do next. We can always use an extra set of hands. The pays crap, but we can give you room and board.'

The tears came in a great waterfall this time as Eva gently washed them away.

'Come on, eat up your soup. I'll show you your room

after and find you something to wear while I wash your other things. They got dirty laying out on the street all night. Jock, can you sort her a basin of hot water and a washcloth so she can clean herself before bed?'

Jock nodded and took a few steps before turning back to me. 'Did you see the face of the guy who did this?'

'Only briefly. But I definitely left a set of teeth marks on his palm.'

'Good. I'll keep an ear out and see if rumour brings anything up.'

'I can't go to the police.'

'If people find out someone's been attacking tourist lassies, you won't have to. We don't take kindly to arseholes here.'

Maybe they would find my documents. Maybe everything would be okay.

I moaned as the first rich, salted mouthful of soup warmed my tongue. Man, someone here could cook.

Staying in one place for more than a day or two was risky, but Eva and Jock seemed like good people. And what other choice did I have?

I'd just have to trust that I covered my tracks well and that Dad would look for Esther McGowan, not Emily Reid. Just another expat in rural Spain. There was no reason to suspect I was in Spain, let alone in the middle of nowhere.

The unease still clawed at my belly as I ate.

TEN
ALEC

The sultry summer air almost immediately brought me out in a light sweat as I walked through Madrid Airport. We'd tracked her flight there, but she hadn't taken any more flights, not under her new alias. If Wee Dave had double crossed me and given her another name, I'd go back and string up the bastard by the balls.

Stretching out my tense shoulders, I looked around the crowded airport. There were a million ways she could have gone, and still, there was no sight of her anywhere. She hadn't logged into anything online, nor contacted anyone. Fuck, she could be dead and no one would even know.

My phone dinged in my pocket, and I pulled it out to read the text. Ellis's name flashed at the top of the screen and I tapped on the message. 'Found her on the airport CCTV. She changed on the airplane by the looks of it and left in blue jeans and a white top with her dark hair in a ponytail. She was carrying a brown rucksack and had dark sunglasses on. Looks like she got on a bus heading south. I'll send you the registration and route details.'

Soon enough, the details pinged through and I headed

through the airport to where the busses terminated. I picked my way through them before finding the one she had got onto. The yellow-striped bus was an airport shuttle and would take me to the city centre. There was little point in quizzing the bus driver about whether or not he remembered her. She'd have ended up in the city station, regardless. Ellis was already on the case, trying to track down and hack the CCTV in the central station to figure out where she went next.

Leaning against the wall of the bus, one hand lightly gripping the bright yellow handrails, I tried to picture her there. Where would she have gone? Would Esther have lost herself amongst the millions of people in the city? Or aimed to stick to a more rural area? She was the spoiled daughter of a millionaire, so I imagined the city would be much more her style. There had to be some financial support somehow. She couldn't have packed enough cash to see her through for very long, especially not in the fashion she was used to existing in. My initial fury after she dropped me in the shit had dulled to heavy, solid anger. Not as fiery, but equally as intense. I'd enjoy dragging her back to Harold. She'd erased my sympathy with the insane manhunt she'd set me up for.

I fingered the wallet in my pocket, it's thick leather exterior clammy against my fingers. Esther wasn't the only one travelling under false pretences. The fake ID I had was more equipped for getting information out of the locals with the Scottish Police info. As long as no one checked into it too hard. Or checked into me too hard. Most of my tattoos were hidden under the lightweight, but dark shirt I wore, the briefest glimpse peeking out near my collar. It was too hot to do the button right up to my neckline. Sure, some policemen had tattoos these days, but I'd never seen one quite so decorated. Mine twisted up my arms and engulfed my torso before dipping down into my waistband. Definitely overkill for an officer.

Tilting my head back, I rested it against the window, watching the city zip by. Every muscle in my body itched to swing into action, to catch Esther and drag her home, but there was so much waiting as Ellis did his thing back home.

Nine days had passed, and with each, the idea of finding her became more unlikely. I scanned everyone around me, wondering whether she'd done the same.

Had she stood in the same spot as me? A memory of her at my feet, staring up at me with those big green eyes assaulted me, making me twitch in my pants.

My knuckles whitened against the yellow handrail as I tried to clear the memory from my mind. Whatever happened if, no, when, I caught her, it wouldn't be that.

As much as I'd love to hate fuck her as she squealed out apologies for fucking with me, it was nothing but a dirty thought. A dangerous thought.

I'd find her and throw us onto the first available plane home.

Then wash my hands of her for good.

FIVE DAYS LATER, my skin was browning after the terrific pink it had taken on from my long-winded hunt around the Spanish countryside. Esther had gone from bus to fucking bus, dotting around the rural landscape like an annoying fly. I groaned as I made my way into the small family-run hotel, the last one in the village where Ellis had traced the latest bus. It was getting so much harder to track her now that we were out of civilisation proper. There was barely any CCTV, and I was relying on the goodwill of bus drivers, locals, and hotel owners to continue my hunt.

A pretty brunette smiled warmly at me as I approached the desk.

'Hola,' she said, her eyes dancing over my exposed arms. I'd soon given up hiding them in the blazing sunshine. My poor little Glaswegian ass wasn't used to hot weather.

'Do you speak English?' I asked, really hoping she did. I'd had partial success with my online translator, but it made conversation difficult, not to mention my spotty internet access the further I travelled into the rolling hills.

'Si, yes.' Did she just blush? Damn.

'I'm looking for a woman who may have stayed here last week. I'm with the Scottish police and she is a fugitive we are trying to locate.'

The woman looked me up and down before reaching for my fake ID, looking from it to my face. After a few tense moments, she shrugged. 'Do you have a picture?'

I nodded and went into the photos on my phone, bringing up Esther's pretty grinning face, her arm slung about her sister's shoulder. 'This one here.'

She tilted her head and considered for a moment. Nerves crept into my chest as I faced the fact that I may have lost the track entirely if Esther hadn't been there.

'Yes. She was here.'

'When?'

A comically enormous book creaked as she opened it, scanning through the last, half-filled page. 'One week ago. See here?'

Her finger ran along an entry. It didn't say Esther or Emily, but rather Amelia Reid. Really, I would have been impressed with the lengths Esther had gone to if I wasn't so fucking pissed at her.

'And it's definitely the girl from the picture?'

'Yes,' she nodded eagerly. 'I remember her eyes, so green.'

Relief. Cold and fresh. *Thank fuck.*

'Do you know where she went?'

'Yes. She took the morning bus up to Cuelle.'

'Thank you.' I could have kissed her. The way she looked at my lips, she may have welcomed it. 'Is there another bus?'

'In the morning, Si.'

'A taxi? Uber?'

She giggled and shook her head. 'Not out here. Bus is it. First thing tomorrow.'

'I guess I'd better take a room then.'

I handed over cash and filled in the form with my details, all while the receptionist fluttered her long eyelashes at me. When she slid the room key, an actual key not a plastic card, into my hand, her fingers hovered over mine for just a second too long.

'Would you like any help in your room?'

My eyes fell from her fluttering lashes to her generous tits. She was pretty. And if I hadn't been so exhausted, I'd have likely taken her up on the offer. My balls were blue enough.

'Not tonight. It's been a long trip.' I gave her a soft smile, hoping it would stop the sting of rejection.

Her face reddened as she pointed to the staircase at the far end of the room. 'Up the stairs, first door on the right. Call me if you need anything.'

The way she stressed *anything* told me I hadn't left her too disheartened.

My room was quaint but clean, looking out over the small pool below. The sun was just dipping below the horizon, sending great streaks of orange light over the sea of hills.

I stripped off my clothes and ran the shower, stepping in under the blistering hot water and groaning. I missed my house. My bed. Hell, I missed Gladys. Tracking people down usually meant hitting a few junkie dens and twisting arms for names, not a thousand-mile-long hunt through the dusty back roads of another country.

Scrubbing the dirt from my blonde hair with shitty hotel shampoo, I let a seed of hope flourish. I was close. I had to be. Esther couldn't be moving to a new village every single day, could she? With each passing day, she'd be feeling emboldened by her escape. She'd have to slow down soon.

My hand stroked at my cock as my mind filled with her. It wasn't the first time I'd fucked my fist and thought of those pretty green eyes. Little did I know that in the flesh, she'd be even hotter than in my fantasies. The way she'd said please when she asked to suck me, her voice so sweet and eager. Fuck, it had got me straight in the crotch.

I leant one hand against the slick tiles of the shower stall as I stroked my fist up my length, imagining her hot, wet mouth over me. Those fuck me eyes begging me to use her. My cum dripping from her lips.

Fuck.

My grunts mingled with the sound of falling water as I let myself go, fully imagining her there, on her knees, begging to please me. Tears on her face as she pleaded for forgiveness. Fuck, I'd make her work for it.

Balls heavy, I jerked my swollen dick. In my head, it was her sweet little cunt engulfing the head, wrapping me up in her heat. She'd writhe against me as I speared her again and again, making her pay for deceiving me. All the while begging for more.

Water dripped down over my face as I came with a heated groan, jerking my hips into my fist as I imagined filling her pussy until she begged me to stop. Her face would blush and slick with sweat. Her cunt swollen and sore and dripping with my cum.

After the moment passed, my cum washed down the drain, and my post-nut clarity returned like a huge slap in the face. Esther was off limits, and when I found her, I wouldn't be getting my dick anywhere near her. I'd been burnt once by her deception already. I'd be a fool to fall for it twice.

I crashed into bed with a sigh, watching the sky turn blue and then black.

If only I'd have been born into a family like Esther's.

She could have been mine.

ELEVEN

ESTHER

As each day passed, my bruises subsided a bit more. The aches that had wracked my body after the attack slowly faded until I felt almost back to normal. With each day's healing, I settled in more to the cosy life at the taverna.

Jock and Eva were sweet, like the grandparents I'd never had. Despite knowing that I wasn't being open about my past, they'd welcomed me with open arms. I'd eaten like a queen. Not the fancy food we had at home, but proper home-cooked Spanish food, which warmed my heart almost as much as it did my belly.

Their taverna didn't seem to make a large amount of money. The locals mostly used it as a watering hole, and Jock and Eva did pretty much everything themselves. But they were ageing. I wanted to help in exchange for the kindness they'd shown me, and after much asking, Eva had eventually relented. Just like that, I had my first job.

I passed the two beers over to the men who'd ordered them, picking up some empties as I passed amongst the tables outside. Initially, I'd been worried that my attacker would show up in the bar, but so far, there was no sign of him. My smiles were coming easier as the number of days since my escape increased. They couldn't look forever, and I could be anywhere in the world. I'd done it.

I was free.

A young couple sat at a table near the door, all entwined and looking at one another with puppy love in their eyes. I smiled as I picked up their empty plates and balanced them on my arm. Would I ever feel that? Arranged marriage was always going to be my destiny, but now that I was free, could I have it? A shiver of hope tugged at my insides as he reached forward and kissed the girl on the nose, grinning as she scrunched it.

I stopped myself from my wistful staring and went back inside, smiling as the herb-laden air washed over me. The interior was a maximalist dream, full of colour and texture, the walls covered in bric-à-brac and mismatched paint. A far cry from our sleek interiors at home.

I fucking loved it.

Shouldering the door, I let myself into the kitchen, dropping the plates off at the sink to wash later before leaning against the counter and taking a drink of water. The heat would take some getting used to, a far cry from Glasgow's dreary rain sixty percent of the time.

Jock came into the kitchen and nodded at me in that gruff way older men do when they don't know what to say.

'Do you want me to do these dishes now? I think most people have had food and Eva's still on the bar?'

'Why don't you take a wee break, go out and see some of the town in the daylight? We can manage here for the afternoon.'

Jack reached into his pocket and pulled out a few euro notes, coming across and stuffing them into my hand.

'Oh, you don't have to--'

'Shush now, lass. You've been a great help these past few days. You'll be needing some essentials, I'm sure.' Jock's wrinkles that framed his eyes deepened as he smiled.

'You are already feeding me and giving me a room. I can't take this.' I tried to pass the money back to him, but he shook his head and put his hands in his pockets.

'You can. You've been working hard, and we have the food and space here, anyway.' He cleared his throat as his eyes misted. 'We've missed having young 'uns around.'

'Your children?' I asked, fingering the notes in my hands as I watched him.

'Aye. I've not seen mine since I left Scotland. Eva's daughter used to help us here. We lost her almost twenty years back, and it's never quite felt the same. But I see how Eva's brightened since you arrived. You've given her a purpose again. Someone to dote on.'

Guilt bit at my insides despite the sweet sentiments. There was no way I could stay there indefinitely, no matter how much I enjoyed the relaxed, homely atmosphere.

'That's sweet. But you know I can't stay?'

'Aye, we know. But the offers there. Someone will need to take over this place when we can't. It could be you.'

I let the idea ruminate for a moment, imagining staying there with Jock and Eva. Already they'd been so welcoming, treating me like one of their own, like family. The taverna was quaint and wonderful, full of life, but without being somewhere where anyone would spot me and report back home. I enjoyed working there. It could be perfect.

Jock sidled up beside me and put an arm around my shoulder, pulling me into a side hug. 'I don't know who the man you are running from is, lass, but I know you can't keep running forever.'

'I know,' I whispered, leaning my head against his shoulder, welcoming the gentle intimacy he offered.

'Don't go running off in too much of a hurry.' Jock coughed and released my shoulders, wiping discretely at his eye. 'Now, off with you into the village. You'll find the market at the bottom of the hill. It has toiletries, snacks, and some clothes. There's a coffee shop too that makes the best churros I've ever tasted.'

I grinned at him and pocketed the money. 'Well, if there are churros to be eaten, it would be rude not to go. Thanks, Jock.'

'Och, it's nothing, lass.'

In the main bar area, I took off my little apron and hung it up behind the bar.

'Off out?' Eva asked with a smile.

'Yeah, Jock's convinced me to take the afternoon off and see a bit of the village.'

'Good. You can't stay cooped up in here day and night. Go, have fun.'

She shooed me out of the bar as I laughed.

Nerves pricked at my tummy as I left the taverna. Standing on the street brought memories of the attack flooding back. Taking a deep breath, I scolded myself. It had been late at night, and this was the middle of the day. People bustled about their daily lives on the stone streets, and it was as safe as it was going to get.

I picked my way down the hill, taking in the hodgepodge of stone buildings almost piled on top of one another, their red roofs visible further down the hill. Grass and tree-covered hills towered over the village, almost encasing it in a geographic hug from two sides. It was breathtaking.

The market was easy enough to find, though I already

dreaded how much my thighs would burn on the way back up to the taverna. If I stayed, I'd have thighs of steel by the end of the summer. I picked up some shampoo and deodorant, a new toothbrush and toothpaste, as well as a pack of tampons. I was still a few weeks off - I thought - but was losing track of the days.

The cafe was adorable, and I sat outside in the sun drinking a strong coffee and munching on the cinnamon-laden churros. I didn't know if they were indeed the best, but they were bloody delicious. Melt in your mouth, groan out loud, delicious.

As I tucked into a second helping, a prickle of warning crept across the back of my neck. I sat up straighter and looked around me. Nothing was amiss. An ancient old lady pulled a trolley up the hill. A couple walked hand in hand with their baby strapped to the mum's chest. The workers in the market milled about busily. I traced my eyes from building to building, but saw nothing out of the ordinary. Was I imagining it? It had to be because of the attack. Subconsciously, my body was still on alert. I took a steadying breath and pushed my coffee away. Perhaps the caffeine had me on edge.

Still, maybe it would be best to return to the tavern. I felt safe there.

I started the long trek back up the hill with my bag of goodies over my shoulder. The unease creeping up my spine carried me the whole way, despite the expected burning of my thighs.

I didn't breathe easily until I was back in my room, surrounded by four sturdy walls and two people who seemed to care about my welfare despite being virtual strangers.

How long would it be until I could relax and feel at ease again?

I sighed as I flopped back on my bed, glad of my new deodorant after that walk back up the hill.

TWELVE

ALEC

I followed the bus in the hire car I'd picked up at the previous village. If Esther was in Cuelle, I'd need transportation to force her back to the airport. Manhandling her onto the bus would raise far too much suspicion.

Seeing a gap in the dusty road ahead, I overtook, wanting to be parked up by the time the bus pulled into the village. I still needed confirmation on whether Esther had been on it. Assuming it was the same driver.

The village rose like a pile of kids blocks teetering up the hill. The houses seemed almost haphazardly stacked on every available piece of land, and no two were the same. A far cry from my cookie-cutter-house back in Glasgow. I'd have liked to be visiting under much less pressing circumstances so I could explore the maze of a town, but there was little time for that. Both Harold and Malcolm had been blowing up my phone, demanding results which I hoped I could assure them of soon.

I parked at the outer edge of the village and hot-footed it to the bus stop, waiting and watching as the bus slowly trundled along. At last, it stopped, its doors opening with a sigh as the few passengers alighted. The driver raised an eyebrow at me when I stalked on, flashing my faux badge at him.

'Do you speak English?' I asked, trying to keep my voice warm and non-threatening.

'Yes.'

'I'm searching for a fugitive from Scotland. She's travelling under the name of Emily Reid? I've reason to believe she was on your bus a few nights back.'

'Slow down,' the driver said, his moustache twitching as he watched my lips moving.

'This woman,' I said, holding up my phone and bringing up the picture of Esther and Maeve, tapping on Esther's face. 'Was she on your bus?'

The driver looked at the picture for a moment, his face creasing with indecision. Eventually, he took another look at my badge before letting his shoulders fall a touch.

'Yes. She was here.'

'Did she get off in this village?'

'She did. She was attacked and is staying at the taverna until she is better.'

I thanked the stars for small village gossip before another feeling crushed my gut. Someone had hurt Esther? Whom? I shouldn't care. If she didn't comply, I'd have to hurt her too, but it didn't stop the twisting in my stomach.

'Who hurt her?'

'A local, they don't know who, or so they say. The police are unlikely to come all the way out here for a tourist who's been mugged.'

Relief swept through me. So that's why she was still here. If she had been mugged, she'd have no access to money, which should make her much more amenable to being taken home. She'd never lived without money, never felt hunger gnawing at her stomach in the night like a pack of rabid rats. She'd never gone without. Maybe she'd even be glad I showed up to take her back.

'Thanks,' I said, stepping off the bus. 'Do you know where the taverna is?'

'Top of the hill.'

Within fifteen minutes, I was across the street from the taverna, trying to spot Esther amongst its patrons. There was an older couple running it from what I could see, but no sign of the green-eyed runaway. After an hour, my muscles were bunching, needing movement. Perhaps the driver's gossip was incorrect. Maybe she'd moved on after all. Either way, I needed a piss and something to drink, but couldn't use the taverna until I'd confirmed if she was there. I headed back down the hill, looking for somewhere to relieve myself.

A smirk stole across my face as I pulled myself into an alcove, spotting a curvy brunette sitting in a cafe. A shiver of excitement stole up my spine as I waited for her to turn. I was almost certain it was Esther. I'd know her freckled skin and the softness of her curves almost anywhere from my years of watching her. At last, she lowered her hand to the table and turned, looking around her as if sensing that she was being watched. My fists tensed as I saw a series of ugly brown-green bruises up her jawline, an old cut healing on her lip. The last time I'd seen those lips, they'd been perfectly pink and set in her unblemished freckled face as they wrapped around my cock. The mugger had done a number on her, and I wish I had time to find him and make him pay. I blinked hard, knowing that it was irrational to care. I was there to drag her back to a life she dreaded enough to leave everyone and everything she held dear behind. Hardly a Prince Charming.

She stood up, brushing crumbs from her clothes as she gathered up a shopping bag and swung it onto her shoulder. With a final, agitated look around, she started back up the hill.

I smiled as I went over to the cafe, dragging a finger along the rim of her cup where her lips had been before going inside.

I found you.

THIRTEEN
ESTHER

The evening had gone by in a flash, with the taverna being busier than usual with a quiz night that Jock hosted once a week. I didn't understand a word of the questions, but I enjoyed watching the excitement bubbling between the patrons.

As the last patrons stood to leave, I smiled over at Jock and Eva, his arm slung around her waist and her head on his shoulder. Their love was like a well-worn leather jacket, comfortable, warm, worn in by years gone by. A pang of want ate at my insides. I would kill to have that simple love with someone. To be the centre of someone's world. Not just in that first all-consuming lust, but in the comfortable love that comes with time gone by.

'I'll do the outside tables,' I said, loathe to break up their sweet moment. Grabbing a cloth and some cleaning spray, I made my way from table to table, wiping up the night's detritus. Then that same prickle from the morning snuck up my spine. Was it the mugger?

Frozen, I looked up and gasped when I saw someone altogether more dangerous watching me.

Alec.

How did he find me?

I stumbled back, dropping the bottle of cleaning fluid, feeling it splash up my leg as the top came off.

'No,' I said, fear making my insides crumble.

'Hello, Esther.' His voice was dark and gravelly, chock full of quiet anger.

'No!' I turned on my heel and ran back to the door, crying out when his fingers grabbed at my arm. Yanking hard as I turned into the doorway, I sent him stumbling over a low plant, his curses filling the air behind me.

Eva's eyes widened as I came dashing into the room. 'What's happening?'

'They found me.' Tears pricked as I tried to survey my options. Run? Hide?

There was no time. Alec stalked into the room, a gun drawn and pointed right at my chest.

Jock slid Eva behind him and straightened his shoulders despite the deadly weapon.

'I'm not going back,' I said, my words trembling as I forced them out of my mouth.

'Yes, you are.'

'You can't make me. I'd rather take the bullet than go back to Harold.'

'You nearly cost me my job. My fucking life!' Alec's nostrils flared as he barked the words at me. 'I'll take you back full of bullet holes if you like, but you will go back.'

Eva gripped Jock's hand as Alec stepped closer, the barrel of the gun staying directed at me. My breath came in hitches. Could I do it? Could I make him shoot me instead? I didn't want to die.

'I can't. I can't go back.'

'I will be fucked if I'm going to let some mafia princess

in a strop cost me everything I've worked for. We're not all born with a silver fucking spoon in our mouths.'

'You know Harold. You know it's not some life of pleasure that awaits me. He will hurt me and beat me and rape me. Every day until I go mad or die. He killed my mum and my brother. How can I stomach it?'

Alec's jaw ticked, and momentarily I saw a softening in his eyes, but all too quickly it was gone again. 'Not my problem. My job's fetching you back. What happens after that has fuck all to do with me. You shouldn't have used me as a pawn to get away, and then I wouldn't be here to drag your ass back. You made me do this.'

'He's old enough to be my dad. I won't shackle myself to him to win my father some syndicate points.' I started walking toward him, my knees quaking with each step. I'd force his hand, see how serious he was. He narrowed his eyes before swinging his gun to point it at Jock. My feet became leaden as I froze to the spot.

'Leave them alone. They have nothing to do with this.'

'They are harbouring a fugitive. I've killed people for less.' Alec's voice was bitter, and it sent a chill to my bones.

'Pretend you couldn't find me.'

'It would cost me too much.'

Eva trembled behind Jock, her hand going to her chest as her breathing became heavy.

'I can get you money.' I was running out of options. I couldn't let them get hurt on my behalf. They'd already done more than enough for me.

'Your father has put a stop on all of your accounts, so unless you're carrying a hundred grand's worth of jewels, you definitely can't.'

Fuck.

I'd have to go with him. I'd run out of cards to play.

'Can I at least say goodbye?'

Alec nodded tightly as I moved over and pulled Eva and Jock into a quick hug, their warmth even under attack sending a jolt straight to my heart.

'I'm so sorry,' I whispered under my breath. 'I didn't mean for this to come back on you guys. Thank you for everything.'

'You're a good lass. If you ever get away, we'd welcome you back any time.' Jock's Scottish lilt washed me with kindness.

'Go out of my window upstairs, across the roof, and down the back.' Eva fixed me with a hard stare. 'Head for the hills and hide there. We'll come find you.'

'I can't,' I said in a breath. 'He'll shoot you.'

'I'll take the risk. I have a feeling that under the bravado there is a boy who wouldn't shoot an old lady if he doesn't have to. Once you're gone, he'll go after you. When he does, Jock can go for his shotgun and protect us.'

'I can't risk it.'

'You will. For me. We've lost too many before their time. You deserve a chance.'

'That's enough.' Alec's voice made me jump. 'I don't have all day to stand here and let you say goodbye.'

'Can I get my things?' I asked, fixing him with what I hoped was a petulant glare.

'Fine. You've got five minutes.'

As I took the stairs, I looked back at Jock and Eva. From her spot behind her husband, she fixed me with a stern nod. Could I do it?

Guilt warred in me with every step. I knew Alec to be efficient, but not cruel. I knew he tortured and killed on my father and brother's behalf, but I hadn't known him to hurt anyone unnecessarily. Then again, I didn't know him all that well. He could be as bad as Harold, for all I knew.

My hand grazed on the door as I made it into my room and stuffed my toiletries and the few clean clothes I had into a bag that Eva had lent me after mine had been stolen. I shucked it on and snuck through to Eva and Jock's room. I'd never been in it before, but it was as cosy and sweet as they were. The bedside table stuffed with happy family photos from their years gone by caught my eye. The people they had loved and lost. It tore at my heart. I couldn't do it. Couldn't flee knowing they'd be at risk.

Then a creak sounded on the bottom stair. Fuck. He was coming. Which would give them time to get their shotgun.

The window slid open with a squeak that made me wince and I fed myself through the gap, my feet sliding against the slippery red roof tiles. I couldn't afford to lose my balance and break something falling off. I'd have to take it slowly.

My heart thundered in my chest as I picked my way over the rooftop, reaching the end, and lowering myself onto another. I needed to find a way down and quickly. Going roof to roof would slow me down way too much.

I took one last look at Eva's window and saw Alec's stony face. My heart all but stopped as he fixed me with a glare. I half expected him to tear through the window, but he turned and left the room.

Which made me all the more terrified.

Minutes later, a loud gunshot sounded in the night's air, taking my breath with it.

I continued on through a veil of tears.

FOURTEEN
ALEC

The little bitch!

She met my eyes as she lowered herself to the next roof and went scampering along it. I turned back from the window and stalked through the upper floor, heading for the stairs.

I would not risk breaking a leg following her, grappling on a rooftop was not my idea of a good time at all. If I followed the rooftops from below, I should be able to catch her when she dropped to the street.

Taking the stairs two at a time, I put my gun on safety, having no actual intention of killing the old folk who owned the place. As much as I'd used it as a threat, it was only to dissuade Esther from trying something stupid. Not that it had worked. Who knew she had it in her?

Halfway toward the door, I heard a cocking click to my right. I'd barely had time to glance at the old guy, his fucking shotgun pointed at my midriff. I cursed and ran toward the doorway, stalling as my gun caught against a table and slid across the stone flooring. A loud bang made my ears ache and my stomach lurch. Crumbling brick tore away from the wall to my left as I ducked out of the room, the shot having only just missed me.

Sweat slicked at my palms as I ran around the building, another shot coming through a window and taking out a plant in a shower of green shards just in front of me.

Where the hell was Esther?

I dodged around the stone buildings, finding a narrow alleyway and making my way through it, all the while keeping my eyes fixed on the rooftops. Finally, I spied a swish of brown hair before it disappeared over the edge of another roof.

Gotcha.

With a look behind me coming up negative for shotgun-wielding maniacs, I darted across the cobbled stones and around the corner of a building, just in time to see her feet hit the ground.

Her eyes widened as she spotted me, cursing as she hightailed it down the hill. But she wasn't quick enough. My legs were longer, and I wasn't tired from hauling myself about rooftops. The distance between us shortened with each step, my heart rate increasing as I closed in on her.

Within a hundred yards, I reached out and grabbed her around the waist, pulling her back against me as I panted. She fought like an enraged fucking badger, nails scratching and legs flailing as I struggled to subdue her.

'Just stop,' I said, reaching into my pocket and grabbing a handful of cable ties - one of my favourite tools.

'You killed them.' The accusation stung as she battered at my face with clawed fists.

'No, I didn't. The old fucker was shooting at me.'

Shock ripped at me as she let out a full, throaty, somewhat demented laugh. 'I wish they'd hit you.'

Her skin was warm as I yanked both hands in front of

her and secured them together with three cable ties, one around each wrist and then one tying them together. Her eyes flashed dangerously as I pushed her back against a wall, holding her secured hands above her head.

Anger mixed with heat as she looked up at me with hatred in those big green eyes. Nothing like a tied-up hottie panting to get me going. Her chest rose and fell as we stood there for a moment, catching our breath.

'Does this turn you on you sick fuck?' she whispered, ire dripping from her voice.

'Maybe it does. Thinking of you with your hands tied and your lips on my dick does.' It was a bad idea to go there, but the last time I'd seen her still flashed into my head while looking down into her freckled face.

'You can't touch me. You know it.'

'Who says I'd be the one doing the touching? Plus, no one said I had to return you in one piece. A few gun holes, knife marks, or filled with my fucking cum. No one cares as long as I hand you over to him in the next few days.'

I saw it hit her; her face crumpling as a tear tracked down her cheek. Good. I wanted her too fucking scared to try any more of this shit. She was exhausting.

'Now we're going to walk down this hill and get into my car and drive to Barcelona to get your ass home as soon as possible. If you fight, I will come down harder on you.'

'I'm not afraid of you.'

'You should be.'

'Why Barcelona? Madrid is closer.'

'Because I can get you on a flight tomorrow night in Barcelona, and I don't want to waste one more fucking minute than necessary on you.'

I turned her and gripped her arm, digging my fingers in

so she didn't doubt my hold on her. The bruises on her face still filled me with a rage that I had no business feeling.

She stumbled as I quickened our pace, wanting to get her secured in my car as quickly as possible. A few locals raised an eye at us as we made our way down the hill and toward the edge of the village, but no one interfered. Thank god. I was too exhausted to fight them all.

As we approached the car, some hooded guy was jimmying the window.

'Hey,' I shouted, startling him as he met my eyes.

That's when I felt Esther stiffen next to me. I looked at her as the man backed up a step.

'What?' I asked.

'I think…' Her face had turned ashen as she stared at the man. 'I think he's the one who attacked me. I bit his hand…'

I walked toward the car, clicking it unlocked with the fob before roughly shoving her into the passenger seat. The guy took off at a run. I locked her in before heading after him. It was stupid. I should have let him go. But if he hurt her, well fuck, I saw red.

He didn't stand a chance. With pure rage fuelling my steps, I caught him quickly, not understanding a word of the Spanish he threw at me.

Esther's eyes were saucer wide through the windscreen as I turned the guy around and made him face her, my knife at his back.

I reached down and pulled his hand up, seeing a dirty bandage covering his palm. The fucker had better hope he'd had an accident with a kitchen knife. With a yank it came off, fluttering down onto the bonnet of my car. I grabbed his wrist and held it up to the soft glow of a nearby streetlight. A perfect round set of teeth marks blazed against his skin, infection setting with raised red and yellowing pus in at one edge.

Every muscle in me tensed as I twisted his hand painfully and held it up for Esther to see. She nodded softly, and it ripped a hole in me to think of his hands hurting her. Pinning her and brutalising her. Sure, I was no hero, but jumping on random girls in the street was deplorable. Especially Esther. I might be furious at her, but I was going to let that fucker feel the full force of my wrath.

He struggled against me as I lifted my knife to his face, dragging it down over his jaw, feeling it slip through his skin as though he were a soft fruit. The squeal he let out paid for the bruises he'd left on her jawline. The tears as I slit the sides of his mouth were for the broken lips he'd given her with his fists.

Esther was pale and still as she watched the blood splatter down on the silver bonnet of the car. When I slipped my sweet, sharp knife to his throat, he wet himself. They so often did. His voice was a babble of pleading. You didn't need to understand someone's words to know when they'd reached the pleading for their life stage.

His body stiffened as I severed the artery in his neck, letting his life force leak out as Esther watched. She didn't revel in his death. She looked sickened.

I let his body slump to the floor, wiping my blade on his coat to clean it off before closing it and slipping it back into my pocket.

Esther might hate me, but I was nothing if not loyal, and I worked for her family. I had a duty to protect them, even if it meant dragging her back to a man she hated.

I told myself it was loyalty and justice that led me to extinguish her mugger, but a tiny little annoying voice at the back of my head mocked me. Told me it was more than that.

Ignoring it, I got into the car and heaved a sigh of relief. What a fucking day.

Esther sat awkwardly beside me, her lip trembling and her face still tear-stained, while she sat forward in her chair, her limp rucksack still jutting behind her. There wasn't a chance I was cutting off the cable ties, so I reached up to her, grasping a strap in one hand and bringing back out my knife. She flinched as it flicked outward, her eyes darting to mine before going back to the blade.

It slipped easily through the old material, and similarly on the other side. I threw it onto the back seat before putting my knife away and leaning across her.

'What are you doing?' she whispered as my face pressed dangerously close to hers.

'Putting your seatbelt on,' I answered, grabbing the belt and pulling it across her torso, fitting it as best as I could around her secured hands. 'Can't have you dying in a crash after all the trouble I've gone to, can I?'

Silence enveloped the car as I backed out of the spot. The mugger's body lay slumped on the floor in a pool of his blood. If anyone else touched her, I wouldn't hesitate to do it again. Fuck, I wished I could kill her husband-to-be for putting her through this shit. But I knew my place in the pecking order. The mugger was fair game. The main man in Glasgow's most influential syndicate wasn't. I had no desire to join the mugger in hell. Not for someone who could never be mine, anyway.

Flicking on the radio to drown out the silence, I settled in for the long drive to Barcelona. With good luck, we should be on the first available flight the following night, and I could pay off my house and put this whole mess behind me.

We'd driven for thirty minutes or so before she muttered a thank you so softly that I almost missed it.

I pretended I hadn't heard it.

How had she been in that village a few days, and found people willing to take her in, to protect her and be willing to shoot a stranger for her? How had she had me willing to kill a stranger for her? I'd spent my life looking for a family, a place to belong, and still didn't have a place I fitted into. She'd left everything behind and found another family within a fortnight. It's all I'd ever wished for.

Which confirmed one thing.

It wasn't impossible to find that love and loyalty. I just didn't deserve it.

I'd stick to what I was good at.

Being a paid killer and torturer for people who had everything I'd ever wanted.

And would never have.

FIFTEEN

ESTHER

My eyes felt like sandpaper lined the lids as I stared at the road ahead. We were already a few hours closer to Barcelona, and with each passing mile, terror gripped me anew. I had to escape, or at least delay our flight back until I could speak sense into Alec. For the years he'd been around my family, I'd been so certain that he wasn't a pile of shit. He was proving me wrong.

I let my eyes close, just for a second or two, sweet relief flooding me. Until the sight of fresh blood hitting the bonnet yanked me back out of my minute-long rest. The mugger was dead. Because of me. Sure, he was trying to break into Alec's car, but it was him hurting me that signed his death warrant. My fault that he no longer breathed.

Mixed feelings assaulted my insides at the thought. Relief. Guilt. Anger. I hadn't asked Alec to kill him for me, and I still wasn't one hundred percent sure why he had.

Sneaking a glance over at Alec, I sighed. His eyes remained steadfast on the road, ignoring me as solidly as he had for the previous few hours. A muscle ticked in his jaw, and his fingers were almost white at the knuckles where he gripped at the wheel.

I'd tried to throw myself from the vehicle twice already. The first I'd opened the door, but he'd grabbed me by the hair and dragged me back into my seat without a word. The second time, he'd activated the child locks, making my handle useless. He ignored that attempt entirely.

I watched as his eyelids fluttered and dipped. Fuck, he was going to get us killed.

'You need to rest,' I said, trying to get my hands comfortable where they sat still fastened in my lap.

'No.'

'A few hours wouldn't hurt. It's the middle of the night, and you're half asleep. If you are going to kill yourself on the way to the airport, you might as well let me out right here.'

Another tick of the jaw and silence.

There were no lights ahead of us, and the villages we'd gone through recently were small and dark; everyone already bedded for the night. There were no Travel Lodges or Premier Inns in sight.

My eyes dipped again as I jolted myself awake. The car veered leftward as he did the same. I pushed my tied hands against the dashboard as my heart thundered in my chest.

'Please?' I asked, not above begging.

Nothing.

Within a few minutes, he'd pulled off of the main road and slowed the car to a halt in a lay-by overladen with trees. He tipped his head back against the headrest and closed his eyes for a few seconds before looking over at me with a half-lidded gaze.

'Only a few hours.'

'I need to pee.'

He groaned and unbuckled his seat belt, opening his door as the chilly night air wrapped around me.

My door wrenched open next as he reached in to undo my belt and pull me up to standing. Prickles ran up and down my legs as the new position brought life back into them. My ass was entirely numb.

Alec pulled me over to a tree and crossed his arms, waiting.

'Can you at least turn around? It's going to be hard enough to pull my jeans down and avoid getting piss on them with my hands tied.'

'I can't trust you not to run.'

'I won't, I promise.'

'Fool me once and all that.'

'Please? What if I sing the whole time so you can hear where I am? I can't run anywhere for long with my hands like this, and we are miles from civilisation.'

I watched as he mulled over my words and looked about, assessing the situation. 'Fine, you have two minutes, Princess.'

I didn't have time to mull over his nickname for me as he leant against the other side of the tree.

Trying to get my jeans down over my hips was a workout in itself. I huffed as I tried to pull them down one side at a time, the material barely budging.

Alec looked at me as I scowled. 'I don't hear singing.'

'I can't get my jeans down.'

I was startled as he turned and walked over, his hands gripping roughly at the waistband and hauling my jeans down over my ass, my underpants going with them.

'Hey!' I shouted, trying to cover myself up with my hands.

'Nothing I haven't seen before.'

'Not on me.'

'No, but it's all the same. Now hurry up before I throw you back in the car and leave you to piss your panties.'

I cursed under my breath as I leant awkwardly against the tree trunk and closed my eyes, willing my bladder to empty.

'Do I need to come back there?'

I growled as I let out a few bars of a tune, my face red as the audible splash of my wee filled the air. But oh, it felt good to let it go.

Peeing was only half the problem, though. I had nothing to wipe with, nor could I pull back up my trousers.

'Do you have any tissues?' I asked, my cheeks burning all the brighter.

'No.'

'I need something to wipe myself.'

Before I could say another word, his footsteps crunched toward me. I shrieked as I looked over at him to see his knife glinting at his side.

'What are you doing?' I stumbled backward as sweat pricked at the back of my neck.

'Wiping you.' His answer was gruff as he reached down into my trousers and sliced at my lace underpants.

'Stop it,' I said as the knife snicked through both sides of the material, my face screwing up as he bunched my panties in his hand. He pulled me roughly away from the trunk where I had supported myself and used my panties to wipe me from front to back in one swift motion.

'Alec, what the fuck?'

'You needed to wipe. It's all that was available. Now stop your caterwauling or I'll use them as a gag next.'

I narrowed my eyes at him as he leaned down and

pulled my jeans up, taking the time to fasten them at my belly before roughly leading me back to the car.

The whole time my eyes and mind went to escape. Could I run? Slip out while he slept? Get his knife and take him out while he snored? There had to be something I could do.

When we got back to the car, he reached into his bag and grabbed a small bottle, putting a splodge of the cold gel into my hands and his. 'Antibacterial gel. It's the best I've got in lieu of a sink.'

'Why do you care if my hands are clean?'

'Because they are about to be awfully close to me.' He stood inches from me as he opened the back door of the car, stopping to tuck a flyaway strand of hair behind my ear. Somehow, that felt a lot more intimate than the fact he'd just wiped my ass. 'Get in.'

He dashed all of my escape hopes when he pushed me into the back seat and climbed in beside me. My pulse increased as we sat in the cramped space like a bunch of awkward teens. In another life, it could have meant something very different between us. Now, all I wanted was to be a million miles from him.

He pulled another cable tie from his pocket and looped it through the ones at my wrists, securing me to his belt loop.

'Very mature,' I said, scowling, as all my plans for the night died. If I so much as struggled, he'd know.

'Lay down and shut up,' he said through a yawn as he settled back against the seat, one tattooed arm slung across the back seat headrests.

The only way I could lie was on my side, with my hands against his crotch and my head on his lap. I wriggled into position, offering a litany of curses upon my breath as I all but snuggled up to his nether region.

'There's a good girl. Now close your eyes and sleep. I'm fucking exhausted.' He reached down and traced a finger over my jaw as I shivered. As much as I hated him, his words filled me with a dash of warmth. I wasn't a bloody pet. He shouldn't be speaking to me like one. Everyone outside of our family had always treated me with nothing but the utmost respect. And my father had never been one to coddle us. So why did Alec's praise feel good despite him being the second worst person in the world to me at the moment?

Why did I want to hear him call me a good girl again? And again?

I had no idea.

As his breath settled into a soothing rhythm, I searched my brain for a way out. A way to grab freedom by the horns. But there was nothing I could do. At least not that night. His musky scent filled my nostrils as I shifted against him. Not unpleasant, but both manly and clean. His arm drifted down from the backrest and settled on my hip, sending warring thoughts attacking me all over again. He was an attractive man with his dark blond hair and his well-muscled and tattoo-laden arms.

Sleep wrapped its inky tendrils around me as Alec's body heat lulled me with its treacherous warmth.

Sleep claimed me quickly, filling my head with images of running and running, but instead of getting away, I always found myself in Alec's arms, with a good girl on his lips.

SIXTEEN
ALEC

I woke up with the sun's first, far too bright rays. Esther snored softly against my crotch in an entirely too distracting manner. It didn't help that morning wood was very much in attendance as her breath heated my dick.

What was I thinking strapping her to my belt loops?

Well, to be fair, it had stopped her from trying to escape and given us both a few hours of rest without me needing to fight with her.

She'd given me far more fight than I'd expected. Her whole life she'd been spoiled with everything she could even think to ask for, and she should have crumpled at being surrounded by strangers, beaten badly, and with none of her worldly goods. She should have been welcoming my appearance with open arms as the vehicle back to her charmed life. But she'd given far more fight than I'd have ever given her credit for. If only it wasn't so fucking annoying.

Travelling with captives was not a skill I'd honed. Far less with one I couldn't afford to incapacitate in any real way.

And definitely, never one who had sucked my dick so fucking well that I still thought about it almost hourly.

Her lips were only a hair's breadth from my hard dick, and I wanted nothing more than to slip it free and have her take it in her mouth, muttering sweet sorries in between tongue strokes for all the shit she'd put me through. The tied wrists were all the hotter. I'd dabbled in the occasional slap and tickle with others, but it had never quite hit me the way it did, looking down at Esther's pink cheeks and thick eyelashes. Utterly at my mercy.

Luckily for her, I wasn't one to just take what I wanted.

Reaching down, I flexed her fingers in mine, checking for any discolouring or coldness from loss of circulation, but while the plastic ties held firm, they weren't causing any issues.

Her hair was soft as I pushed it out of her face, threading it behind an ear. She stirred, confusion wrinkling her nose as she tried to move her arms but found them still fixed to my belt. Her eyes blinked open as she looked around, remembering where she was.

'Is your dick hard?' she asked, her eyes widening as the back of her hand moved against me.

'Morning wood, nothing out of the ordinary.'

Esther licked her lips before slowly blinking, fixing those green eyes on me. 'I could help you out with it.'

Surprise made me cough to clear my throat. The thought of her pretty pink lips wrapped around my shaft was more than a little tempting. Last time, it had been sinfully good. It was a dangerous path, though. 'No.'

Her brow furrowed as she shifted, sitting herself up as much as she could with her hands still attached to me. 'I'd do anything to be let go. For you to pretend, what would it take? My mouth? My pussy? Hell, I'd let you fuck my ass if it would make a difference.'

My dick hardened even more as images of her succumbing to me, moaning and writhing beneath me as I filled each hole one by one, filtered into my head. The images were hot and vivid, and they fucking wrecked me. It would be no good to let her see how the idea of her on the end of my dick affected me.

'Not even your spoiled ass is worth losing my reward for getting you back,' I said, shifting so I could get my knife from my pocket and slipping it through the cable tie that held us together, leaving the ones securing her hands intact.

A quiet fury marred her face as she sat up and glared at me, stretching out her shoulders as much as she could. 'I would make it worth it. You could do anything you wanted to me. A perfect little sex pet to use however you liked.'

Dirty words from such a perfect, prissy little mafia daughter. Fuck, they did bad, bad things to me. It wouldn't take much to pick her up and seat her over my dick, to remove the clothing between us and slide right into her. Within a minute or two, I could be balls deep in her heat. It would be the most expensive fuck I'd ever have. No woman is worth a hundred grand. No matter how filthy the sex.

'As sweet as the offer is, Esther, I've got a better offer from your brother. There's plenty of pussy out there, but money doesn't just throw itself at you every day. Well, maybe it does for rich daddy's girls, but not for people like me.'

She remained quiet; the anger bubbling just beneath the surface of her face.

'Plus, you can't live out here with nothing. There's a family who cares about you enough to send me to track you down waiting at home. You are used to getting everything handed to you on a silver platter. The real world is tough, and it's difficult to scrape by. You already lost everything, and that mugger could have killed you. He could have raped you, or kidnapped you and not a soul would have known. You can't go to the authorities without documents. You can't tell anyone your real name. You failed. Face it.'

'I was figuring it out. You know nothing about me. Your head is so far up your ass you only see what you think to be true.'

'What's that supposed to mean?'

'It doesn't matter. Let's get going.'

Within twenty minutes, we were back on the road, her livid silence gnawing at me from the passenger seat.

A LOUD RUMBLING came from across the car. Esther steadfastly ignored the absolute racket coming from her stomach. But I couldn't.

We had time to make a stop, and I'd need to fuel up, anyway. I'd just need to make sure she couldn't leave the car while I did. A few miles later, I pulled into a roadside fuel station. Her eyes darted from one spot to another, always eagerly looking for a way to escape. I smirked, knowing there wasn't a hope in hell she'd get away.

Silencing the engine, I looked over at her. She avoided my eyes entirely. Using two cable ties, I attached her belt loops to her seatbelt. Without a knife to free herself, there was no way for her to break through them.

'Overkill, don't you think?' she muttered, finally meeting my eyes.

'Can't have you slipping out of the car while I'm in the

shop. I've a feeling you couldn't behave yourself if you tried.'

'I'm pretty sure avoiding Harold is behaving in my best interest.'

'Mmm.' I reached into my bag and grabbed my wallet, pocketing a handful of cash before getting out and stretching while locking the car. My back was in bits from sleeping sat up. I consoled myself that within a few hours, we'd reach the airport. By the following night, I'd be back in my bed.

I filled the car up with diesel before heading into the shop and scanning the food on offer. It was mostly junk food, easy to eat while driving. What did Esther like? I pushed down the concern, telling myself she should be happy with whatever she bloody well gets. But I couldn't ignore the fact that I wanted her to at least have something she liked. Every few seconds I'd glance back up to the car, making sure no one approached it, and that she didn't do anything stupid like yelling at a passer-by. The fuel station exterior remained blissfully deserted, thankfully.

Ten minutes, and one laden basket later, I paid for the fuel and food, heading back to the car. Esther sat still in her seat, looking straight forward as I opened the door. I sighed and heaved my bag into the spot between our seats.

'Hope you're hungry,' I said, grinning as her stomach responded when she failed to.

SEVENTEEN

ESTHER

I looked around desperately for something to separate my belt loops from the seatbelt when he left me in the car. There was nothing that would cut through cable ties. I puffed and panted and tried to pull at the ties with my bound hands, but all it did was hurt.

Frustration zapped my energy as I struggled uselessly. I needed to get away. Within hours we'd be in Barcelona, being shoved onto a plane bound for Glasgow. Within a day, I could be in Harold's clutches. Dread clawed at me at the thought. No fucking way.

Alec had taken the keys but left his wallet. I opened it with one of my bound hands and grinned as an idea formed. I might not escape, but if I could slow down progress enough so he'd miss the flight, and destroy his capability to book another... well, that might buy me time.

To hinder him from booking more flights, there were two things I'd have to remove: his funds and his communication. He'd taken his phone with him, but usually placed it in the centre console as he drove so it didn't dig into his ass. I'd deal with that later.

Stealing a look at the shop, I saw him still browsing. I had to work quickly.

I pulled out the cards in there. There were a few. My fingers ached as I turned them painfully against my bonds, until, at last, one by one, they snapped. Using the sharp edge where he'd cut the long strips from the cable ties, I scratched into the chip's surface on each broken card, doing my best to make every single one unreadable.

My fingers trembled as he walked up to the counter in the store to pay. Shoving the cards back in and sitting them just so, so they looked intact unless you pulled one out, I paused when a photograph fell into my lap. It was a little Alec; I was sure. His face was younger and sweet, and he smiled like I'd never seen him smiling before. A real, open, sweet smile. He was sitting on a woman's lap, while a man who looked a lot like Alec slung his arm around him. Alec couldn't have been more than three or four. What had happened to the cheery soul who beamed? Nowadays, Alec rarely smiled, and never with such openness. He was careful, measured, and cold. Mostly. With my brothers, he was a touch warmer, always looking for their validation. I had always presumed that it was for business reasons. Maybe there was more to it?

I cursed as he left the shop, shoving the photograph back in and placing his wallet where he'd left it, praying he wouldn't check the cards for a while. The phone would be my next mission, and then delaying tactics. I just had to make him miss the flight.

The door opened, and Alec thrust a very full bag of food into the middle of the car, sliding himself in beside me.

'Hope you're hungry,' he said, grinning at me as he closed the door behind him.

'I'm not.' Mostly because nerves were tumbling around my stomach, filling it to the brim with butterflies.

'Too bad. You need to eat. I won't let you starve yourself.'

I hadn't eaten since the churros the previous day, and my stomach growled despite me.

'What do you want? Crisps? Chocolate? Fruit? A sandwich?'

He took item after item out of the bag, looking entirely too pleased with himself.

'Can you cut my hands free? The rice dish looks good, but I'll make a mess if I try to eat like this.' Anything for a step closer to freedom.

'Don't worry, I'll feed you Princess.'

Heat flushed upward at the very idea. 'You will not.'

'Your choice. You can just watch me eat if you prefer.'

I pursed my lips as he opened a packet containing a hot, meat-filled pastry. Steam wafted up from it as he broke a piece of flaky, buttery pastry off and put it in his mouth. The bliss that washed over his face was enough to tell me it was good. As the spiced smell filled the car, my stomach gave a great, angry growl. Looking at the front window, I did my best to ignore him, but with every bite he took, my stomach revolted more aggressively.

When there was only a small bite of the pastry left, he held it out to me and waited.

Swallowing hard, I dragged my eyes from the morsel of food to his face. Heat filled my cheeks as I gave in and turned toward him, leaning forward and accepting the food from his fingers.

'Oh my god,' I mumbled as the butter-filled pastry hit my tongue. The meat was spicier than I'd been expecting, and my mouth watered. Fuck, I really was hungry.

Shame caressed at the edges of my mind, telling me I shouldn't be eating from my captor's fingers. That it was dirty and demeaning. But as he broke apart a sweet nut-filled pastry, I kicked those feelings to the side. It was by and large the most weirdly intimate thing I'd done with a near stranger, way more intimate than the rushed blow job I'd given him before escaping my marriage.

His pupils dilated as I took the food from him, licking a piece of the nutty mixture from his fingers and groaning with delight as the sweet, creamy flavour suffused through me. My stomach fluttered at the intensity of his gaze as he watched me eat, giving me more and more of the food until he was hardly eating at all, just feeding me.

'When you stop fighting, you can be delightful,' he muttered, bringing out the rice dish and offering me it from his fingers.

I should have fought it or felt disgusted, but we'd moved beyond just eating to something that left me wanting to see him smile with those blown pupils fixed on me. There was something addictive about being looked at the way he fixated on me. I hadn't ever had anyone look at me with such rapturous attention before, and it was making me feel dangerous things. Making me want to climb up in his lap and lick the food from his lips. Making me want to know what it would be like to be under that gaze with less space between us, fewer clothes between us. Have him call me a good girl again...

'So pretty,' he mumbled as he dragged a thumb over my lower lip, wiping away an errant piece of rice and tucking it into my mouth as I captured the thumb between my lips. 'But so much trouble.'

With that, I caught myself and shook myself from the lusty little trance I'd given in to. What the fuck was I doing?

Alec was dragging me home. Would have me delivered to Harold by the morning. I was reading far too much into a look. He was just a horny guy taking advantage of a situation. He was an ass for keeping me tied up. I could bloody well feed myself.

I sat back and stared out of the window, clearing my throat and breaking the moment. 'We should get going.'

'Eager to go home? Does that mean you are going to stop fighting me?'

'Yeah. I give up.'

'Good. Because you will not get away from me again.'

A whisper of need gripped at me with his words, imagining he said them because he wanted to keep me—imagining a man wanting me so badly, he'd do anything to keep me.

But I had that in Harold. Unfortunately, it wasn't love making him crazy for me; it was power, revenge, and a need for control.

The scenery soon sped by as we hit the road again, heading far too quickly toward Barcelona. I hoped he believed me when I said that I gave up.

It would make it easier for the next part of my plan to go smoothly.

FORTY-FIVE MINUTES HAD PASSED before we reached the perfect spot alongside a quickly flowing river that had trees interspersed near the shoreline. Open enough that Alec might let me go down to the tree on my own to wee.

His phone still sat in the centre console, and I itched to grab it and run. Slowly, Esther, you need to do it slowly.

'Alec,' I asked, keeping my voice soft and unhurried, 'I need to pee.'

'The next village is only a couple of miles away. Just wait, and I'll find a rest stop.'

I moved in my seat as though I was getting desperate. 'I can't wait that long.'

'You can.'

'I really don't want to sit in a puddle of piss for the next few hours. The car would stink.'

Holding a breath, I waited as he scanned the view outside. I blinked through wide eyes when he looked at me and attempted to employ my very best poor little lamb face. It was becoming obvious that he enjoyed being dominant in some form, and enjoyed the sweet sub thing, so I worked to amp it up.

'Please, Alec?' I wheedled, shifting in my seat and pressing my bound hands between my thighs. Satisfaction rushed through me as I saw the exact moment he caved. His shoulders dropped, and he ran a hand through his hair with a sigh.

'Fine. But make it quick, and don't start any funny business.'

'Thank you.'

He pulled the car into the side of the road and got out, coming round the back to open my door. With my stomach in my mouth, I quickly grabbed his phone and slipped it into the waistband of my jeans. My heart thundered as my door opened, hoping he didn't look for his phone. He cut me from the ties that held me to my seatbelt.

'Can you do these too? So I can pull down my jeans myself?' I held out my hands.

Alec looked around once more, clearly deciding we were far enough from anywhere I could successfully outrun him. I was no cross-country runner. Speed was not on my side.

'Fine, but try to run and I will use so many cable ties you won't be able to move, and next time, I'll let you sit in your piss.'

I could have cried when the knife split the ties, freedom feeling that bit closer. Rubbing at the pressure marks they left, I smiled up at him, getting myself out of the car.

'Thanks,' I said, touching his arm gently and trying to keep my cool while it felt like his phone was burning my waist. With every second, I was sure he'd discover what I was up to. 'I'm just going to go over behind that tree there.'

He clenched his teeth as he followed where I pointed before he nodded tersely. 'Fine. Be quick. We're already cutting it fine for making it to the airport.'

I picked my way over the dry grass toward the tree and smirked to myself. We'd be a hell of a lot later, soon.

The tree was close enough to the water's edge that I'd only need to dash down a few steps and launch the phone. I considered just running down and doing it quickly, not caring if he saw, but I needed him not to realise until I got back to the car at the earliest.

I turned around and shouted back to him, 'I'm going to wash my hands in the river after, is that okay?'

'If you like.' Came the reply, and I had to stop myself from squealing with glee.

It was working!

He'd regret trying to drag me back to Glasgow.

EIGHTEEN
ALEC

The car's exterior was warm against my back, where the sun had heated it. The countdown was on to get to the airport, and every minor delay was making me antsy. I shifted from foot to foot while keeping my eyes fixed on Esther.

Trusting her not to run was playing on me. When had I become so soft? Prisoners were prisoners, no matter how much they turned on the charm. I hated to admit it, but she was carving a soft spot inside of me as easily as she could punch one into a peach. It was stupid. Even if she wasn't running from a shit marriage to an awful person, she would never pick me. Esther was rich, beautiful, and apart from the mafia rules, could do what she liked.

Undoing another button on my shirt, I shifted as Esther momentarily ducked out of view. Tension infused my thighs as I stood up from my place against the car, ready to go after her if she dared to run. But she didn't.

Before I could take a step, she was walking toward me, those full hips dipping with each step as she wiped wet hands against her jeans. Her dark hair floated in the breeze, glittering under the high sun, and as she came closer, each of her perfect little freckles came into view.

What I wouldn't do to have all the drama back home disappear. To be on the side of a road with a beautiful girl, the sun shining on me, and nowhere to be, no one to answer too.

That life wasn't for me, though.

Maybe I'd reward myself with a holiday after I paid the house off. Go somewhere where people don't give a shit if you're a loner.

'Thanks,' Esther said as she came up to me with a saccharine smile. Like butter wouldn't melt. 'Needed that.'

She kept flicking her eyes to the car behind me, looking more nervous than I'd expected. What had her so antsy?

'No worries. We should get back on the road.'

'Wait--' Before I could breathe, she was up against me, my pulse quickening as she blinked up at me with those Bambi-like eyes. 'I want to thank you properly.'

'It's fine.' Every muscle in me quivered as I tried to ignore the honey-like promise her voice held. I turned to open her door but froze when her fingers slid down my back, grazing over the muscles and leaving me numb in their wake. The intimacy of it sent my brain into meltdown. How long had it been since someone had touched me gently? Fuck, I had no idea.

'Esther.' I couldn't decide if her name was an invitation or an admonishment. Was she interested, or was it another delaying tactic?

'You are always so tense,' she murmured, smoothing her fingers over the knots in my neck and then slipping her hands down the length of my spine. I closed my eyes as goose pimples adorned my arms.

'I've always got a good reason to be tense.'

'Yes,' she said. 'I know.'

Her answer was odd, but her warm hands on me were far too heavenly to ignore. What would she do if I turned and gathered her up in my arms? Would she let me kiss her? Would her tongue be eager and wanting, or would she reject me? Would she come apart under my fingers, or was is just another way to delay the inevitable?

But then there was nothing but air behind me. I turned as she slipped away from me. Then I heard the familiar click of my knife. The little fucker had robbed me. And now she was armed. She held the knife in her fist, my eyes darting between the gleaming blade and her face.

'Are you going to stab me?' I said, narrowing my eyes at her. Pain danced in my chest as I realised it had all been a ruse again.

'No. I'm going to stab this.'

Before I could reach her, she stabbed my knife sharply into the tyre, leaving it embedded deep into the rubber.

'You little bitch.' She took off at a run, but she wasn't quick enough. I tore my knife from the tyre and ran after her. With each step I gained on her, my fury grew until it was a molten, bubbling, uncontainable thing.

Her feet hit the ground with a steady thrum, her hair whipping out behind her, and I almost laughed at the ridiculousness of the situation. We were in the middle of nowhere. She knew she couldn't get away.

I seized a fistful of her top and yanked her back as she let out a yelp, toppling the two of us to the floor in a tangle of limbs. Esther fought like a hellcat, limbs flying, nails scouring, and curse words littering the surrounding air.

'Stop fighting,' I said, pinning her beneath me with my legs over hers, and my hands gripping her wrists above her head. Dry, dusty mud smudged on her face as she finally gave in and lay there beneath me, her chest raising and falling rapidly as she caught her breath.

My knife was still open and gripped in the one hand that held her. She looked at it and swallowed hard. Good, she could be done with a dose of fear.

If I thought she'd been cow-towed, I was entirely incorrect.

'We're going to miss our flight, aren't we?' she breathed, a smirk crossing her petulant face.

'Not if I can help it. Even if we do, there will be another one in the morning. All you're doing is delaying the inevitable.'

She shifted beneath me, sending warring feelings into my groin. She was making my job difficult, and making me look like an idiot, and anger still bubbled through me, but her soft body pressed beneath me was a fantasy in itself. If only she wasn't such a pain in the fucking ass.

'I'm not going back,' she said with enough intention to show me she really believed that was a viable option.

'You're going back if it's the last job I do. I will not be fucked over by a spoiled brat.'

'That's what this is about, isn't it? You think I'm not worth real love because I had a privileged upbringing? That I deserve this shitty marriage.'

It cut because it was partly true. She had a much better life than I did, and she was going to throw it all away because she had to marry some fucker she hated. He'd probably be dead within a few years anyway with the amount of enemies he'd wracked up.

'I don't care about you or your marriage or any of the shit behind this job. I've been paid to do a job and I will do it. I care about my reputation.'

She deliberately ground her hips upward, sending a jolt

through me as she grazed against my cock. 'There is more to life than your reputation. I could give you the time of your life and then we could go our separate ways and you can say that you couldn't find me.'

'You are nothing but a fucking brat. You're lucky I don't take a finger for stabbing my tyre. I'm sure your father wouldn't begrudge me one or two for the shit you are putting me through.'

'You wouldn't.'

'Stop testing me or you'll find out.'

I heaved myself off of her and secured her wrists behind her back with some more cable ties, dragging her roughly back to the car and launching her into the back seat.

Pulling up the floor of the car's trunk, I punched the back of the headrest in front of me, needing an outlet for the frustration building inside of me. There was no spare in the gap at the back, only some foam to limp the car to a mechanic. My knuckles smarted as I pulled out the can and attempted to fill the tyre, the foam bubbling out of the slit she'd made.

I'd call ahead to the next town and see if there was someone there who could fix it today, and just take it slow and hope we could get it there.

When I opened my door and leaned into the car to grab my phone, it wasn't there. I slapped my pockets but came up empty. Reaching into the back, I pulled out my rucksack and upended it in my seat, shifting through my clothing and toiletries. Nothing.

Esther was lying in the backseat where I'd thrown her and blinked away when I tried to meet her eyes.

'Where is my phone, Esther?'

She ignored me. I threw my body over the seat and

grabbed her by the throat, digging my fingers into the sides as she tried to wriggle away.

'Where the fuck is it?'

She wetted her lips as she smirked, not knowing when to stop pushing me. 'In the river.'

I saw red. I wanted to hurt her. To lay claim to my threats like I usually would with an uncooperative prisoner. My fingers dug further into her flesh as her face reddened. She replaced the smirk with genuine fear. Fear that stopped me in my tracks. I may have been fucking livid, but deep down, I didn't want Esther to fear me. Some tiny part of me, way deep down, liked the brat. Admired her tenacity and her willingness to do whatever it took to get her way. Unfortunately, she used that against me.

She drew a sharp breath as I let her throat go, tears stinging at the edge of her eyes.

'I'm not sorry,' she said.

It took everything in me to temper my anger to a workable level, from deep breaths to digging my fingernails into my palms. There was no way we'd make the flight, but I'd just have to get to the next town and book another one. Staring out of the window at the road unfurling before us, I sighed. There was nothing for it but to try to limp the car to the next village and hope someone would contact a mechanic for me.

NINETEEN

ESTHER

Alec's anger was palpable, even from the back seat where he'd thrown me. The silence inside the car was brutal, contrasting with the awful noise from the wheel with the flat tyre. The small town was finally coming into view as the last golden rays of the setting sun lit up the buildings.

Alec locked me in the car, slamming the door on his way out as he headed into a ramshackle motel. Carrying his wallet. Containing all the cards I had destroyed. I moved to try the door for good measure, but with my wrists now secured behind my back, it was a pointless endeavour. I waited for the inevitable fallout.

It came soon enough.

He stalked over the parking lot toward me, his eyes ablaze as he neared me. I shrank against the backseat, trying to make myself as small as possible, as if that would help me.

The door groaned as he wrenched it open, and before I knew it, he was on top of me, my arms pinned awkwardly beneath him.

'What the fuck did you do, Esther?' His voice trembled as his eyes bored into mine. His fingers moved up into my hair and twisted painfully at the back of my head. 'Do you think you can just fuck with me and there won't be consequences? That you can destroy my property and I won't care? I am this close to fucking ending you and leaving you out here. Saying I never found you. They'd never know. You'd just be another Jane Doe.'

My breath rasped as he spoke, the thought of disappearing forever plaguing me. I didn't want to die.

'I'm sorry,' I said, a tear escaping down one cheek as I closed my eyes, trying to avoid that intense stare. 'I just don't want to go back.'

'You don't know the meaning of sorry. You're just a spoiled brat who has never been told no. Too used to doing whatever the fuck you like, no matter how it affects others. I've every mind to teach you some respect.'

'Will it make you less angry with me?'

Alec froze for a full minute, his eyes never leaving my face as his face went through a series of emotions. Finally, he swallowed hard and asked, 'What are you offering?'

'Whatever it is you think I deserve.' I dropped my voice, aiming for sultry, hoping his mind would go to sex rather than his usual method of torturing people.

'Oh, I know exactly what you need.'

THE AIR WAS thick in the small hotel room, charged with fear and expectation. Sitting on the edge of the bed, I watched as Alec paced backward and forward. His footsteps were rhythmic as I waited, wondering what his plan was. Was he going to hurt me? Fuck me? Take my mouth? Make me sleep on the floor like an animal? I had no idea where his mind was.

Then he stopped and looked at me, his eyes narrowing.

'I know exactly what you need, Esther McGowan. You need to be taught that there are consequences for ruining things that don't belong to you. I bet no one has ever even reprimanded you for touching things that don't belong to you.'

'I'm not spoiled,' I said in a whisper, dropping my eyes to my lap under the intensity of his stare.

'Oh, but you are. You've always had everything handed to you. You've never gone without, you've never been taught that you can't have everything you please.' He stepped closer to me, crouching down so his face was level with mine, and reaching out to touch my jaw, gently pulling it upward until my eyes met his own.

'I didn't believe you when you said sorry earlier. But I'm going to make you apologise properly. With tears, snot, and a hot arse.'

My eyes widened as I stared at him. 'You can't spank me.'

'I can, and I will. You've been a deceitful, spiteful little brat. And brats need to be punished. Trust me, I know.'

'You've done this before?' I asked, my mind whirring at the image of his tattooed hands on my ass.

'Yes. But never to someone who needed it, or deserved it, so much.'

'What if I say no?'

'I wasn't asking your permission. You've already told me I could give you what you deserve, and a spanking is way, way less than I'd be giving anyone else. I'm fairly certain you want to keep all your digits, so let's not beat about the bush.'

I shivered as I nodded. I could take a few slaps to the ass. If it would dispel the anger in him, then it would be worth it. How bad could it be? I'd employ my British stiff upper lip and get it over with.

'Stand up.'

My knees trembled as I did, my arms still fixed behind me. My cheeks reddened as he walked around me. God, what was I doing? Why was I doing this? To appease him? Or did the idea of his tattooed arms wrapping around me and pinning me to him do something else in my brain? I became hyperaware of every inch of my body as he took his time, eyeing me from head to toe, scrutinising me in a way no one had openly done before. My mouth dried as he stepped closer, tension gripping at my stomach.

'I'm going to take your jeans off.' His voice had taken on a deep gruffness that made me want to squirm. I didn't. I held my head high and gave a slight nod. I wouldn't give him the satisfaction of thinking he affected me.

My breath caught in my throat as he knelt in front of me, his fingers tugging at the button of my jeans until it popped open. Flutters filled my stomach when he leaned in close, his warm fingers grazing my hips as he pulled my jeans down, taking them off along with my shoes and socks. I could almost feel the heat burning from my cheeks as I stood there in my dirty top, from our tussle at the roadside, and nothing else, before he rifled through my broken bag and slid a pair of clean underpants up over my hips. He stood back up and tipped my chin.

'Eyes on me.'

I complied as I swallowed hard.

'I'm going to give you a safe word. I want you to only use it if you have to.'

'I thought you were punishing me, not playing?'

'I am. But I want you to know that you have an out. I can always find another way to make you sorry.'

'Okay,' I whispered.

'Your safe word is home.'

I ground my teeth as I stared up at him, his blue eyes darker than usual. He'd given me an out. I could say it before he even started. Why?

Then he was walking around me and sitting on the corner of the bed. He tapped his lap, and I hesitated. We'd been close a few times, but never like this. Once when I tricked him, and then when we'd slept in the car. The other times had all been in fight-or-flight modes. I walked over to him and stood by his legs, gasping as he reached up and grabbed the back of my head, forcing me over his lap.

It was difficult not being able to see his face as he pinned me with one arm on top of my hands and wrapped around my waist. I bit my lip as his hand kneaded at the round flesh of my ass, the tender touch almost worse than the pain I'd been expecting.

'You have been a pain in my ass since the moment you were engaged.' He spoke softly, but with a sharpness that sent flutters of guilt into my belly. 'You have used me, tricked me, and destroyed my property. You have derailed our trip and caused me more headaches than any woman ever has.'

I hung limply over him as he spoke, trying not to let the disappointment in his voice affect me. I shouldn't care. He was an asshole sent to drag me back to hell.

The first slap of his firm hand against my rear had me let out a long breath as I flinched. Heat rippled from my ass as I bit my lip harder, determined not to let him see me cry out.

'That was for spitting cum on my trousers.'

Another sharp slap resounded in the small room as my

eyes widened. I had never been spanked as a child, or as an adult, and it was more painful than I'd given it credit for.

'That was for running from the taverna.'

When the third slap came, I kicked a leg up, trying to protect my poor sore arse.

'That was for my phone.'

Then he placed two spanks almost simultaneously. The loud cracks were followed by a whimper that I couldn't hold in. It hurt. My ass was on fucking fire and a thread of anger mingled with something that I was far more ashamed of.

'That was for my cards, and my tyre.'

Tears pricked as I considered saying home, considered making it all stop. But something in me wanted to show him I could take it. That I wasn't just the spoiled little rich girl. That I was tougher than he thought. I also didn't want it to end because as the pain subsided, a deep-seated pleasure was building inside of me.

I writhed as the next spank came, my side grazing his dick, which was hard against me. More heat filled my cheeks as he caressed my burning ass.

'That was for taking my knife.'

'Please,' I whimpered from beneath the curtain of hair which fell over my face. 'I'm sorry.'

'I don't believe you, Esther.' Another hard spank brought the tears falling over my cheeks as I groaned deeply against him. 'You'd do it again.'

I choked on a sob as he continued to lay hard strokes of his palm on my ass, the pressure and heat beginning to overwhelm me. I gave up on the idea of taking it quietly, my sobs mixing with moans as he began alternating between spanks and caresses. The spanks heightened the pleasure of his fingers grazing over the heated flesh, the contrast between them dizzying.

Alec's breathing was almost as ragged as mine as he continued to spank me, his fingers getting closer to the pressure between my thighs with each caress in between. My whole body quaked as I lost control of it.

'Are you enjoying this, Esther? Are you enjoying someone finally taking you in hand? Finally putting you where you belong?'

'Yes,' I moaned as his hand rounded my ass and fingers grazed the spot where my butt met my thighs.

'Are you wet?' he asked as I squirmed against him, my face as red as my rear.

'I think so.'

Then his fingers were against me, tenderly exploring against my crotch.

'You're not just wet, Esther, you're drenched.'

My face burned all the more, but I gave into the shame and moved my hips to press against his fingers.

'Such a dirty girl. Desperate for me to touch you.'

Another spank brought a guttural moan tumbling from my mouth, my hips writhing as his fingers left my pussy. If my hands weren't restrained, I would've shoved one against me and ground against it, but I couldn't.

I moved my hips until his knee slipped between my thighs, my legs splaying slightly as he continued to spank me, each becoming more spread out as he spent more time kneading my ass and dipping his fingers down over my wet knickers.

'I'm sorry,' I cried, sobs mingling with moans as I laid apology after apology at his feet.

His dick pressed firmly into my side as I wriggled over his lap, wanting it. Wanting him. His anger seemed to have dissipated a little as I gave into the sensation of his hands.

'Good, you should be sorry. God, your arse is even prettier with my handprints all over it. Maybe I should give you a spanking more often.' His voice was thick with lust as he spoke, sending shivers down my spine. I'd long imagined dirty things with Alec, but never any like that.

I shifted against his thigh, grinding down as he continued alternating between spanking and teasing, but I couldn't get the friction I so desperately needed. The sensations were making me quiver and whimper against him, losing all control of any dignity I may have wanted to keep hold of.

'Do you want to come?' He pulled my hair until his lips met my ear. 'Do you want my fingers, Esther?'

'Yes,' I moaned, turning my head so my lips were only a hairsbreadth from his. I heard him swallow as his eyes flicked from my eyes to my lips.

'I'm not sure you deserve it.'

'Please?' Every nerve ending in my body was on fire, all frayed and edgy and desperate for release.

'Are you going to be a good girl from here on out?'

'I'll try.'

'I don't believe you. I think you are just thinking about your wet little cunt. You'd say anything to get me inside of you, wouldn't you?'

'Yes.' My voice caught around the word. He was right. I couldn't think clearly at all. The world had reduced to the absolute fire going on in my knickers.

'Ask me nicely, Princess.'

I stuttered as a last wall of defiance remained steady in my mind, and when he felt my hesitation, he let go of my hair and slipped his fingers roughly over my wet underpants, grinding them against my swollen clit. My whole body reacted with a tremor of pure need.

I closed my eyes as he toyed with me, running his

fingers around my engorged flesh before pulling my knickers down and exposing my wetness to the cooler air of the room. I cried out when he slipped a finger inside of me, my head swimming as I bucked against his finger.

So close, I was so close…

And as I rode the wave toward orgasm, he pulled his hand free and placed another resounding slap across my ass.

Tears of frustration joined the ones from the pain as I growled at him.

'Only good girls get rewards. I could do this all night.'

And he meant it.

I fought against the onslaught of another near orgasm, until he snatched it away again at the last second, leaving my pussy gripping at nothing. My breaths were short and hard as I tried to grind against his thigh, pure want leaving me totally desperate for relief. Then he laid another flurry of harsh slaps across my ass before starting all over again.

Being denied made me furious, and desperate, and needy. Most guys had always just been happy to get me somewhere near orgasm, never mind stealing the orgasms back before I had them. It was deliciously cruel.

I stiffened as he thrust two fingers inside my aching pussy, his thumb reaching under to circle my clit.

'You've never been hotter than you are right now, Esther, with your cunt dripping and your face covered in tears. Your arse redder than your cheeks and your body so desperate for release. You should see yourself, see how fucking delightful you are when you aren't being a brat. When you give in.'

His fingers drove me insane until he stilled them inside of me when I was so close to coming. I whimpered and gave in. I didn't just want the orgasm. I needed it. My whole body strained with the tension gripping at my core.

'Please let me come, Alec. Please?'

'There's a good girl. That wasn't so bad, was it?'

I cried out as he curled his fingers inside me, thrusting them languidly as he stroked at my clit with his thumb. The sensation of him inside me had me back to the edge in seconds, but this time he didn't pull back, this time he increased the pressure until I blew. A ragged scream tore from my lips as my orgasm overwhelmed me, crashing around me and filling my head with fuzz as I quaked on his hand. The squelch of his fingers inside me continued as he made me feel every second of the earth-shattering orgasm.

'Yes, Esther. Beautiful. Such a sweet girl giving in to my fingers. You did so well.'

I tried to smile, unsure if it registered at all. His praise filled me with warmth, filled a little pocket of me I didn't know needed filling. If out-of-body experiences were a thing, I was sure I must have been having one. The trembling of my body gave way eventually, drifting from the absolute high. I went limp across his lap as my mind stayed up in space, disconnected from it all.

My body didn't even feel real as he picked me up and cradled me against his chest, reaching behind me and cutting the ties that held my hands still. I wouldn't have been able to fight or run even if I'd wanted to. He'd turned my whole body to jelly with the intensity of the orgasm, like I'd done so much feeling, that there were no feelings left. I was vaguely aware of him filling the bath, removing my clothes, and seating me in the warm water. The heat enveloped me as I leaned heavily against Alec's arm. I moaned softly as he washed my hair with one hand, his fingers sending tingles from my scalp running down my spine. Happily, I would have stayed there in that bath with him touching me forever. Vaguely I thought I should have been caring that I was naked, and he remained clothed, or that I'd come and he hadn't, but I just had nothing left in me to give.

Goose pimples prickled my skin as he wrapped me in a towel and sat me on the bed, hunting through my bag and finding a brush. He took care not to pull too much against the tangles, working gently and silently until my hair was smooth once again. I leaned into his touch as he brushed for longer than needed, the movement through my hair sending glorious sleepy tingles through me. Then he fitted me with a t-shirt from his backpack and a pair of his boxer shorts, before tucking me into the bed.

'Thank you,' I breathed as he tucked a piece of hair behind my ear. 'I've never come so hard before.'

'Get some sleep.' There was a hitch in his voice. Then he grabbed some more cable ties and tied my wrists in front of my body.

'Still don't trust me?'

'Not even a little.'

It was fair enough. I fully intended to make sure they did not repair the car in the morning. I only hoped he kept to these consequences. I'd happily submit to more of them.

I saw him in the bathroom, stripping off his clothes and tossing them into the bath, along with mine. His tattoos carried on up his arms and down over his back, finishing just above his muscled ass. It was a mighty fine ass. As he turned, I got a full frontal view of him that made my mouth water. While he was muscled and thick, he still had a bit of softness about his belly that made me want to bite it. He clearly worked out but didn't look like he shied away from the odd pizza, either. His cock had softened from the hardness I'd felt against me, sitting thick against his right upper thigh. A warmth gripped me between the legs as I imagined crawling over there and taking it in my mouth.

He leaned down and started hand-washing our clothes in the tub.

I smiled as I snuggled down in the bed, feeling a little more myself as I came back into my body bit by bit.

Planning the next part of the escape could wait until the morning. Sleep was coming fast, and I was powerless to resist it.

Later, I was vaguely aware of Alec joining me in the bed, wrapping his arm around my waist and dragging me against him, his thumb looping over one of the cable ties that held me.

I should probably have moved away, but the weight of his arm over my waist was a welcome addition to my sleep bubble.

'Just in case you get any ideas about running,' he said before yawning and burying his face into my hair.

TWENTY

ALEC

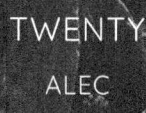

The chitter of birds woke me up early, groggy as I came to. Sweet shampoo scent filled my nose as I shifted against Esther, who lay gently snoring under my arm.

Fuck. I'd been an idiot. I was supposed to be bringing her back to her husband-to-be, instead I was getting in too deep. I'd kept my dick in my trousers, at least. Small concessions. But she felt glorious against my chest. Soft, silken skin and delicious curves. I skimmed my hand over her hip to the dip in her waist and over the gentle swell of her stomach. Maybe I should just forget home, and my job and just hole up in the shitty motel with her, I thought. But other than lust, what was there? Assuming she even felt lust for me, it could all just be another delay tactic. I had turned her on the previous night, whimpering and trembling and writhing under my fingers, desperate and needy and utterly wonderful. She'd been into it in a way only a few women I'd slept with were. And we hadn't even gotten to that part.

My mind flashed with red lights and wailing sirens. I needed to back off, get us to the airport, and move on. The situation was too messy, and I needed to keep a professional level of personal space between us.

As I sat up on an elbow and looked down at Esther, she sighed softly and brushed her arse back against me. My morning wood was already in attendance and reacted with a twitch. Fuck, I was still right on edge from the previous night. Her sweet moans were still fresh in my mind.

You're still mad at her. She tossed your phone in a river. Broke every one of your cash cards and stabbed your god damned tyre.

My cock didn't give a flying fuck. He was straining against her and desperate for action.

She moved again, a deliberate grind back against me. I stifled a moan, my fingers gripping against her hip to hold her still. It only seemed to urge her on.

Soon enough, I was grinding against her, my hands pulling her against me with each of her movements.

'Fuck me? Please?' Sleep still laced her voice as she spoke.

'No,' I said, while a chorus of yeses careened about in my skull.

'Why not? I can feel that you want to.'

Because I might fall too hard. Because even though I should be livid with you, I just want to make you happy.

I didn't reply, instead rolling onto my back and grabbing her, seating her above me, her heat right above my rigid cock. Dark tresses sat tousled about her freckled face, her restrained hands on my chest as she looked down at me with surprise.

'Take what you need, Princess, but we are both keeping our clothes on. Show me how badly you want it.'

Her face warred with emotions as she glanced from my face down to where our bodies connected. Would she be horny enough to grind herself against me? To allow herself to go there?

She bit her lip in a way that made me want to reach up and grab her, taking her lips and devouring them myself.

Then she moved, and my world lurched with the sensation driving through me. Her hips rolled at first, slowly, sensually, and shyly. I watched her, rapt, as she closed her eyes and trembled as the tip of my hard cock rolled against her clit. My chest seized at the delectable sight of her giving into her baser needs.

'Eyes on me, Esther.'

Her cheeks reddened as she blinked them open, those green eyes hooded from either sleep or lust. 'That's it, I don't want you disappearing somewhere else in your mind. You'll stay with me as you fuck yourself against my dick.'

A sweet whimper left her lips as she continued to rub herself over my length, bringing me to an unbelievable stiffness. Fuck, it felt good. Far too good. I hadn't had a girl dry hump against me since I was a virgin and hadn't yet known the delight of fucking pussy. Once I had breached that layer, there was little use for humping. Or so I'd thought. Because seeing Esther hornily seeking an orgasm against my erection was insanely hot. My t-shirt hung off of one of her shoulders as she writhed against me, her movements picking up pace as our clothes moistened between us.

Coils of pleasure wrapped their way through me, and I watched as she ground her cunt against me, hearing her gasp as the tip of my cock arched against her clit.

My breathing grew hoarse as she continued, losing herself to the sensations rippling from her wet cunt. Fuck, I wanted to be inside her so badly. To spread her open and dive in.

I held her bound hands against my chest as she rocked

her hips, holding her gaze as her thighs took on that telltale tremble.

'Look at you, riding me. Such a dirty little thing.'

She bit her lip as I spoke, her eyes never leaving mine as she rode me faster, her clit focused right against the tip of me. It sent shuddering pleasure through me.

'Fuck, you feel so damn good, Esther.'

I dropped my hands to her hips, digging them into the boxer briefs that she still wore and shifting her more vigorously against my dick.

'Oh god...' she moaned as she quivered and closed her eyes.

'Eyes on me, or I'll stop and leave you with a needy cunt and no way of coming.'

She snapped them back to me as I crushed myself against her, using my hands to grind her against me.

With a groan, I flipped her over onto the bed and pushed myself up against her. I needed more leverage. Pushing her bound hands up above her head, I pinned her beneath me, spreading her legs wide and thrusting myself against her.

'That's it, spread wide, baby. Such a needy thing, aren't you?'

'Yes,' she moaned as I ground my hips in a circle against her. There was no way I could come like this, right? The pressure building in my balls said otherwise.

My breath was heavy as I continued to grind against her, revelling in every whimper and moan she gave me, smiling as a red flush crept up her neck. I yanked up the loose t-shirt and exposed her breasts. I leaned down to take one brown nipple into my mouth, circling it before nipping it harshly. She arched against me as she let out a cry, her hands straining against mine.

As I took her other nipple into my mouth and continued to lick and suck, she tumbled into an orgasm, her thighs gripping tightly about my waist as she rocked against me. I should have stopped there, but I couldn't; I was too close. I growled as I bit down on a nipple, grazing my tongue around it. She whimpered beneath me as I continued to grind myself against her, sliding the tip of my engorged cock up and down her soaked underpants. Prickles of pleasure rippled at the base of my spine as I neared my orgasm, closing my eyes and focusing everything on that spot where our bodies connected.

'Eyes on me,' she said with a ragged pant. I looked up at her, surprised to hear my words mirrored, and as I did, my dick exploded against her, streams of hot cum soaking my boxer shorts as I bucked my hips, crushing her wet cunt. All the while, she held my gaze, licking her lips and moaning as she felt me come.

'Fuck,' I groaned through a stuttering breath as I collapsed against her. My heart thundered in my chest as we stayed there for a few minutes, my head groggy and my skin slicked with sweat.

'Hopefully, you will next time...' she said against my neck, her breath tickling me.

'Don't be a brat. Otherwise, you'll be over my knee again.'

'Promise?'

I groaned as I dragged myself upright. She lay spread on the bed, my boxers dark grey where she'd been so wet, her hair tousled about her, cheeks flushed beneath her sexy freckles. It was enough to make my cock twitch back to life. Never had I thought I'd see Esther like that. I'd always seen the prim, poised side of her. It was a fucking sight to behold.

'I'm going to go clean up. The tyre guy will be here in

an hour. I'll get you showered after me, and then we can eat whatever we have left from yesterday.'

A dark look crossed her face as I brought her back to reality.

When I got out of the shower ten minutes later, she was gone.

TWENTY-ONE

ESTHER

The minute the bathroom door closed, I was on my feet, my legs still unsteady from the blissfully tortuous orgasm he'd ground into me. Who knew I could orgasm humping him like my pillow? It had been far hotter than I could have imagined, desperation building until I came hard, grinding against him. His blue eyes had grown more intense as he came, and it left me feeling powerless to anything but lust. I'd wanted nothing more than to kiss him, to reach toward him and capture his lips with mine. To taste him, to swallow his groans. But whatever this was, it wasn't romance. It wasn't kissing and sweetness. Just two stressed people dealing with it in the least sensible way. A spark of solace amongst the whole sordid affair.

I pulled on my jeans, unable to do them up but lacking the time to care. I had to get to the car before the tyre guy fixed it. Hunting around for his knife, I let out a frustrated groan. Where was it? My hands would have to stay tied, which would slow me down.

As I checked the last drawer on the taped-together desk,

I found a box of matches with the motel's name branded across the pack.

Fire.

Fire was perfect.

But how the hell did you set a car on fire? I needed fuel, air, and ignition. I had the matches, but what about the fuel?

Glancing around the sparse room, there was nothing I could see that would help. There would be petrol in the car's tank, but I needed to get it into the interior for it to burn quickly. There was no tubing around that I could use as a syphon.

Shit. I was running out of time.

Then I spotted an abandoned bath towel, thinned from years of use. There was even a small hole at one end. I stood on the towel and used my bound hands to rip a long strip. God, I hoped it would work.

Taking a deep breath, I unlocked the hotel door and grabbed Alec's keys from the side. The car sat in the car park a little distance from the building. Far enough, I hoped. I didn't want to burn the hotel down. Mass murder was definitely not in my life goals.

My bare feet hit the tarmac, making me wince as small stones bit into the flesh. I got to the car, unlocking it, and finding the button to ping open the petrol cap. Stuffing the strip of towel into the tank until only a tiny tuft poked out, I glanced back at the door to our room. The towel slipped as I looked away, and I cursed before reaching in with my fingers and grasping it.

The smell of petrol burned at my nose as I took out the sopping towel and ran it over the material of the back and front seats before leaving it in the driver's seat and winding a window down. Fuel and air. All I needed was the ignition.

My wrists ached where they remained bound by the

plastic ties as I groped into my pocket and pulled out the matches.

'Esther!' Alec's voice carried over the car park, and I dropped the matches, sending them skittering over the ground. Dipping down, I grabbed one and struck it against the box, throwing it into the car right as a heavy impact hit me from the side.

The tarmac burned against my side as we hit the ground, Alec's weight bearing me down as he gripped my face painfully between his fingers.

'What the fuck are you doing?' he asked, fury spilling out with his words.

For a moment, I thought I'd failed until I heard the lick of flames behind us. A relieved laugh escaped my mouth as he looked up, his face falling as he cursed.

'You burned my car? Fucking hell, Esther. I thought you were done with this?'

His words burned into my chest as he spoke, his displeasure sending a thread of guilt through me. But I had to do it. He left me no choice.

With dwindling cash and no transport or communication, he'd have to ditch me and go home. Surely?

'I wouldn't forgive myself if I didn't try everything to dissuade you from taking me back.'

His fingers dug painfully into my arm as he got to his feet and dragged me with him. Flickering orange flames were engulfing the seats, plastic and foam melting and dripping in a fiery waterfall onto the tarmac below.

'You are going to regret it. We will get to the city and onto a plane if you have to walk until your feet bleed.'

'You didn't seem so keen on delivering me to Harold when you grinding your dick into me this morning.' He scowled at me as I raised my voice to a higher pitch.

'That was a mistake. One which I won't repeat.'

Somewhere inside of my chest, a pain pricked me. Why should I care if he rejected me? I didn't want Alec. I'd simply given into stress relief. Nothing had changed. He was still the scumbag sent to drag me home to the shit that awaited me.

'Come on,' he said gruffly, dragging me by the upper arm toward the motel. 'We need to get our shit and get out of here before the authorities arrive to deal with the mess you made.'

'Why? They could get us home faster. That's what you want, right?'

His jaw tightened as he pulled me toward our door. 'Yes. That's what I want. But I don't want to deal with any authorities.'

'Why, got something to hide?' I laughed then, a bit manically, with the chaos of the morning bleeding into me.

'I'm a fucking criminal. Of course, I have something to hide.'

My side ached where I'd grazed it against the tarmac as he threw me onto the bed, still rumpled from our morning activities.

He started stuffing items into his bag, dumping my own belongings out, and adding it to his bag. With my cut straps, it would be difficult to carry. Then he grabbed me roughly and slit the bindings at my wrist, rubbing at them roughly before shoving a light jumper over my head. The long sleeves were made for his arms, not mine. He avoided my eyes as he did up my still-open jeans and then took out more cable ties from his bag, attaching one hand to each of the belt loops on my hips. The long sleeves covered up the ties, but my arms sat awkwardly attached to my hips.

Far off sirens sounded, and Alec's eyes flicked to the window. 'Time to go.'

'I haven't eaten or been to the bathroom.'

'Tough shit. You should have thought of that before fucking everything up.'

Then he was manhandling me out of the door and down past the inferno of the car. Other people were gathering at their doors and windows, watching the fire rip through the vehicle. The heat warmed my left side as we hurried away from the hotel, hoping that no one would stop us. The last thing I needed was the police taking me in with no documents. Going to prison would be awful, being sent home would be worse. And with Dad's strings, that's exactly where I'd end up.

A bus sidled up to a stop a little way up the road, and Alec hastened us toward it. It was only going locally to a few towns over, but it would have to do. Alec handed over some of his dwindling supply of euros before pushing me past a few passengers toward the back of the bus.

I squeezed into a seat, sitting uncomfortably with the way my arms bent. Alec slid in next to me, blocking off the route to the aisle as he sandwiched me between him and the condensation-clad window.

Anger thrummed from his body, from his tight muscles and the white knuckles as he gripped his bag on his lap. From his ticking jaw to the way he stared straight ahead, utterly ignoring me.

Turning my head, I focused on the window as the bus trundled forward, taking us away from the scene of my crime. The condensation gathered as we moved, before dripping down in quick rivulets that cascaded to the seal of the window.

Escape was looking futile. Alec would not give up, and

now I'd just made the journey a thousand times harder on myself.

For the first time in a while, doubt filled my head. Was I stupid for running? Was I just delaying the inevitable? Would I end up chained to the monster regardless of what I did? It looked that way.

Even an orgasm hadn't softened Alec towards my plight. Fuck, it had been good, though. And we hadn't even gone beyond horny teenager levels. What would it have been like to actually have him inside me?

A glance at his furious face made me sure I wouldn't be finding out anytime soon. Nausea gripped my stomach at the thought of Harold being the next, maybe the last, person inside me. I knew my pleasure wouldn't even be on his radar. If anything, he'd take pleasure from me hating every minute of sex with him. There would be no praise that sent flutters straight to my core, or words of encouragement as I came like a good girl. There would be no passion or desire, or looking after me afterward. Why couldn't it have been a guy like Alec? A guy who was the criminal on the outside to fit in with my world, but underneath this hot, simmering sex fiend who, even when furious with me, wanted to make me have earth-shattering orgasms. Why wasn't that in my future?

I'd always known I'd be a pawn in my dad's games. I didn't understand how much I'd be missing out on, though.

How much I'd want to be cherished.

How much my pleasure would mean to me.

Despite my family, I'd always be expendable to Harold. Useful to make a deal and to fuck, maybe even to add some more kids to his family, and then I'd just be another inconvenience. Another millstone to his plans. And when another offer came his way, he wouldn't hesitate to get rid of me. Likely with a bullet to the head.

A tear slid silently down my cheek, mimicking the condensation on the window.

I left them to fall.

None of it mattered anymore.

TWENTY-TWO

ALEC

The bus pulled into the terminal a few stations over, but we couldn't afford to keep still when the police would undoubtedly hunt for the car's owner. Thankfully, the roadside hotel was shitty enough that it didn't seem to have CCTV, which would hamper their search until they tracked down that it was my hire car.

'Come on,' I said as we stepped off of the bus, linking my arm through Esther's left arm, still bound to her belt loop at her waist, and guiding her quickly away from the other people and back onto the open road.

'We can't walk to Barcelona.' She tried to yank herself away from me before digging her heels into the floor when I wouldn't let her go.

'We've hardly got any money left thanks to your fucking with any means I had of getting more.'

'I know my card details...' she said.

'Your Dad has cut you off. You no longer have card details.'

Like a belligerent donkey, she refused to move. If I had to drag her every step, I would.

I pulled her along beside me, her shoes kicking up dry dirt as she tussled against me. Gritting my teeth, I kept moving until she had no choice but to give in and walk reluctantly beside me.

Tyres crunched on the road beside us, and I felt the intake of breath in her chest against my arm before she could make a sound. Her mouth opened, ready to scream out at the passing vehicle, but I turned us away from the road and clamped a hand over her lips.

'Try any of that shit and I'll start taking fingers. Harold won't give a fuck as long as you still have a mouth and your pretty pussy to use.'

It was harsh, but I needed her to stop the fighting. I was exhausted. Drained. Angry. The job was feeling like I should have charged a lot more money for it. She was proving a difficult charge. I'd never had anyone get up in my head before, and it made being the harsh, no-fuss, torture-laden enforcer near on impossible. I didn't want to torture Esther. I didn't even want to bring her back to Harold. I just wanted to get on with my life and be financially independent so that I could pick and choose the jobs I did. Or maybe find something else to do entirely. There had to be something else I could be good at. I'd seen the way things played out for guys like me. We were useful until we weren't, and then we ended up washed up without work, or worse, dead. Torturing people on your boss's behalf didn't exactly ingratiate you to the other criminal networks around.

She sniffled as I let go of her mouth once the car was well out of sight and continued down the road.

'I know you have to take me home to do your job,' she said after a few minutes of walking in silence. 'But please, just give me as much time as you can before we go back. It's going to be horrific, and I'm scared.'

I steeled myself against her words, but they still left sharp little stabs of pain in my chest. She was tenacious, passionate, and stronger than I'd ever expected. Hearing her pain sucked. Knowing I was the one hauling her back there sucked even more.

'We have little money. What else can we do? I need to get to the city and contact your father so he can sort out some new flights and some money. We don't have the means to take longer.'

'You could still just let me go.'

'And what will you do? You've been spoiled your entire life. You've never needed anything. You've never had to scrimp to get by or struggle alone. You have always had a family to watch your back and support your lifestyle. Do you really think you'd last out here on your own? You're just a spoiled mafia princess with no clue.'

Those green eyes burned into me as she stopped walking and stared at me.

'You don't know me at all, do you?'

'I've been around you enough to have seen it.'

'You saw what you wanted to see. I've never wanted that lifestyle. I hate it. I hate that we are constantly under threat because of the things our fathers do. I have been promised to a man that killed my mother and okayed my brother's death. And everyone thinks that's fucking fine. They'd all come to our wedding and toast to a long and happy marriage, despite knowing that I was going to be hurt every fucking day with him. They all know who he is and what he does. They know that I'm younger than his son, but no one cares. My own father has promised me to him. Do you know how much that hurts? I'd rather struggle and starve than have that be my life. He'll impregnate me and then I'll be forced to watch him mentally torture my kids, probably physically torture them too. And what? He'd never let me take them. He'd never let me leave. His last wife got away and had to abandon her children to do it. I don't want that life. I want to be happy, to be with a man who adores me, and to have children that are loved. Treasured. I may have been brought up with privilege, but what has it gained me? Nothing but misery.'

I let her spill her words out, fast, tumbling, and thick with emotion. Each one struck against me anew, making me hate myself a bit more. My arms itched to wrap around her, to comfort her and tell her it would be okay. But it wouldn't be okay. So I did the opposite and added fuel to her fire.

'At least you have a family. No one has cared about me since I was four years old. You'll have to excuse me if I don't give in to your pity party. Lots of people have shitty marriages to shitty people.'

Her mouth drew into a sharp line as those pretty green eyes flared with fury. She pulled herself free of my arm and turned away from me, walking off along the road as I tailed her.

After a few paces, she turned around and glared at me.

'You're jealous that I have a family, and that makes you willing to ruin my life. You're a piece of shit Alec. I can't believe I used to like you.'

Then as she turned back to the road and stalked off, I hear a fuck you on her breath. I sighed and followed behind her, giving her a bit of space.

She was right. I was jealous that she had so many people who loved her. I was mad that she would turn her back on them all. I'd never believed I was anything other than a piece of shit, either.

She was wrong about me wanting to ruin her life. Giving her as much pain as I was didn't bring me an ounce of happiness. The flood of joy I'd felt seeing her writhe against my fingers and my dick had been the highest points I'd experienced in years. With each day I spent with her feisty, bratty, troublesome self, it got harder and harder to justify doing my job.

My job was the one good thing I had going for me, though. It wasn't worth throwing it away to let her disappear back into the ether.

We walked on into the bright day; the road stretching endlessly before us.

Neither of us said a word.

For hours.

TWENTY-THREE

ESTHER

My feet burned in my shoes, every step like walking through hot coals at a slow, blistering pace. Aches gripped at my arms from their painful position attached to my hips, and every part of me was bone weary.

The hours of silence had washed away my anger, leaving me an empty shell. I needed to sleep, shower, and eat, and it was driving me out of my mind.

Every step was torture, and Alec had slowed beside me, keeping to my pace. The sun was dipping, and I wanted to crash down along with it.

For the first time, I regretted my rash decision to cut us off from the world. To cut us off from money, transport, and communication.

I stumbled as I took another step, my foot catching on a tuft of roadside grass. My arms were useless in catching myself as I fell, and when I hit the cooling grass, I welcomed it like the finest feather pillow. If I closed my eyes, I could just have a little nap…

'Esther,' Alec said, worry lacing his words as he knelt and turned me over.

'I just need to sleep. To leave for a bit.'

'Not yet, Princess. Come on.'

He slipped his arms beneath me and lifted me, groaning as he stood. He had to be just as exhausted as I, and I didn't know how he found the strength to pick me up.

His eyes grazed over me as he frowned, concern furrowing his brow.

As he walked us away from the road, I heard the gentle babbling of a brook. Leaves cascaded overhead as trees welcomed us into their midst. My head lolled against his chest as I let relief sweep over me, glad to be off of my painful feet.

A few minutes later and he was setting me down at the edge of the river, removing my shoes and socks with sure hands and inspecting my feet. I watched him quietly as he placed each foot into the cold water, making me moan as the chill swept over my burning feet.

'Oh god, that feels good.'

'You should have told me how bad they were.'

'I didn't think you'd care.'

The blue of his eyes was steely as he looked up at me. 'I care.'

He rooted through his bag and pulled out a cloth, wetting it in the river and then coming over to me and wiping down my face and neck, removing the dust that had clung to my sweaty skin. It was glorious. Each swipe of the rough material made me feel a little more human. His tenderness caught me off guard, the nearness of him making my insides turn to jelly as he fussed over me. I sighed with relief as he cut my hands free from the restraints at my waist, stretching them out overhead as tingles shot from my shoulder to my hands.

He washed out the cloth and washed himself down too.

Then took off his shoes and joined me, dipping his feet into the water before rooting through his pack and bringing out two apples and some sort of power bars I couldn't read. I didn't care. I was hungry enough that I'd have eaten just about anything.

The crumbly chocolate bar filled my mouth as I ate without reservation.

'Slow down,' Alec said, leaning over to wipe a smear of chocolate from the side of my mouth. 'It's all we've got left. Take your time.'

I nodded and slowed down, watching the sky go through its colourful dance as the sun set.

'After we eat, we can sleep until morning. It'll be cold, but I'll see if we can find enough branches for a fire.'

'Are you going to tie my hands again?' I looked down at the red marks that wrapped around my wrists. The skin chafed where the plastic ties rubbed.

'I don't think you could run if you tried tonight.'

'You're not wrong.'

He stood up as I watched him, the muscles of his arms flexing as he stretched out. His blonde hair stood mussed up from the chaos of the day, and he looked as tired as I felt. He started gathering up broken sticks and I braced my hands against the grass, intending to join him.

'Sit down, Esther.'

'I can help.'

'Soak your feet longer. You need it.'

'No, it's fine. I don't need you to--'

Alec turned and glared at me, sending a quiver of need deep down into me. Fuck, how did he elicit that reaction?

'Sit your ass down. I will not take no for an answer.'

I gave in, my feet finally becoming numb as the water rushed over them. It was kind of nice having someone fuss over me. My father had never been very involved with my upbringing, and my series of nannies had never been motherly. After Harold killed Mum, we'd had everything we needed financially, and had all the material belongings we could have wanted, but there had always been a lack of care. As long as we behaved publicly in the way Dad expected, he was happy. We'd grown up as a feral little band of siblings behind closed doors, the mansion being a super-sized playhouse.

Alec worked quickly and quietly, gathering sticks into a small but well-stocked pile. Pulling a lighter from his bag, he set to encourage them to light.

'I still can't believe you burned my car,' he said as the flames eventually bloomed.

'I'm sorry for what it's worth. I just couldn't face going back yet.'

'I know.'

'Are you mad?'

'Yes. But I get it too.'

The burn of tears pricked behind my eyes as I focused on the rippling water surrounding my feet. I'd fucked everything up for him, and he still didn't hate me. It was more than I deserved. As the hours passed with my stomach churning for food and my body aching for sleep, reality was setting in fast. I had no choice but to go back. But the thought of giving in to a life I dreaded tore my insides apart.

'You okay?' Alec asked as the warmth of the fire heated my side.

'Yes,' I said, the hitch in my voice belying the truth.

'No, you're not.' Alec joined me and slipped his arms under my thighs and around my waist, picking me up and pulling me into his lap near the fire.

The tears sprung free and cascaded down my face as

my future came crashing down around me. The running had given me a few weeks of limbo, but I would never be free. I should have known.

'Hey,' Alec said, tipping my chin up to look into my face. 'It's going to be okay.'

'No, it isn't.'

'He'll get bored fast. He's the kind of guy who wants what he can't have. When the games are over, he'll find others to chase.'

A sob ripped from my throat as the situation overwhelmed me. 'I don't want a husband who I'm hoping will get bored with me quickly. I don't want a life praying that my husband doesn't come home.'

Alec pulled me against his chest as he let me spill out the emotions I'd been squashing down. 'You're strong Esther. I didn't see it before. You were like this quiet, stony mountain. Cold and untouchable, I thought. But I was wrong. So wrong. You were a volcano, dormant and quiet, but with all this heat beneath it, this passion and fury just waiting to be unleashed. I see you now. And you can survive him, I promise.'

A mixture of emotions hit me. Dread clawed at my stomach as the idea of having to survive someone terrified me. Yet, Alec made me feel seen. For the first time, someone was seeing me as something other than one of the McGowans. People always saw me as a prize to be won for their own benefit, a friend to make to increase your standing in the crime community. Someone to fuck for brownie points amongst your friends. But Alec saw me, and that put a spark of that fire right back in my stomach.

'I don't want to just survive. I want all the things other people have. I want to be loved fiercely. I want someone who is desperate to be with me because he wants to be, not just because I'm his enemy's daughter. I want passion. Fuck, what if I never have passion? What if I never know what it's like to be kissed by someone who just needs me that badly they can't help it?'

My tears washed down my cheeks as panic rose in my chest. I'd been with enough guys to have enjoyed sex, but none of them had burned for me. And now they never would.

'Don't I deserve that? To know what it's like before being tied to a sadistic, horrible man for the rest of my life?'

'You deserve the world, Esther.'

Then I looked up at him, to see his eyes burning with an intensity that sent shivers down my spine and stole the breath right out of my mouth.

He lifted a hand and dragged his thumb across my lower lip, gathering the tears that fell there. 'You deserve passion. You deserve a man who will worship the ground you walk on.'

Alec leaned in, his lips just a breath from my own. 'Can I kiss you?'

'Are you trying to kiss me because you feel sorry for me?'

'No. I want to kiss you because I've been forcing myself not to since the moment we met. And if I don't do it now, I might never get the chance.'

Did I want Alec to kiss me? The thundering of my pulse told me that yes, I did. It would make things even messier and likely break my heart all the more. But he wanted me, and I wanted to feel the burn of his mouth over mine more than I cared to admit.

'Yes,' I whispered against his lips, my tongue wetting them lightly as I waited, my heart beating impossibly fast.

His fingers trembled as he placed a hand under my jaw and held me firm.

'Fuck, I've wanted to taste you for so fucking long.'

A tremor made my breath hitch as his words sent heat to that spot between my thighs. He'd already made me come twice in the previous days, but this felt like far more dangerous territory. Like we were putting much more on the line.

Then his lips skirted mine, deftly placing a tentative brush of a kiss on me. I breathed him in, smelling the chocolate we'd eaten on his breath as I melted against him. The gentleness caught me off guard, I'd expected him to rush into it, but Alec took his time and savoured the seconds.

His lips slipped to my jaw where he kissed away the tears, following their tracks up my cheeks, kissing away my sadness as I lost myself in him. It wouldn't fix the situation, but it could make me forget it for a time. If that was all I could have, I'd take it.

'You're so beautiful, Esther. I've wanted to kiss these fucking freckles for months.' I smiled as his lips brushed over my cheeks, closing my eyes as his hands reached down and pulled me over him so I straddled his legs as he moved his back against the tree behind him. Goose pimples stole over me as his hands worked their way around my waist, gripping me near the spine and pulling me hard against him.

I moaned as he wound me up, his soft kisses both delightful and infuriating. I needed more. So much more.

Pushing my hands into his hair, I pulled his mouth back to mine.

'Look at you Princess, so needy aren't you? So impatient. I love that you need me so bad.'

I whimpered as he kissed me again, this time giving me

a little more of him. My mouth opened as his tongue slipped against my own. When he groaned against my mouth, I lost my shit entirely. He had been telling the truth. I could feel it in the way he touched me, in the grip of his fingers about my hips and the vibration of his moan against my tongue. He'd come here to bring me home despite the feelings that he'd been burying. Now that we'd breached the wall, there was no denying it, no tempering the want that flowed between us.

He deepened the kiss, claiming my mouth with a fire that I could have only dreamt of. I was floating on the heady sensation of the ravenous strokes of his tongue against mine. The world could disappear entirely for all I cared, as long as he kept kissing me with the heat he poured upon me.

His hair was soft against my fingers as I twisted them in the strands, holding him firm in my grasp. We kissed like we were starving; dirty, needy, and hot. When I felt him straining against me between my thighs, I pressed into him, angling myself so that I could grind myself against his rigid cock.

Losing any sense of dignity, I gave into the crashing cascade of sensation washing over me. When he pulled his mouth from mine to graze it along my throat, I greedily snapped it back and bit his lower lip before kissing him hard.

'Look at you, Princess, giving in. Letting yourself burn for me. So desperate for my tongue, aren't you?' He shifted his hands into my hair and pulled firmly so he had access to my neck and ears as he spoke. 'Where else would you like my tongue, sweet one? You like my teeth on your nipples, and like me to soothe the bites with my tongue, don't you?'

I murmured as he swept his tongue the length of my neck before nipping at my earlobe. My hands fell from his hair to his chest, tucked between us as I gave into his firm hold.

'Would you like my tongue on your pretty pussy too? Lapping up all the wetness that I know is gathering there? Maybe I should have you ride my face the way you ground against my cock.'

A moan escaped as I imagined him between my thighs, his tattooed fingers holding me tight as he drove me wild. Yes. I wanted that. So. Fucking. Bad.

'I've dreamt about your sweet lips taking my cock every night since you left. About fucking that pretty mouth until I bruise it. You were so perfect, knelt there on your bedroom floor with a mouthful of my cock. The image is burned on the back of my eyelids.'

I squirmed at his words. I'd never had anyone speak to me in such a dirty way and it was making my pulse quicken and my insides heat.

He gripped my hips as he hungrily kissed my mouth, the absolute heat driving me wild. I needed so much more.

'Please, Alec, I need you. I need to forget everything else,' I panted against his lips as he pulled me tightly against his hard dick, driving waves of desire from my clit shooting up into my body.

'I don't have a condom. We can't.' His voice sounded pained as I moved against him, stealing some pleasure from the sensation of rubbing myself against his length.

'I'm clean.'

'What about pregnancy?'

'I'll deal with it when I get home if it happens. Harold wouldn't let me keep another man's kid. I need this. I need this heat between us before I'm denied it forever. I want you so bad Alec. Please?'

He hesitated as those blue eyes took in my face. 'This isn't some sort of trick?'

I couldn't blame him for asking. Every other time he'd given into temptation it had ended with me burning him.

'No,' I murmured as I took his jaw in my hands and dragged my lips over his, moaning softly. 'I've thought about what this would be like so many times when you've been in my home, working with my brothers. I've imagined sneaking you into my room and having my way with you. When you pinned me over your knee and spanked me, you opened up something in me I didn't even know existed. I want to get to have this. Even if it's only for a few days.'

Alec let out a growl and flipped us over, the cool grass beneath me contrasting with the warmth from the fire licking across my side.

His hands were at my waist, and then he was yanking off my jeans with an almost frenzied need that drove mine even higher.

As my pants joined my jeans on the floor, I blushed. We'd been walking all day, and I hadn't showered. I'd been so wrapped up in his mouth that I hadn't considered our situation to quite that level.

He must have felt me tense up and seen the hesitance in my face.

'What's wrong, Princess? We can stop if you don't want to.'

'It's not that. It's just… I haven't showered.'

A wicked grin passed his face as he stood, leaving me half naked on the grass, and walked to his bag, picking up the cloth and dipping it into the river. Water dripped from it as he walked back toward me, twisting the material.

'Spread your thighs for me.'

Heat flushed my cheeks as I did what he said, the cooling night air whispering over my heat.

Then he was there between my legs, my back arching as he wiped the cold cloth over me in long, agonisingly decadent swipes. The rough material grazing over my clit made me see stars as I leant my head back against the grass and tipped my hips toward him. Never had someone had such vivid access to my pussy before, and while it filled me with a dirty desire to be spread so, it also made me a little self-conscious. Things weren't perfectly tucked in down there like the girls I had seen online. Would he care? When I'd been over his knee, he wouldn't have seen me like this with nothing to hide behind.

'Look at you, Esther, with your cunt spread wide for me. I want to see you touch that pretty pussy for me.'

Heat flushed my cheeks anew as I circled my clit, his eyes darkening as I did. He unbuckled his belt, and I whimpered as he took his cock out, already fully erect and the tip bulging against his hand as he cleaned himself with the cloth. Seeing him knelt between my thighs with his cock thick and veined in his hands made me forget all of my own insecurities. I wanted to feel him inside me.

I reached up and pulled him down on top of me, claiming his mouth and kissing him with desperate need. His muscled back rippled beneath my nails as I dragged them down to his ass, trying to pull him inside of me.

'Patience, Esther.' He pushed a hand beneath my neck, sliding his fingers into my hair as he kissed me deeply until I was whimpering and arching against him. Each stroke of his tongue made me want him all the more, and when he pressed his length against my clit and ground it in a circle, I cried out against his lips. 'I love to see you so fucking needy. Your whimpers do ungodly things to me.'

'Please?' I moaned, trying to slide myself down to capture his cock inside of me, but he kept it maddeningly just out of reach. He knelt up and pulled my hips up onto his lap so I could see myself spread for him. One hand dug fingerprints into my hip, while the other grabbed his dick and smeared it through my wet folds, the swollen head pressing against my clit as I trembled.

'Oh god.' The taunting was dirty. Most guys would have been inside and fucking with fury, but he held off, driving me more and more crazy for him. I wanted his dick worse than I'd wanted just about anything.

'Such a sight, Esther. Spread out in the grass and almost crying for my dick. You'd do anything to have me inside of you, wouldn't you?'

'Yes,' I whimpered as he moved his hips, his cock sweeping over my entrance. I held my breath, waiting to feel him push inside. When he slid back up to my clit, I growled. He laughed at my frustration and when dimples appeared, I melted. I'd never seen him laugh. It was glorious. His entire face lit up, and he looked so much less severe, so much more free.

'I could tease you for the entire night and never get bored with it.' He did it again, this time circling my entrance before moving back to my clit. 'So wet and willing.'

When I was trying to find words to cuss him out, my frustration reaching a peak, he slid inside me sending my brain to absolute mush as I stretched out around him.

Fuck.

Fuck.

FUCK.

He filled me so perfectly that I could have cried, the sensation of fullness sending me half into a daze.

'Yes, there's my good girl. Look at your pretty cunt flared around me, sweetheart.'

I looked. With the way he had my ass positioned in his lap, I had a perfect view of myself speared by his cock. It wasn't a sight I'd ever seen before, and it sent a quiver right through me. I groaned as he shifted inside of me, the way my lips spread around him looking positively filthy.

He gripped my hips with both hands and pulled me harshly onto him, the strokes slow but firm, his body colliding against my wetness with each one.

When my eyes flitted closed, he reached down and pinched a nipple harshly, making me cry out. 'Eyes on me.'

I watched as his tattooed torso worked, the muscles in his arms bunching as he lifted me again and again, driving hard into me. My thighs trembled against his waist, and when I met his eyes, I whimpered. The intensity he looked at me with should have burned me up. He looked like a cat who had got the cream, revelling in every second of fucking me.

Waves of pleasure washed over me, building steadily as he picked up the pace, my back sliding against the grass with each thrust. Then he was on top of me, claiming my mouth with a hunger that sent my head spinning. A clash of lips, teeth, and tongue, his thick cock driving me higher and higher. His mouth moved to my tits, licking and biting, sucking my nipples into his mouth and torturing them with his tongue. I lost myself entirely in a world of sensation, every part of me so full of him, so surrounded by the heat of his body.

Then his fingers were between us, finding my clit and making me lose any semblance of control I may have thought I had.

'That's it, give in to it. I want to feel your cunt squeezing my cock as I fill you up with my cum.'

Then I tipped over the edge, an orgasm ripping through me as I cried into his neck, clinging onto him desperately. It was a harsher, stronger orgasm than I knew I could have. Every muscle in my body thrummed as he rode me through the waves of crushing intensity, my thighs bruising against his waist as I shook beneath the onslaught of his cock.

'Fuck, Esther. You beautiful little fuck. What are you doing to me?' he groaned into my ear as he pressed hard against me, his ass clenching beneath my feet as he lost control. His balls bunched up against me as he came, his mouth finding my neck and his hands pulling my hair tightly in his fist as he filled me up.

We remained entwined as we panted against one another, our skin slick where we touched. My body felt like jelly beneath him, his cock still inside of me as I blinked up at him.

'I didn't know,' I said groggily, my mind feeling a million miles away from my body.

'Didn't know what, Princess?' he asked, his lips grazing over my neck as he did.

'Didn't know it could feel like that.'

'Me either.'

TWENTY-FOUR

ALEC

What a momentous fucking idiot.

Sleeping with the boss's daughter was a surefire way to get my balls lopped off. I'd cleaned us both off and stocked the fire up with bundles of fallen branches and twigs, dressing us both in our remaining clean clothing.

My stomach rumbled as I laid down on the grass near the fire, the sky above the deepest indigo as stars started twinkling high above. Before I could protest, Esther wriggled in beside me, looping my arm about her shoulders and laying her chest on my shoulder.

'Got to keep warm,' she said with a bratty grin as she pressed close against me. It felt too damned good to have her there, slotting in like it was where she belonged.

'Yeah, it's going to be a chilly night. Not a cloud in the sky.' The stars above may be pretty, but they didn't keep the warmth in like a blanket of clouds would. 'How are your feet feeling?'

Her nose wrinkled, the fire throwing a warm orange cast over her freckled face. 'Honestly, I think I'd forgotten I had feet for a while there.'

When a blush tinged her cheeks, it sent a dart to my chest. Fuck, she was the full package. Why did she have to be a McGowan? If she was anyone else, she could have been mine. I could have swept her off her blistered feet and taken her home to keep her for good.

She'd fit so perfectly in my arms, around my dick. Her kisses were like a salve to my stupid, broken heart and while her mouth was on mine, I wasn't just the man you called when you had a problem to take care of. I was needed. She melded to my touch with that intense passion she'd been hiding so well. If I could bottle up the feeling that had poured through me, setting every nerve alight, I'd lose myself in it every second of every day. Esther could become an addiction, of that I was sure.

'You were perfect,' I said, smiling as she bit her lower lip. 'Just perfect.'

'You weren't half bad yourself,' she joked, her fingers brushing against my collarbone as she grinned.

'Not half bad. I'll have to try harder next time.'

'I'm not sure I'd survive coming any harder.'

'You would. You will.'

'Until I go home.' Her eyes dropped to my chest as I sighed.

'Yes, until you go home. I can't change where you're headed, but I can make your journey more exciting if you want me to.' God, I hoped she wanted me to.

'Why do you want to take me back so badly? What difference does it make to you?' There was no anger behind her voice for once, like she'd finally accepted that she would go back, regardless of what happened between us while on the road.

'I value your family's trust in me. They are the first people who ever believed in me. They made me who I am.'

'By giving you a job?'

'No. By pulling me off of the streets and taking a chance with me. My parents died when I was young, only four, and no one ever adopted me. I bounced from one shitty home to another, causing more and more trouble wherever I went. I'd learned that fists often followed honeyed words once we were behind closed doors. That the nicest people on the outside could be some of the worst when no one was looking. I spent years terrified. Not everyone was bad, but by the time I got out from the worst of them, I was too far gone. Too hurt to trust anyone, knowing I could be given up at the drop of a hat and thrown back into the group home. I wasn't trouble when my parents died, but the system tortured me until I didn't care anymore.'

'That's awful,' Esther said, through a sharp breath.

'I did okay from it. It hardened me. Made me able to do what I do. Made me worth something to people like your father. Like your brothers. People who need others to send in and do the dirty work. It took a while to build up to the point I wasn't just instructed by the lower rungs of the gangs, but the big guys themselves.'

I lifted my hand and slid it into her hair, toying with the strands as I spoke. 'Then I saw your brothers together, and fuck was I envious. The little boy inside of me, the part that never really grew up, was wildly jealous of them. Of all of you. I didn't know what I wanted more, to ruin you all or join you. They treated me with respect, and I tagged along, desperate to belong. It's sad. I know.'

'It is sad, but not for the reasons you think. It's sad that people did that to you. You should have a place you belong, a family.' Esther said it without pity, just in that matter-of-fact way she had. 'We would be lucky to have you.'

'You barely even know me. I do bad, bad things to people for money. I'm no prize.'

'I've grown up in that world. Condemning you would be condemning just about everyone I know.'

'I know. But knowing about it differs from seeing it. Seeing what happens behind the money and the mansions. Seeing the people involved in keeping you guys at the top. It's dirty, damning work.'

'I watched you slit a man's throat for hurting me. I'm not as weak as you think.' She scowled up at me until I pushed her head back down against me. 'You didn't have to do that, by the way.'

'I wanted to. He's one of the few people that I've killed that I cared about seeing dead.'

We lay quietly for a time, staring at the blanket of stars while the fire warmed us. Comfort lulled me as she toyed with the collar of my jumper as the gentle babble of the river filled the surrounding air.

'Did you know I had the biggest crush on you?' she said sleepily, a yawn stealing over her.

'On me? Why? You could have anyone you wanted.' My pulse quickened at her admission. I'd spent many moments in her home wishing I could touch her, taste her, kiss her. All the while, she'd been thinking the same.

'I guess you weren't like the guys around me. So many are just spoiled, entitled jerks who think that because of their dad's name or the stacks of cash in the bank, they can do whatever they like. I guess they can, a lot of the time. They are whiney and demanding, and act like they own the world, but when things don't go their way, they run straight to their parents like spoiled children. When I've given in and had a fling with one or two over the years, they've been just as selfish in the bedroom as they are out of it. You've always had this air of needing no one to back you up. Being the one in control. And that piqued my interest. You are stoic and steady and not at all spoiled. I like that.'

'I'm also not someone who would ever be an acceptable option.' Her father would have a conniption if she wanted to date someone like me.

'I know. I know you think I'm one of those spoiled brats too, and I am in some ways, but I've never revelled in the lifestyle. I've never wanted to be a part of a crime family. I wanted to backpack across Europe without an entourage of my father's men. I wanted to get myself into stupid scrapes and have to get myself out of them. I wanted to know what it was like to make a name for myself, without it being because of who I was marrying or giving another family babies to carry on another generation of spoiled mafia kids. I was mugged and had everything I owned taken from me, and although I was scared and hurt, I'd never felt so alive. Serving people's coffee was probably the most useful thing I've done in my entire life. I wanted for nothing materially, but equally, I've been wanted for nothing. A doll to sit on the shelf until I became useful enough to pass onto someone else who needed placating. And I almost put up with it. Until he chose Harold. The worst fucking option out there.'

It pained me to know I was going to have to hand her over to him. To know I'd be instrumental in letting him crush her spark, wipe out her beautiful smile, and force her to become a shell of the bright, effervescent person she was showing herself to be.

'You seem to have accepted that you are going back, though. Is that another trick?' I asked.

'No. I'm just so tired of running. I ache all over and I know they will never stop and just let me go. I'd hoped that Harold would get bored waiting and move on.'

'Your sister is next in line if I can't get you home.'

Her face crumpled as she blinked up at me. 'They'd give Maeve to him? But she's too young, too sweet. I can't let him have her.'

'It didn't cross your mind that Harold would want her?'

'Yes, but it didn't cross my mind that my father would actually stoop so low. She's the baby of the family.' Her eyes flared with anger as her mouth drew into a worried line. 'You don't think they'd have done it already?'

'No. Not until they've heard from me. If I went back empty-handed I'd be out on my ass without a job, and they would stuff Maeve into your wedding gown and tumble her down the aisle.'

Esther sat up and looked around. 'We need to get back on the road.'

'Princess, come here.' I pulled her back down against me, soothing her back with the palm of my hand as she trembled against my side. 'Walking any more tonight won't help. It'll be too cold and your feet are ripped to shreds. I won't let you damage yourself anymore. Tomorrow we will hitchhike to the next big town and try to find an internet café, or someone who will let me get online. I can get access to cash and let your dad know we're coming. With money, we can get to Barcelona and get another flight.'

It would be much simpler now that she wasn't fighting me.

At the same time, the idea of bringing her home for a bank full of cash was becoming more and more sour in my mouth.

Stupidly, I wanted to keep her.

TWENTY-FIVE

ESTHER

All morning we'd tried to catch a lift towards town, but people were wary of stopping to pick up two raggedy strangers.

My feet burned as we limped along the road, each step like walking through a sea of lava as my blisters tore anew. Alec had done his best to wrap my feet in strips of a torn t-shirt to try to give me some relief. It had worked for a little while.

A sharp intake of breath gave me away. I'd tried so hard to hide the pain.

'Esther? Are you okay?'

'Yeah,' I said through gritted teeth, taking another biting step with a wince.

'Don't lie to me.' Alec pulled me up into his arms, the muscles of his forearms bulging beneath my knees. The relief was instant until the guilt pricked at me.

'You can't carry me to town.'

'Watch me.'

The day's heat already burned at my skin and we were both tired, sticky, and exhausted. Not to mention the grumbles that kept tearing from my stomach. We needed food, sleep, and a hot shower. I winced as Alec held me close, very aware of needing that shower.

'Put me down, I'm sweaty and gross and you're too tired to carry me.'

'Princess, I wouldn't care if you'd just walked out of a swamp. I won't let you wreck your feet any further.'

We made our way down the road, glacially slow. It had barely been ten minutes and the veins in Alec's neck were bulging. We couldn't go on for long like this, not as tired as we both were. His jaw soon clenched with every step, his arms trembling beneath me.

'Put me down, Alec.'

'No.'

'Listen, I won't let you hurt yourself, either. We can rest for a little. It's so hot and we're both too tired. Walking when it's cooler will be easier.'

Those icy blue eyes closed for a few seconds as he took a ragged breath. His shoulders slumped before he walked over to a shady spot beneath a tree and set me down. Fire shot up my legs as my feet connected with the ground.

'God, what a state we are,' I said, sitting and pulling off my shoes, moaning with relief as I pulled the crushing material away from my bloody feet. 'I'm really sorry for burning your car. It was stupid.'

Alec sat down heavily next to me. 'You were desperate, and desperate people do desperate things. I still can't believe you had the balls to try it.'

'I thought you liked me desperate.' I raised my eyebrows as I dropped the last word into a sultry tone.

'I'm too tired to deal with your bratty ass right now. But don't think I won't keep track for later.'

'You love my bratty ass,' I said with a smirk before realising what I said. I stuttered as I tried to backtrack. 'I mean, not love. Obviously. Just... You know... Like...'

Alec laughed, giving me another glimpse of those glorious dimples. My face heated as he pulled me against him.

'It's a mighty fine ass. I won't lie. Even better when it's as red as your cheeks are now.'

'I still can't believe you spanked me.'

'You needed it. Look how well behaved you were after it, mewling in my lap like a kitten.'

I squirmed next to him, trying to bury my face in my hands. He gripped my wrists and pulled them from my cheeks, tilting my chin up toward him. 'Never be ashamed of enjoying yourself, Esther. You were perfect.'

I swallowed hard as he brushed his lips against mine, electricity jolting through me. Leaning into the kiss, I opened my mouth, hunting for a swipe of his tongue. Despite the exhaustion, his kisses instantly set me alight, making me need more of him. It was dangerous how crazy he made me feel for him with the barest of touches.

He broke the kiss and leant his forehead against mine, his breath as quick as my pulse. 'Fuck Esther, I'd love to pin you down here and fuck you until we both can't take any more, but I'm too hot, too tired and I need a shower pretty bad.'

'Me too,' I admitted, a little disappointed that his claiming my mouth had stopped. He was like a drug that I just couldn't get enough of. Was it because I knew our time together would be short-lived?

Alec pulled my head down into his lap, toying with my hair as I closed my eyes. The touch soothed me, connecting us even if he was too tired for anything more.

'Talk to me, Esther. Tell me about your dreams. What do you want out of life?'

'I didn't have any.'

'You must have had something you wanted to do when you grew up?'

'Dreams aren't for women in our family business. What's the point in a dream when you will just get shuttled off to wherever the men in your family want to put you? We are mostly ornamental. There to shop, host parties, and say the right things to the right people. To charm but be aloof. To let people think we could be attainable, but we have no actual choice in who will be the one to claim us. Careers are out of the question. Charitable work can be seen as favourable, but knowing that half of the charities are owned by my father's corrupt pals kind of ruined my desire to help them raise funds.'

He continued to play with my hair; the sensation sending delicious waves of pleasure down my spine.

'What about you?' I asked.

'I was chock full of dreams. I'd get out of care and become an actor, or an astronaut, or a lawyer. I'd have my own home with my own belongings that would fill more than a trash bag. I'd be successful and have a place to call my own. I'd have a picture-perfect family who I'd love fiercely and protect with everything I had. I didn't realise that most people who became those things had people helping them, backing them, and supporting them. I failed school pretty miserably because I was rarely there. I fell into the only crowd that would accept an isolated orphan with ill-fitting, dirty clothes and anger issues. They welcomed me because they could use me to do the things they didn't want to, and I did them because having someone need me was addictive. Then my dreams fell away. I couldn't get a respectable job. I couldn't expect a woman to attach herself to me when I spent my days torturing people for money. She'd just be another target. I couldn't have children knowing that any day things could go wrong and I could be taken out, leaving them like my parents left me. It's probably better to have never had dreams. They just sit in the back of my mind like discarded, long deflated balloons. Reminding me I was a stupid kid with no idea.'

'You should make them pay, the people who did this to you.'

'I've thought about it, but there are too many to count, and it's too easily tied back to me. Going forward is the only way. And I have my house. It's the one thing I've achieved.'

We fell back into a peaceful silence as my eyes grew heavy, the caressing of his hand in my hair lulling me into a daze. I must have drifted off as I startled awake when I heard voices. Through groggy lids, I saw a car, and an older woman chatting to Alec.

Sitting up, I watched as they spoke with the odd word of understanding and a fair amount of gesticulation. I rubbed at my eyes to clear the sleep from them as I stood, my feet aching all over again.

'We've caught ourselves a lift,' Alec said, gathering up my shoes and his bag and taking me by the arm, helping me toward the car. 'I think she's going to the next biggest town, but I'm not a hundred percent sure. It's got to be better than hobbling, though.'

Soon enough the world trundled by us as the older woman babbled at us in Spanish, neither of us understanding but both entirely thankful for her hospitality.

THE TOWN she dropped us in was a good-sized one, but despite our best searching, there was no sign of an internet café, being that everyone used their phones. Alec used the last of our money to pay for a crappy hotel room above a seedy-looking club. Normally, I would have turned my nose up at such a skeevy place, but when I saw we had a bath, a shower, and a big, soft bed, I could have cried. Even better, Alec had wrangled us both breakfast and supper for both days, and as it was a two-day minimum stay, I could rest my feet properly. Two days longer until I had to go home, too.

I had a quick shower while Alec washed our clothes above the bath, the cheap shampoo feeling wonderful as I scrubbed it into my dirty hair. The hot water cascaded over my shoulders, washing away the days' worth of dirt and grime, and left me feeling like a new person.

I left Alec to shower after me, towelling off my hair and finding my brush in his bag, pulling it through the tangles as I flicked on the TV. The only thing I understood was the music channels, so I put one of them on, filling the room with noughties tunes. The street beneath the window was fairly busy, the night filled with people eating at the outdoor tables that dotted the sides of the road. Music drifted up and mingled with the songs from the TV.

When Alec emerged from the shower with a towel wrapped around his waist, a whole heap of tingles shot through me. His tattoos wrapped around his torso, dark against his fairer skin and I wanted to touch each and every one.

'Put your eyes back in their sockets, Princess,' he said with a laugh as a loud knock sounded at the door.

Food. Finally. My stomach somersaulted as the smells wafted into the room.

Alec thanked the man and took the tray to the bed, setting it down as I leaned over to inspect our feast. The burgers looked cheap and greasy, the fries about drowning in fat. I had never been more excited to shove something in my face.

The fries were salty, greasy, and fucking delicious. 'Oh, my god.'

Alec joined me, watching me practically drool as I gulped down the food, not holding back in the slightest, each bite calming my angry stomach.

'Slow down, you'll give yourself a bellyache.'

'Sorry,' I mumbled through a mouthful of burger. 'Not very ladylike.'

'I don't give two shits about ladylike. I just don't want you to puke it all up again afterward from inhaling it too fast.'

I slowed down, taking my time to savour the burger. It may have looked like someone had assembled it in the dark, but it really was delicious.

We ate silently, listening to pop songs and filling our tummies until they were near bursting.

When there wasn't a single fry left, I put the tray outside of the door before slumping back on the bed, finally satisfied.

'Take your towel off and get your ass in the bed,' Alec said, draping his over the back of the chair and giving me a delightful view of his rounded ass. I lifted my eyebrows as he smiled and shook his head. 'Not for that.'

I pouted as he climbed into the bed, slipping under the covers and obstructing my view of him. Two could play at that game. I walked over to the chair, my back to Alec as I slowly dropped the towel, my damp hair tickling at my spine as I let the towel fall to the floor.

'Oops,' I said, bending at the waist to pick the towel up, taking my time to give him a full view of my behind as I did.

'You'll end up going to bed with a hot arse if you keep that up,' Alec growled behind me, bringing a smirk to my lips.

'Promises, promises.'

I laid the towel on the chair before taking a seat and facing him, spreading my thighs. He swallowed visibly as I pressed my fingers against myself, moaning softly. It was by far the most brazen thing I'd ever done, and the way his eyes darkened made me squirm.

'You are being a brat.'

'I am. What are you going to do about it?'

Alec was on his feet before I could take another breath, lifting me to the bed and throwing me over it, one of my legs on either side of the bottom corner, spreading me wide. One hand tangled in my hair, holding me firm and pressing my face into the bedcovers. He laid a series of harsh slaps across my ass, making me cry out and writhe with each smack. Warmth emanated from my ass, each sharp smack making me wetter.

But then he stopped. Running a hand over my heated arse as I whimpered.

'You want me to touch your wet little cunt, don't you?'

'Yes. Please?'

'Not tonight, Princess. Brats don't get rewards. If you go to sleep like a good girl, I'll make it worth your while in the morning. I fully intend to have you for breakfast.'

I turned when he released my hair, fully frustrated, only to be met with his firm, fat cock. I leant forward and licked my way up its length, meeting his eyes as he groaned. Taking the head into my mouth and running my tongue along the flared head, I held his gaze. His fingers trembled as he fought against the feeling.

'No. We both need rest.' He pulled me off of him and threw me into the bed, sliding in beside me and tucking me against his chest, his hand pinning my wrists and his arm trapping me against him. His cock sat proud against my ass and I tried to wriggle against him, his cock sliding against my wet folds.

'Enough, don't make me cable tie your thighs together. I love you so needy for me, but I am going to make you wait until morning. I want you fresh and rested when I finally taste your pussy. You'll need your energy for what I have planned for you.'

I pouted against the pillow as his hardness drove me mad. But a yawn stole over me. He was right; I was tired. Tired and horny and with a hot arse to boot.

Giving into sleep was my best option, because I desperately wanted to feel him between my thighs and see if he could live up to his promises.

With his cock nestled between my legs, I gave in and let sleep take me.

TWENTY-SIX

ALEC

Every minute I spent with Esther was as titillating as it was agonising. She antagonised me in a way that made me need to conquer her. In truth, she was stepping all over my stupid, weak heart with every move she made. Every word she said. Every twist of her smile. They all cut me to the core. I wanted to package her up and take her far from the world, lock her up, and keep her for myself. It was just a stupid infatuation, and putting my walls back up was the answer. It was.

When I awoke tangled in her nakedness, all reason went out of the window. A slave to my dick. What a fucking stereotype.

Esther lay on her back, her freckled face tipped toward me, those green eyes hidden beneath her lash-lined lids. Her dark hair spilled out around her, sitting a bit crazily after going to bed with it damp. The blankets had ridden down in the night, my arm slung across the soft curve of her belly, her tits free for the taking. I ran a finger gently over her right breast, watching in fascination as goose bumps broke out over her skin, her nipple growing more pronounced as I grazed over it. Still, she slept on.

It was hard to grasp the fact that she was really in my bed. That she had been begging to have me the night before, despite us both being dog-tired. I was finally beginning to realise that her heated passion wasn't a trick. She'd have to be a hell of an actress to pull that off.

She shifted against the pillow, the pink tip of her tongue wetting her lips as she arched into my touch, still in that half-awake-half-asleep space.

I lay my head down next to hers, my lips lining up with her ear as I continued to toy with her nipples, touching, teasing, and pinching them. Her eyes blinked open as she suppressed a whimper.

'Good morning sunshine,' I said, my breath against her neck before I leaned forward and kissed her jawline.

'Morning.' Her words were a breathy whisper that had me fully erect within seconds.

'Did you sleep well?' I asked.

'I certainly woke up well.'

I twisted a nipple, delighting in the way she arched her back.

'Mmm, that you did. What a sight you are, Esther.'

'Hardly,' she groaned, tipping her face to mine and capturing me in a slow, decadent kiss.

I stood up as her brows furrowed, displeased at my pulling away. 'Come, sit in my lap.'

She sat up, sending a cascade of dark hair tumbling down over her shoulders as she looked at me. 'You come back to bed.'

'Now, Princess. Otherwise, you'll be having cornflakes instead of cock.'

When she stood up and stretched I watched her

hungrily, it taking every ounce of willpower not to take her where she stood. With the limited time we had together, I wanted to make every second count. To take my time and indulge in Esther. Not to rush to orgasm. Hell, it had taken everything to peel her mouth off of my dick the night before, but tired and haphazard wasn't my jam. I wanted to make sure she'd never forget having me between her thighs.

Turning her to face the wardrobe's mirrored door across from the bed, I pulled her down into my lap, her back grazing against my dick as she settled.

I looked over her shoulder at our reflections, her creamy freckled skin against my ink-stained torso. Her hair was dark while mine was blonde, her features softer where mine were sharp. She was nothing like me. Maybe that made it hotter, maybe the contrast made having her in my arms all the sweeter. Seeing her naked and desperate for me when the rest of the world saw her as prim and proper was intoxicating, and making her plead for my cock made my head light.

Roughly, I pulled her thighs apart, dropping them over my thighs until she was splayed before us.

'Look at you. Such a feast.' I captured her arms behind her, pushing them into the small of her back and clasping them in one hand, forcing her to display herself all the more lewdly. 'I can see how wet you are already. You like this, don't you? Being seen properly.'

She swallowed hard as she nodded, her cheeks turning that familiar shade of pink.

'You'd let me do whatever I liked to you, wouldn't you?'
Another nod.
'Fuck your mouth?'
Nod.
'Your cunt?'

Nod.

'Your ass?'

There was hesitance there as she met my eyes in the mirror. The blush deepened.

'Never had a dick in your ass, sweetheart?'

'No,' she said, squirming against me. 'I want to, though. I don't want there to be anything left for Harold to take first.'

His name on her lips made me see red. The thought of him touching her had me holding her all the firmer.

'Noted,' I said through my teeth, knowing it wasn't her fault. She didn't want to be touched by him, either.

'Are you going to do that now?' Her eyes widened in the mirror.

'No. Not now. It's not something to be hurried. It takes patience, at first.'

Her eyelids fluttered as I ran my free hand up her stomach, teasing her nipples as I made my way to her neck. The thrumming of her pulse quickened as I fit my hand around her throat, tilting her mouth back to me and taking her lips with my own. Her muscles relaxed as I deepened the kiss, bracing her against me but without cutting off her air supply.

'That's it, Princess, forget about everything else and just feel,' I said against her lips, continuing to kiss her until we were both lost in a sea of lips and tongues.

'You are so beautiful.' I moved the hand from her throat to her hair, pulling sharply and grinning at the gasp she gave. 'Look at yourself.'

I slid a hand down between her thighs and used it to spread her pussy wide. 'Nothing to hide. I can see everything. Touch everything.'

'Yes,' she moaned, writhing back against my dick. It slid

against the cleft of her ass with each movement and made me bite my lip. If I wasn't careful, I was going to blow before I had three seconds inside her.

My fingers found her swollen clit, circling it lazily as she panted. 'Do you want to come, baby?'

'So badly.'

'Ask me before you do.'

'Or?'

'Fuck around and find out.'

Her ass was a royal distraction as I picked up the pace, circling her clit again and again, occasionally stopping to slide my fingers deep inside her. The guttural noises she made drove me wild.

'Please, can I have your cock in me? Please, Alec? I need it so bad.'

Well, I'm only a gentleman.

'Yes, Princess. You can have my cock.'

I shifted her in my lap, her heat engulfing the head of my dick in a way that made my eyes roll back. Fucking hell, she really was the perfect fit. I thrust fully into her, our legs both still spread wide, giving the most delectably lewd image in the mirror. I watched her eyes fixed on the spot where I sunk inside of her, her chest raising with each quickened breath as I continued to tease her clit.

'Do you see what you do to me? Look at that hungry cunt eating me right up. You'd like more though, wouldn't you greedy girl?'

Her hair fell over her face as she nodded. I let go of her arms and pushed a fist into her hair, gathering it back from her face and holding it firm.

'I want to see you. I want you to see you. To see how fucking exquisite you are.'

I pushed two fingers inside of her alongside my dick and

grinned as her eyes rolled back in her head at the delicious stretching. 'You take me so well. Fingers and dick. You'd take it all, wouldn't you? Anything I gave you.'

'Yes. Anything.'

My cock was ready to burst inside of her, every movement she made reverberating down my length. But I didn't want to fill her. Not yet. Using the palm of my hand, I ground against her clit, my fingers moving against her g-spot as my dick filled the rest of her up. She was a goner within seconds. Her thighs trembled, pulling roughly against my legs as she fought to close them.

'Watch yourself,' I said roughly against her ear, bringing her eyes to my face as she quivered, the sensations ripping through her. Her cunt jerked around me, tightening maddeningly as I fought the urge to fuck her properly.

Trembles shook her entire body as she went to pieces in my lap, losing control as she thrashed against the palm of my hand. Utterly wild. Wonderful.

Fortunately for me, she'd forgotten to ask for permission to come. When her body slackened against me, the orgasm subsiding and leaving her spacey, I picked her up and put her on the bed. Grabbing my trusty cable ties, I fastened her right wrist to her right ankle.

'What are you doing? I thought we were past tying me up.'

'Oh sweetheart, this isn't to stop you from running. This is for fun.'

She let me attach the other wrist to the other ankle, leaving her spread on the bed, and unable to do much about anything.

'You forgot to ask to come.'

Her eyes narrowed as she looked up at me. 'I didn't think you were serious.'

'I'm always serious.'

'So what now? Another spanking?'

'Not this time, Princess.' I knelt at the edge of the bed and pulled her roughly toward me, so her ass was right at the edge, right in front of my face.

'Oh god,' she whimpered as my breath taunted her glistening pink cunt.

'You might not be calling me that by the time I'm through with you.'

'What are you going to do?'

'Have my breakfast. You are going to take it like a good girl. Understood?'

'You say it like it's a punishment.'

'Oh, it will be.'

TWENTY-SEVEN

ESTHER

Holy shit.

The way Alec had me tied had my brain fried as I tossed between mild panic and not-so-mild desire. It felt dirty to be so vulnerable, spread open, and unable to do anything but take whatever he was going to give me.

He'd made me come hard, and I expected him to do the same before we got on with the day, but he clearly had other intentions.

A smirk crossed his lips as he pulled me to the edge of the bed, the position feeling precarious if it wasn't for his tattooed hands supporting me. The fucker actually licked his lips.

With my wrists attached to my ankles, there was little I could do but watch and wait, breath bated. How was eating me out going to be a punishment? It was one of the best things a guy could do.

He reached out and slid his fingers down the length of my pussy, slipping them inside and curling them upwards. I clenched around him, tipping my head back as tendrils of pleasure flitted through me.

'I could watch you all day.' Another twist of his fingers inside me. 'The way you whimper and moan makes me so fucking hard.'

Then his tongue was on me, licking over my clit and wringing a stuttering gasp from my lips. He explored every fold with his mouth, licking, sucking, and nipping until it was all a blur of pure lusty need. This time, he didn't hold back or keep me waiting. He attacked my clit with a full-on tongue assault, driving me wild beneath him, his fingers thrusting inside me. Sweat gathered at the nape of my neck, and the cable ties dug into my wrists as I twisted beneath his mouth, wanting more and more as he drove me over the edge.

I came with a body-quaking rush, the world spinning around me as I squeezed my thighs hard against the sides of his head, his stubble digging into my skin and heightening the sensations. The bed covers dampened beneath me, whether from sweat or my own moisture, I didn't know.

'There you go, darling. That's it. You ride my fingers until you're spent.'

Before I'd had the chance to recover, he was on his feet, pushing his hands roughly against my thighs, pinning me back into the bed as he slid into me. He didn't hold back, fucking me with punishingly hard thrusts, his cock disappearing into me with each solid piston of his hips.

'Oh my god,' I squealed as he used his forearms to crush my legs back against the bed, his hands looping behind my neck and forcing me to look at his dick claiming me.

'Look how red your cunt is. Swollen, wet, and covered in my saliva. This is how you should be. Spread around my dick.' It felt like he was going to split me in two, my pussy lips flaring with each harsh thrust. This wasn't sex. It was pure, lust-driven fucking. His eyes darkened as I met them, his lips crushing against mine as he slowed his thrusts, each one ending with a twist of his hips that made me whimper.

'You feel so fucking good, Esther. I want to fill you up and watch as my cum drips from your well fucked cunt. But you haven't earned that. Not yet.' His voice was deep and growly, laced with desire.

'Please,' I groaned, wanting him to keep going. When he pulled out, I let out a string of curse words as he laughed.

'Never would I have dreamed about seeing you like this. Seeing you so desperate for a good dicking. You are a fucking delight, Princess.'

Then his hot mouth was back on me, dragging another orgasm from me, whether or not I wanted it. When I came writhing amongst the sheets and screaming his name, I was sure he'd be done.

He wasn't.

He kept going, alternating between filling me with his dick and fucking me harder than I could have imagined possible, his hands in my hair or pressing against my throat as he ripped orgasm after orgasm from me before soothing my swollen, too-sensitive pussy with his tongue until I stumbled toward orgasm time and time again.

As I came hard against his face, I finally broke. 'Please? No more... I can't take any more.'

'You can't, but I can. I can take and take until you crumble into a pile of worn limbs. Are you asking for a break for your pussy? Ask me nicely, and I might use your mouth instead.'

His cock was outrageously stiff, dark, and veiny since he'd been on edge for hours. I didn't know how he held back. I couldn't even count the orgasms he'd given me as they rolled into one another, yet he hadn't even had one.

'Please let me suck your cock, Alec. Please? I want to please you so badly.'

'You'd better be a good girl and take it all. Otherwise, I'll be right back to punishing that pussy of yours.'

'Yes, I promise.'

'I'll never tire of you begging for my cock.'

He flipped me around so that my head hung off the edge of the bed.

'Open up, Sweetheart. Let me see that tongue.'

I did, sticking my tongue out as he smeared the head of his dick against it, his other hand pinching at my nipples as he toyed with me.

'If you can't breathe or need an out, make two fists, okay?'

I nodded as I closed my eyes, concentrating on wrapping my tongue around him, feeling for the ridge and licking at it.

'Say yes. I need to know you understand.'

'Yes, I understand,' I said breathily. With that, he slid his cock into my mouth, slowly and gently. At first. I had little purchase with the position I was in to move how I normally would, but I needn't have worried, Alec treated my mouth like another pussy, fucking it with sure strokes, filling my mouth with the taste of myself and the salt of his pre-cum. When I moaned, he gripped the side of my face and fucked me with more vigour. Saliva streamed as I gagged on him, unable to take him fully without it making my stomach heave.

'You are taking me so well, baby. Keep that tongue moving against me. Yes... god, your mouth is good.'

His words spurred me on as I relaxed, accepting his dick as it nudged at the back of my mouth again and again. Then he pressed forward until the head of his dick slipped into my throat and held himself there. My body fought the invasion, my stomach heaving and my chest fighting for air as he pressed his body firmly against my face. Then he pulled back as I coughed, sending saliva dripping as I gulped in air.

'Beautiful,' he murmured, looking down at my face. He reached down and slid his fingers into me, grinning, and he held them up before wiping them across my lips. 'Look how wet you are. You really are a dirty girl, aren't you?'

I nodded, before finding my mouth full of cock again.

Every time he praised me for taking his dick, it sent shivers of pleasure rippling through me, and before long, despite how puffy and sensitive I was, I wanted him inside me. To feel the stretch as he fucked my swollen pussy. I needed him again.

He pinned my throat as he fucked my mouth, his strokes becoming more erratic as he neared his own orgasm. When he pulled out to let me breathe I spoke through a gasp.

'Please, fuck me, Alec. I need you.'

With a groan of pleasure, he flipped me over on the bed so I was face down and ass up, his fingers digging at my hips. I cried out as he slid inside me, my well-fucked pussy protesting despite wanting him there so badly.

He picked up his pace before reaching over to his discarded jeans and pulling out his knife, freeing my hands with his dick still deep inside of me.

'Touch yourself for me. I want to feel you come around my dick as I fill you up.'

My fingers slid against my clit, which was more pronounced than I'd ever felt it. The bed sheets stifled my moans as he thrust into me, while his fell loosely around me as he thrust deep. Tears pricked as I circled my clit quickly, bringing me shaking toward another orgasm. Everything was so sensitive, I wasn't sure I could handle it. But I wanted to feel him fill me with cum so badly. Every thrust of his dick seemed to say you're mine. Mine. Mine.

And for that moment, I was. All his. He imprinted all over me. Inside of me. For a while, I could lose myself in the what-ifs. What if this was my life? Having someone who would pleasure me until I begged him to stop?

My body lurched as an orgasm ripped me apart, sending me screaming into the bed as he gripped my hips firmly and ground me down into the sheets, fucking the orgasm into me. His mouth was against my ear as he came hard, filling me with rope after rope of hot cum.

'Yes. Good girl. Fuck, you're the best girl.' His voice felt distant as he spoke, hot and heavy against my ears, his breath ragged as his heartbeat thumped against my back.

He turned me over as he slipped off of me, gathering me up against him and kissing my wet cheeks. 'You did so good, sweetheart. So good.'

My whole body felt loose and numb, like I'd spent so much feeling that I was just an empty shell. Like he'd fucked the stuffing out of me.

'Are you okay?' he asked, sitting up and pulling me into his lap as he caressed my hair and my back, slowly enticing me to come back into my body from whatever realm he'd fucked me into.

'I think so. I feel kind of floaty. I don't know why I'm crying.'

'It can happen when things get intense. Was it too much?'

'No. Not too much. I think you might have fucked my brains right out of my head.'

He lifted me up and walked us to the bathroom, depositing me on the toilet with the instruction to pee. After a few moments, he came back and filled the bath up, tipping in the full mini hotel bottle of soap.

The air swirled with the scent of the floral soap as I sneaked looks at Alec's naked self. Who could have known he was hiding in plain sight all this time? Sure, I'd had a crush on him and joked with Maeve about it from time to time, but look at what I'd been missing out on. A man who didn't hesitate to put my pleasure front and centre in bed, but would scoop me up and care for me too, even when he was mad at me. How the hell was he even single?

Taking my hand, Alec helped me into the bath, smiling when I sighed happily as the water encased my body. My blistered feet stung slightly, as did my swollen vulva, but within seconds the heat obliterated all my aches.

'Are you going to come in?' I asked.

'Soon, I'm going to grab us something to eat before breakfast closes.'

I closed my eyes as the room door clicked shut, trying to clear my racing mind as I came down from the high of our bedroom activities. As the water soothed my body, the thoughts I'd been pushing from my head came tumbling down over me. I'd failed to run, and I hadn't at all considered that Maeve would truly be at risk if I didn't come home. I'd put my little sister at risk, and it left my stomach feeling hollow. What if Harold had already taken her? What if I was luxuriating on Alec's dick while she was being tortured by the man my father had promised me to? A wave of nausea swept over me as I sat up in the bath, the idea sickening. I didn't want to be Harold's, but I definitely didn't want to subject my sister to him, either.

What if I could maim him? Or kill him?

His men always hung out near him, so it would be difficult. There had to be times when we'd be alone, though.

Where he'd set his gun down to get naked. I swallowed hard at the thought of being naked within five feet of him. Maybe I could play the willing wife and then finish him once and for all. I definitely couldn't spend years submitting to him. It was the only way.

The room door opened, and Alec let me know it was him. He shouldered his way into the bathroom with a mammoth plate of diced fruits and some delicate pastries.

'Not quite the full English, but it should fill us up before we go out.'

'Where are we going?'

'To track down some internet access so I can book some more flights.'

It was like someone placed a rock in my stomach, weighing it down. I knew it was what had to come next, but hearing it left a nasty taste in my mouth.

'I'm sorry, Esther. But time is running out, and as much as I want to hole up in this room with you, we can't.'

'I know,' I whispered, watching as he pulled his top over his head before removing the rest of his clothes.

'Shift up.' He slid in behind me, pulling me tight against his chest, my ass sandwiched between his thighs. Closing my eyes, I rested back against his chest, our skin slick between us in the hot, bubbly water.

He alternated between popping pieces of sweet fruit in his mouth and mine. I didn't fight it, licking the juice off of his fingers even as he grew hard against my back.

When I tried to reach behind me to touch him, he gently redirected my hands back in front of me. 'Not now. You've had enough for now. Sex can't soothe everything, as much as I like to think it can.'

When we polished off the plate of fruit, he wet my hair before lathering it up. Every sweep of his fingers against my scalp felt like heaven. Hairdressers had washed my hair a thousand times, but never had it felt so decadently intimate before.

'You don't have to do that,' I murmured as I closed my eyes.

'I want to. I enjoy looking after you.'

'I should have eloped with you instead.' The words tumbled out before I'd realised what I was saying. His fingers stilled in my hair as there was nothing but the gentle slosh of water around us.

'You wouldn't want me for keeps, Esther. I'm a fuckup.'

'Aren't we all?'

'I don't have a family to offer, no in-laws, no siblings. Nothing except a half-paid-off house and a knack for making unwilling people talk. I'm no catch.' His fingers worked down to my neck, rubbing against the knots I'd gathered there.

'You are sweet and caring and just need to be loved. We all need to be loved. Your worth can't be measured by whom you bring to the table, but by the person you are. You are enough, just as you are.'

Alec audibly swallowed behind me, and the need for levity weighed on the conversation.

'Plus, you fuck like an absolute beast. That trumps in-laws any day.'

His throaty chuckle soothed me as he wrapped his arms around me, idly running his fingers over my chest as I tipped my head back against his shoulder.

'You're something else, Esther.'

'In a good way, I hope?' I teased.

'In the best way.'

TWENTY-EIGHT
ALEC

The library we'd found had a computer. A frustratingly slow, entirely in-Spanish computer. Eventually, I logged into my bank account to get my card details and then manoeuvred around a site for flights. There was one that left for Barcelona the following morning. I could use the last of my cash to get us bus tickets and have us home by suppertime. There were multiple flights with seats available for each day, if I was honest. Glancing over at Esther, where she was browsing a small section of English books, flipping between them and smiling to herself, I chose one three days out.

I had to take her home. But selfishly, I wanted more time with her first. As soon as we were home, she'd be off limits. The thought of Harold claiming her made me want to vomit. She wasn't the spoiled mafia princess I'd believed her to be at all. She was sweet, sassy, passionate, and no-nonsense. And I wanted to keep her with every fibre of my being. If only I'd realised before she knew she had to return, and before her sister had to fill her spot. Then we could have disappeared together, spent our days wrapped up in one another, and forgotten that our world back in Scotland ever existed.

Three days.

It wasn't enough. Nothing short of forever would be.

I waded through more sites, trying to find somewhere that I could purchase a phone in the town using my details online. No luck.

Esther had tucked herself in a chair, reading a book as she twirled a dark strand of hair around her finger. Adorable.

Pretending to keep battling the internet, I stayed quiet about being finished and spent the next hour basking in her. Soaking up every moment from my spot across the room. Like an absolute creep. I'd spent months watching her from afar, and never dreaming she'd be mine, even if only for a few days.

She flicked from page to page, her cheeks reddening every now and again. Eventually, she looked up and blushed furiously.

'You're just flicking through and reading the dirty bits, aren't you?'

She stammered and quickly shut the book. Her face was beetroot as I laughed. 'Don't worry, baby. I don't mind you doing a little research.'

'Research?' she said.

'For later.' I smirked as she squirmed in her seat.

WE WALKED THROUGH THE TOWN, spending the afternoon looking every bit like a pair of tourists. At some point, she'd slipped her hand into mine to drag me toward a shop window. My heart had skipped about twenty beats, leaving me breathless as I looked down at our entangled fingers. The gentle intimacy shook me far more than any of the sexual connections we'd had. When she'd noticed me staring at our hands, she'd blushed and tried to pull her fingers away. I took them right back, gripping her hand in my own and leading us down the street, enjoying every second of her touch.

For the rest of the lazy afternoon, I let myself imagine we were the sweet, love-struck tourists the rest of the world could perceive us as instead of the perverse situation we actually found ourselves in.

Using the last of our money, other than the bus fare I'd set aside, we shared a large portion of Patatas Bravas at a tiny café as the street flowed with people around us. Esther moaned as she bit into one of the crisp potato bites, catching a drop of the spicy tomato sauce that threatened to fall from her fork.

'Oh, my god. It's so good.'

I tucked in, the savoury flavours exploding in my mouth. 'It puts chips, cheese, and gravy to shame.'

Her laugh filled me with a honeyed warmth. 'Let's not get hasty.'

'You've had chips, cheese, and gravy? With your chefs on board, I wouldn't have thought you would have stooped so low on the culinary ladder.'

'I may have had chefs, but I didn't live under a rock. I still went to Uni, and I still had drunken nights out with pals. We just had men with guns tailing us while we ate the takeout.'

People watching always made me both curious and lonely, seeing the lovers, the families, and the joy surrounding me as I sat alone. That day it felt different. Esther's thigh pressed up against mine as she chatted away, smiling as though there wasn't a problem in the world. It was glorious to be one of the happy people, even if it was only long enough to get a glimpse of what could be.

'Man, I'm going to reek of garlic from this sauce. You'll not want to kiss me after this,' Esther said with a grin.

'As if a little garlic could stop me.'

I turned toward her, slipping my hand along her jaw and pulling her lips to mine. Her mouth opened with a soft moan as I kissed her slowly, savouring every second of her tongue tentatively exploring my own. I loved the way she leaned into my touch, so open now that we had temporarily dismantled the walls between us. My fingers skimmed down her throat, feeling the thrum of her pulse quicken as I nipped at her lower lip.

The clearing of the waiter's throat broke us apart as he checked if we wanted anything else. There was not a single thing I needed more in that moment than Esther.

We finished the plate, neither of us willing to leave a crumb of the divine treat. By the time we made a move, the sun had sunk below the horizon; the street bathed in the yellow glow of window light.

'There was something else we used to do in Uni on the rare occasions we escaped our henchmen for long enough. Although we had our accommodation, food, and anything for university paid, we never had that much fun money, so we got creative.'

'Doing what?'

'Sneaking into strip clubs and taking a turn before high tailing it with a thong full of cash.'

'You stripped?'

'Yeah,' she said sheepishly. 'Stupid, right?'

The thought of her on stage, surrounded by men and women panting over her, should have flared jealousy in me, but it had my cock thickening in my pants. 'I'd have loved to see that.'

'Really?'

I nodded as we walked, her fingers back in mine. 'I'd love to see your face as all those people's eyes were on you. See you move in a way that makes them salivate over you. I can't guarantee I wouldn't want to drag you into a private booth afterward, though.'

'Other people looking at me like that would turn you on?'

'No. You expressing yourself like that would turn me on. Seeing your reactions would turn me on. Fuck, there isn't much you could do that wouldn't turn me on. It's enough of a battle for me not to get an erection watching you eat fucking potatoes.'

She laughed, a throaty sound that I wanted to thrust into my pocket and take home with me.

'Should we do it? I'm pretty sure the place below the hotel is a strip joint?'

'If you want to?'

'This is going to be my last few days of freedom. I want to do anything that feels crazy.'

A sliver of pain. Was I included in that? Another crazy thing to do while she's in limbo between her old life and her new one. I shook it off. It could never be anything more. I knew that going into it. With every touch, every smile, and every kiss, it was like I was piling little pieces of my heart up in her arms, expecting that she'd hold on to them when eventually she'd drop them, leaving me shattered. I had to believe that it would be worth it, though. That this short time with her would leave more good than bad behind.

'Then let's do it. What will you wear?'

'I'll borrow something from one of the other girls. There's usually a closet of clothes backstage and makeup and such.'

'What should I do?'

'Enjoy the show,' she said with a devilish smirk, 'and if any of the bouncers get antsy, then create a distraction to let me slip out.'

'Is it a good idea?'

'No, but since when were you on the side of good?'

She had a point.

NERVES PRICKED at my belly as we sidled around the back of the building, looking for a way in. Esther had assured me someone would be out back to smoke, and we could slip in there.

Sure enough, a woman opened the door shortly after we arrived and didn't question Esther when she confidently thanked her and waltzed right in. I followed, dumbstruck by her absolute brazenness.

The back corridors we found ourselves in were old and dingy, dirt gathering in corners and cobwebs stretching across the upper corners. It wasn't my first time in the back rooms of strip clubs. Many of them were owned by crime organisations and used to launder money. The McGowans didn't own any as far as I was aware, but they owned a sex club. Albeit, a much cleaner one than the strip club we'd just walked into. It hid the screams of the people I needed to extract information from well enough in the backrooms of the club.

Esther grabbed my fingers, pulling me along behind

her as she peeked into the rooms that we passed. The occupants didn't seem in the least bit phased they didn't know who we were, more than one smiling at Esther. Music thrummed louder the deeper we got into the building through the warren of tiny rooms. Finally, she found the one she was looking for, a room that was more like a closet than a changing room. It overflowed with all manner of clothes. From tiny sparkly numbers to dress-up clothes.

'What look should I go for?' she said to me as I squeezed in behind her.

'What do you like wearing?'

'It's more what will make the most money in the shortest amount of time before someone questions who I am. Something with multiple pieces I can take off. Delayed gratification and all.' Esther grinned at me, moving foot to foot with an excited little hop. She really loved it. Whether it was the sneaking about or the fact she was going to be watched, I wasn't sure.

'You'll look amazing in any of them,' I said, reaching out and pulling her toward me. Running my hands up her stomach to her throat, I pinned her back against my chest, dragging my lips over her neck. 'Tell me, Esther, does it get you hot thinking about all those eyes on you?'

She swallowed hard, her throat bobbing against my fingers as she nodded. 'Is that okay?'

'More than okay. I like that you like being watched. I like it even more that I can take you upstairs and be inside of you after, when you are all wet, wound up, and needy.'

A soft moan made me grin as I nipped at her neck, loosening her jeans and sliding my hand down into her underpants. Soaked already. My dirty girl. 'You're going to go up there and dance with a wet cunt, aren't you?'

'Yes,' she whispered, grinding against my hand as her head tipped back against my shoulder.

I toyed with her clit idly, enough to wind her up, but not with enough pressure to get her to come. A perfectly maddening amount.

'Please,' she moaned as she tried to move against me faster, to make me pick up the pace.

'No, darling, not until after. I want to see you up there with those lust-crazed green eyes. If you are a good girl, I'll make you come after. As many times as you can take.'

I reached out and picked an outfit out, still wrapped in plastic. The picture on the front showed a black bra and a black thong, with some sort of fishnet enmeshment to go over the top with a matching skirt and thigh-high stockings. Even the thought of her in it had me rock solid.

'You like this one?' she said, taking the packet and running her fingers over it. I mimicked the touch against her with my other hand still between her thighs.

'I do. You'd look killer in anything, but you can tear that one off.'

When she looked over her shoulders at me, her eyes gleamed. 'I like that you aren't jealous. Most guys wouldn't be so cool with me doing something so crazy.'

'Why would I be jealous when I'm the one dragging you upstairs after and having my way with you? Fuck it, if it was a different kind of club, I'd get up there with you and take you right there on the stage.' Her whole body quivered when I spoke, a gasp falling from her lips as I circled her swelling clit.

'That would be... so fucking hot.'

I opened my mouth, ready to promise that one day we would, when reality kicked me in the stomach. I couldn't promise anything because she wasn't mine. We only had a few days left. So I turned her in my arms and captured her lips, pouring every emotion that ripped through me into her mouth. The kiss was heated and messy, desperate and decadent. I groaned as I pinned her back against the wall, knocking into a dresser that had a stack of unopened eyeliners and lipsticks in it.

With rough hands, I grabbed at a thigh, lifting one of her legs up to my waist as my dick pressed against her through our clothing. Tipping my hips, I ground the head of my cock against her, eliciting the sweetest sighs. 'Atta girl, you just remember how good it feels to have me there. I'll see you out there, and if you are very good, I'll feed you my cock later.'

'Yes, please,' she said against my lips, her arms wrapping around my neck as she claimed a last kiss.

'I'll be watching.'

I left her there, trepidation clawing at me as I walked out, finding a door to the back of the main room, by the toilets. no one batted an eye as I strode purposefully toward the stage, slipping into a padded chair and subtly eyeing the other patrons seated within touching distance of where my girl would dance. It was packed. A woman was on stage, finishing up, her attention focused on one particular individual, an older guy with a whole wad of cash in his lap. He leaned forward and pushed another euro note into the waistband of her thong, smiling up at her as she moved so that her tits all but grazed his face.

Scanning the room, I made a note of the security staff. There were four of them, two on the doors, one roaming, and one placed next to the private rooms. The club was pretty packed, with a mixture of single men, couples, and even a few groups, two of which looked and sounded very much like British stag parties.

One of them was getting a little handsy with one performer, very much a no-no, but the perfect distraction for the security staff.

The woman on stage stooped to scoop up the money that the patrons had tossed on stage, flashing me a grin as she did. I only had eyes for one woman, though, and I shifted in my seat as I awaited her. Who knew how long it would take before she could wangle a spot? It was early in the night though, so the newer girls would likely be up first, making it more likely she'd find a way.

Then I saw her, at the back edge of the stage near the door, talking to the DJ, who looked absolutely smitten with her. She coiled a piece of hair around her finger as she spoke, coyly smiling at the young guy, leaning in close and whispering in his ear.

It would be a lie if I said that I wasn't jealous at all. A wisp of envy wrapped around my chest as I watched them. I replaced it with a smirk as I scanned her body, knowing it would be beneath me soon enough. Let them pant over her, let her have her night of sticking it to her family and revelling in her sexuality. I was on tenterhooks waiting to see her dance. Did she even know how? The prim mafia princess I'd watched at arm's length was so far from the woman Esther actually was. Confidence brimmed from her, mingling with the way she allowed her sexuality to ooze from her. She was sweet, bratty, and smart. I wanted to stay in her orbit forever, needing her heat and light like she was the sun itself. My sun.

Then she was striding toward the stage, a pair of black high heels completing the outfit I'd picked out. She looked fucking incredible. She'd teased her hair into soft waves, which framed her freckled face perfectly. Her lips were a deep red that made me almost lose myself to imagining them wrapped around me, my dick blurring the edges. She'd lined her eyes in the darkest black, making the green irises pop. So fucking sexy.

She brought her full brat persona to the stage, flicking those fuck me eyes from patron to patron as the music kicked in around us. The fishnet grid of the skirt dug gently into her hips and ass, making me want to crawl up there and feel it beneath my tongue. The contrast between her soft skin and the harsh nylon would be perfect.

Then she was moving, her body twisting to the music. When she dropped to her knees and flicked her head up, sending her hair cascading down her back, I was already back to full attention. I split my time between watching her and watching the others watch her. They were already baying for fresh blood, a new girl to fantasise over.

Arching her hips as she gasped, her chest raising with each little pant. She was sex on fishnet-covered legs. When she reached up and tore the fishnet top, biting her lower lip and making eye contact with the older man, she breached their walls. They cascaded notes at her; the floor littering with them. She crawled toward me, eyes on mine, and I added the last of the money I had, our bus fare to Barcelona, to the other offerings. I leant forward and slid the notes into the waistband of the fishnet skirt, muttering a low good girl to her. Her pupils dilated as she heard me, her tongue darting out to lick her lips. Esther looked like she was in heaven, enjoying every second of having all eyes on her. She tore the skirt from behind, her round ass looking perfectly biteable as she did. When she slipped her bra off, the stag party cheered, sending her cheeks the most glorious shade of red. Her nipples were hard as she brushed her fingers down over them as she danced. She seemed to be thirty seconds short of slipping her fingers into her thong and fucking herself right there when the music came to its crescendo.

The crowd was wild, lust heavy in the air around us as people pressed closer to the stage, men taking the chance to shove note after note into the paltry amount of clothing she had left.

When the music ended she stood there, revelling in the attention for a moment, cheeks aflame but eyes sparking in delight. Then she stooped to gather up the piles of notes scattered around the stage. To my surprise, pride swelled in my chest as I watched her up there, claiming something for herself in the world that restricted her so much. Her family would go fucking ape shit if they knew she liked to strip, not even for the money, but because it got her revved up. Not that I'd ever let her secret be known. It was ours now.

I stood as she alighted from the stage.

'Meet you in the alley out back,' she whispered as she passed me, arms full of notes. I watched her head toward the door and froze as a guy from the stag party blocked her way.

'I want a private dance, luv,' he slurred, his eyes unable to fully focus.

'No, thank you,' she said, her voice reaching me as I sidled closer to them.

'You've got no choice. I've got the money and I want those tits in my face.'

'I said no.' Esther went to move past him, and he reached out and grasped a nipple hard between his fingers.

She yelped and tried to pull away, only making him smirk as he dug his fingers into her flesh even harder. There wasn't the time to wait for security to see amongst the crowd of people.

Within two steps, I was on him, my fingers gripping into

his throat and entirely cutting off his air supply. He let go of Esther, who took one look at the situation and scurried off toward the back room to gather her things.

I pushed the drunken idiot backwards until I sandwiched him between the wall and myself, his face turning a delightful shade of puce as he sputtered desperately.

'What gives you the fucking right to touch her?' I asked, my voice hard. I let him have enough air to reply while keeping him pinned in place.

'Fuck off. What are you, a fucking white knight? She's a whore. Who cares?'

'I care.'

His nose crunched as I punched him, my fist aching from the collision with it. Blood spurted out of him as he crumpled.

'You broke my fucking nose!' he wailed through the torrent of blood as I turned to walk away. He was lucky there were too many witnesses for my trusty knife to make an appearance.

His friends crowded around, looking like they'd make trouble, but made way when I didn't give any leeway. I'd learned as a kid that the cat's defence mechanism would do me well. It didn't matter how big the other guy was, if you still went in claws a-blazing and looking crazed, the others would soon back down. Most of the time. When intimidation doesn't work, a lot of enemies lose their muster.

I'd almost made it out of the front door when a hand gripped my shoulder. I twisted, ready to deal with whoever it was. I came face to face with a security guard who said something in Spanish.

'English,' I said between my teeth.

'Ah, yes. I wanted to say sorry. One of my guys should

have been there to get in between them. We take the safety of the girls important here.'

My shoulders relaxed as I smiled at him. 'No worries, mate.'

Then I was out in the cool evening air, walking at speed around the street to the back alley, needing my girl in my arms.

TWENTY-NINE
ESTHER

Kicking off the heels and shoving my feet into my trainers, I grabbed an oversized hoody someone had left on the back of a chair backstage and dragged it over my head. I stuffed the wads of cash into the front pocket and picked up my discarded clothing before heading for the back door. I needed to get out fast before someone started asking questions about who I was.

Cold air hit my legs as I burst into the alleyway, the door shutting with a snap behind me.

'Hey, pretty girl,' Alec's voice was gravelly as he appeared from a nook a few steps down the alley.

'Hey.' I grinned as I walked over to him, throwing my arms around him. Excitement still coursed through me from my time on the stage. I hadn't felt so alive in a very long time. 'Are you okay?'

'Yeah. Just drunken punks. Are you okay?'

'I'm fucking great.'

'Yes, you are. What a sight you were up on that stage. no one could take their eyes off of you.'

Heat crept up my chest and into my cheeks. He looked at me so intensely I thought he might burst. 'So you enjoyed it?'

'You bet your sweet ass I did.' His hands pushed up into my hair as he kissed me hard, his tongue sweeping over mine as I moaned into his mouth. His kisses were like crack. No matter how many he gave me, they were never enough to appease the need that gripped me.

'God, I'm so fucking horny,' I whimpered as his lips grazed my neck, his hands slipping under my hoody, touching the torn fishnet skirt.

'You kept it on...' his voice cracked as he lost control, pushing me toward the alcove he'd come out of until my back was pressed up against the cold stone. Then he was on his knees, his mouth there above my thong, the heat from his tongue rasping against the already wet material.

'Someone could see,' I gasped as his fingers dug into my ass, pulling me hard against his mouth.

'Then let them enjoy the show because I need to taste you right now, baby.'

His hair was soft between my fingers as I entwined them through the strands.

'Fuck,' I moaned as he roughly pulled my thong to the side and slid his tongue against me.

'You taste so good, darling. That's it, take my tongue, sweetheart.'

Alec mumbled half of his words against my pussy, sending vibrations through me. God damn, this guy. I twisted my fingers, gripping his hair tightly as he licked at my clit, sending torrents of pleasure mounting through me.

When he growled against me, lifting one thigh over his shoulders for better access, I saw stars. When he roughly slid his tongue inside me, I arched my hips and whimpered; the sensation sending me to outer fucking space. When he slid three fingers deep inside me and fucked me slowly with them while tonguing my clit, he catapulted me into a whole other universe.

I came loudly, gyrating against his face.

'Oh my god, Alec, yes. Fuck, your tongue is insane.'

'There's my girl. Take it all sweetie,' he said against me, continuing to lick as my whole body quaked.

'Told you she was a fucking whore.'

The English accent broke me out of the reverie I was floating in as I looked up and saw the guy who had pinched me standing a few metres away. Alec was up on his feet in front of me within a second as I pulled my hoody down to cover myself.

'Just wanted her for yourself, didn't you?' Another one of the guys piped up.

'What did you call her?' Alec's voice was laced with pure rage as he wiped his face on the back of his hand and pulled himself to his full height.

I counted them, all seven of them.

'I called her a whore.' The bloody-nosed guy took a step toward Alec as I ducked behind him, the hairs on the back of my neck standing to attention. 'You broke my fucking nose, and now I want my turn on her. She looks like a screamer, and she'll take my dick for getting my nose burst.'

'I'd get your drunk fucking ass out of here before I cut your dick off.' Alec's fists bunched at his sides as he moved forward, making the guys step back.

'What do you care? We'll pay her well enough if she takes all seven of us.'

I shrank back against the wall, pulling my hoody down

lower over my thighs. Sweat pricked at the base of my spine as I looked for another way out. There wasn't one.

'Last warning,' Alec said, his fingers slipping into his back pocket. 'Is it a fight worth dying for?'

The ringleader laughed. 'Alright. Hard man. Do you really think you can take all of us and come out on top?'

Alec drew the knife from his pocket and held it out at his side, the blade flicking forward with a snap that drew more than one set of eyes.

'Fuck this,' one of them said, holding his hands up and retreating from the alley, quickly followed by another.

'I'm not getting killed for some pussy, mate. Let's go.' One of the others grabbed the blood-covered idiot by the arm and tried to pull him away from us.

'He's all talk. He's not going to stab me.' He looked a lot less cocksure than he had a few minutes prior.

I stepped forward, lifting my head and feigning a confidence I absolutely didn't feel.

'The last guy who touched me without my permission had his throat split in two with that very knife. He wouldn't hesitate to send you to hell right along with him.'

He narrowed his eyes, looking from me to Alec and back to me. 'I don't believe you.'

Then Alec was on him, knocking him to the floor as he squealed. He dragged up the guy's bloodied shirt and set his knife to his skin. Blood seeped from the spot where he sliced the point into his pale flesh.

Alec stuffed a hand over the guy's mouth as his friends stared wide eyed. Even his friends weren't willing to defend him. I really hoped Alec didn't intend to gut him. He was a dick, but I didn't need anyone else dying.

Within a few seconds, Alec stood, wiping the bloodied

knife on the man's shirt. I looked at the red-coated skin and raised my eyebrows. Alec had scored a great big cock and balls into the guy's lower stomach.

'Thank your lucky stars. It's only skin deep. Now whenever you go around trying to force yourself on women, hopefully you'll think better of it.'

One of the other guys took his phone out and tried to take a photo of Alec, yelping when Alec strode over to him and snatched up the phone. 'What's the code?'

The man stammered but didn't answer.

Alec grinned at him. 'I can take your PIN or your thumb. Your choice.'

'Eight-zero-zero-eight.'

'Like boob? How fucking mature.' Alec typed it in to test it. The home screen popped up, and he pocketed the phone.

'Get him cleaned up and back in his hotel. Try the police, and I'll come after anyone on your phone who means anything to you.'

With that, Alec grabbed my hand and took me back to our hotel.

'I'm sorry you had to see that side of me,' he said, not meeting my eyes.

'Hey,' I said, slowing down and pulling him toward me so that we were face to face, forehead touching. 'That side of you doesn't scare me off. You make me feel safe. Protected. I wouldn't change it.'

He closed his eyes and inhaled shakily. 'You're perfect Esther. So fucking perfect.'

The kiss he gave me was tender and chaste, so unlike the ones usually filled with blistering heat. So sweet that it made my insides turn to jelly.

I was falling for him. Too hard.

And it was going to break me to go home and never be able to explore what could be.

But I had to go.

For Maeve.

She didn't deserve Harold any more than I did.

THIRTY

ALEC

We took the first bus toward Barcelona in the morning, just in case the drunks had gone to the police after all.

As we settled into our seats at the back of the bus, I gathered Esther up with her head in my lap, and her legs stretched out over the rest of the back seat. There were so few people up and out that early that we were alone at the rear of the bus, with a few hours to go before we hit the city.

I'd used the stolen phone to book us into a luxury hotel for our remaining few nights in Spain. The suite looked out over the city, with an eight-seater sunken hot tub on the rooftop terrace accessed only by our suite. I'd also instructed them to leave champagne, condoms, and a generous amount of lube. I hadn't forgotten her last request to go back to Harold with none of her holes remaining virginal.

But for now, I was glad to just have her in my lap, a bag stuffed full of snacks, and nothing to do but luxuriate in her for a few hours.

'What did you tell them about where you found me?' Her question was out of the blue, drifting up toward me as I toyed with her soft hair.

'I just told them I found you in Spain.'

'Good, can you avoid telling them where?' I lifted a brow at her question.

'Why? Are you going to run away again?'

She shifted to look up at me and fixed me with a sad smile. 'No, but I don't want anyone coming down on Eva and Jock. They were good to me.'

'I don't think anyone's going to bother coming all the way out here for that.'

'Then you are underestimating Harold.'

'Okay, I'll let them think I tracked you down in the city.'

'Thank you.' Her smile sent a wash of light into my chest. 'What will you do when you've freed yourself from me?'

My fingers stilled in her hair as my stomach roiled. Being free of her was the last thing I wanted. I wanted to stow her away and take her home with me, telling the McGowans and Harold to fuck right off if they thought I was going to let him have her. But then we'd both have to run. Was it too early to know if this thing between us could last? Esther felt so right in my arms, so utterly perfect for me, but was it just proximity and desperation driving her into my bed? I feared so.

'I'll go home. Keep working for your dad for a bit, and maybe decide to start my own business.'

'What would you do? Freelance killer for hire?'

I looked around the bus wide-eyed as she said it, only to be warmed by her laughter.

'No. Something legitimate that I don't have to hide. I've been lingering in the underbelly of Glasgow for so long, I thought I was stuck there. But what if I didn't need to live under the radar, avoiding the real world? I've never known normal, but with every passing year, I want it more. Want to have the house and the family and be doing bloody school runs without worrying that someone will snatch up my family for some sort of revenge.'

Esther turned in my lap so she was fully looking up at me, her fingers toying with the seam on my t-shirt. 'And who is the lucky lady who has your kids in this dream?'

You. But it couldn't be you. We'd never be given the peace to live together. We'd be hunted down, and you'd be dragged back to him. And me? Well, I'd be dealt with permanently.

I needed to change the subject before emotion dragged me into its grasp, and left me teary-eyed in front of Esther.

'Let's not worry about the future. Tell me about growing up. Your life is so wildly different from mine that I can't even imagine your childhood in that big ass mansion.'

'It was pretty good when we were little. My bed was a fancy bespoke princess castle with a tower, a slide, and everything. I loved that bed. After Mum was killed, Dad lost any sense of frivolity he'd ever had and had it all torn out and replaced with beautiful, but very sensible rooms. Mum lit up his universe, and when she went, it just crushed him. They used to pack us up and take us to the beach at a moment's notice if the sun dared shine. We'd eat soggy sandwiches, buy ice cream, and stay there until the sun dipped in the sky. They were so in love, and seeing it made me want that for myself. That love you'd just do anything for.'

'Why didn't he look for revenge?'

'He did, at first. Until Harold killed my eldest brother. Malcolm Jr thought he could blaze into Harold's place and just shoot to kill. He learned that someone like Harold expects people to be trying to kill him due to him being an utter cockwomble of a human being. It broke Dad when

Malc died, and he just wanted to keep us all out of Harold's way.'

I stroked along her jawline, smiling as she turned to kiss my palm. 'Why does he hate your family so much?'

'Because he was in love with my mum, and she chose my dad. They were thick as thieves as teenagers, building up from the low rungs in other gangs to forming their own together. They were ruthless together and soon amassed a crime organisation that rivalled any of the others. Then Mum appeared, and they were both instantly smitten, both vying for her attention. And she revelled in it, going from one to the other and even both at the same time. I think she thought they could all be together, but both my dad and Harold were much too jealous to entertain that. They both liked to conquer completely, and although they shared a business, sharing a woman was too much. Harold gave her an ultimatum, and she chose dad. It left him furious and wild and erased any moral compass he once held.'

'Why wait so long for revenge?'

'They still worked together for a while, and then Harold met his wife, and Dad distanced from him, creating his own empire. For a while, Harold seemed happy, at least externally, but his wife could never live up to the image he had in his head for her. From what I've heard, he was horrifically cruel to both her and his two kids, to the point she abandoned them and disappeared. Harold seems to have that effect on women.'

I sighed and closed my eyes, the bus jostling us as the rural landscape swept by. 'Why did your dad agree to let him marry you, knowing all that?'

'I'm collateral damage. Risk the one to save the many. I'm pretty sure he hates himself for agreeing to it too, but he's already lost his wife and his eldest son. He wants to avoid losing any more kids to Harold's bullets. Not to mention how unstable things have been recently, Harold is powerful, much more so than Dad. He has his fingers in so many pies that it's beginning to strangle Dad's hold in Glasgow, and marrying me off will theoretically end this war between the two of them. Not that I foresee it working. Harold just wants to twist the knife.'

'You don't deserve this,' I said, my thumb drifting over her cheek.

'I know. But if it's me or Maeve, then I have no choice. She's my baby sister.'

We ran out of words for some time; the bus lulling us into silence as I wracked my brain, trying to find a way out for Esther. Trying to find the possibility of a future for us. Every which way just ended in death, hers or mine. Harold wasn't a man to mess with, even for someone like me who killed for a living. He was well aware of the pile of enemies waiting for a chance to destroy him, so he gathered men around him who would shoot first, question later.

My jaw tightened as I looked out of the window, anger tearing at my innards. I was fucking useless, and I would be the one to deliver Esther back to the monster awaiting her.

I should have left her in the taverna when I had the chance.

THIRTY-ONE
ESTHER

The masseuse finished rubbing her oiled hands across my legs as I sighed happily. Alec had booked a fantastic hotel, all marbled flooring, floor-to-ceiling windows, and even a luxury spa. We'd pretended for two days that this wasn't the beginning of the end and just ate good food, walked about the city hand in hand, and fucked like a pair of people possessed. Between using his card online, and my ill-gotten dancing cash, we'd lived like kings.

It had been the best few days of my life. I couldn't decide whether it was because I knew our time was limited, so I didn't have any of the holding back that oft came with new relationships, or the fact I'd seen him cut a dick into a man's stomach to defend my honour, but the barriers between us had evaporated.

The masseuse pulled a warm towel up over my back before stepping out of the room, leaving me with the gentle tinkling of music coming from the in-room sound system. I placed my head on my arm, spying on Alec where he sat on the roof terrace. His chest rose and fell smoothly as he cat-napped in the sun, his blond hair peeping out from the hat he'd pulled down over his face. Warmth filled my stomach as I watched him, mulling over everything I knew about him. What would he do when we went back, and I was out of his hair?

Loneliness clung to him as surely as his shadow, leaving visible chasms around his heart. I hadn't seen them before, but I'd never been looking past his sexy bad boy shell. Inside, he was sweeter than I'd ever imagined he could be. Protective. Dare I say it, loving. He thrived off of my touch and my attention, and never had I felt so needed. So wanted. It was killing me. This glimpse of what could be was a curse as much as it was a blessing, because I'd know its absence all the more keenly when he was no longer within reach.

I took a quick shower before sliding open the door to the rooftop and walking naked to the jumbo-sized hot tub.

Alec murmured his approval as I walked past him, putting a little more wiggle in my step for his benefit.

'Keep wiggling that thing at me, and I'm going to have to take another bite,' he said, sliding his hat off and putting it on the table beside him.

'You wouldn't dare.'

'Oh, but you know I would. I'd get it good and red first, too.'

'Promises, promises,' I sighed with an overly dramatic flair, hitting the button by the pool that kicked the bubbles to life.

The water was glorious as I sank into it; the jets soothing against my muscles. I closed my eyes and leant back against the side; the sun warming my face. Until a shadow stole the heat.

His hand was in my hair before I could even open my eyes, pulling me up and over the edge of the hot tub so that my arse was on full display. Thankfully, with the height of the hotel and our top-floor suite, it was unlikely anyone could see.

Three sharp slaps rang out loudly as his hand connected with my wet skin. I muffled a cry into my arm as I writhed against the edge of the tub.

'I don't break promises, sweetheart. If you get all bratty on me, I'll tan your arse until it's double the size, and you can't sit down when I take you to dinner.'

'I'd like to see you try,' I said, smirking until he landed me with some more stingy slaps.

'All mouth, aren't you? Well, Princess, you know what they say about idle mouths, don't you? Open up, baby.'

He pulled me to my knees, my bottom half submerged in the water as he straddled the side of the tub in front of me, his shorts already gone and his dick filled to bursting.

I licked my lips and looked up at him.

'I said open.'

I did as he asked, opening my mouth wide and sticking my tongue out.

'Yes, that's it, sweetie. See, you can behave so well when there's some dick in it for you, can't you?'

I nodded, trying to swallow as drool built up on my tongue. His thumb slid over my lip before he thrust two fingers into my mouth. My stomach lurched as he pressed them far against the back of my tongue. When I coughed, he grinned. 'I love it when you get all desperate, Esther. Do you want my cock now?'

Nodding again, he grinned, running his hand over the head of his cock before positioning himself so he could drag it against my lips.

'Get your cunt against one of those jets. I want to feel you struggle as you suck me down.'

Separating my knees slightly, I shifted until one jet hit me just right. Holy fuck. I'd always been a huge fan of the shower head for a bit of me time, but doing it while Alec fisted my hair and pierced my mouth with his dick was something else.

The first orgasm rolled over me as I let him slide his cock into my mouth. My cheeks burned as he laughed, holding my gaze as the tremors shook me. 'Already, baby? Fuck, I love how turned on you get.'

I hadn't always come at the drop of a hat with a partner, but with Alec, it took everything not to just orgasm at the first touch. The way he was in bed had me forever teetering on the edge of excitement.

When my body calmed down, he used his fist in my hair to guide my mouth over his cock. 'How do you want it? Are you in the mood to worship my dick or to be fucked by it?'

'Fucked,' I said without hesitation. I loved when we slowed down and sex turned into something closer to lovemaking, but I couldn't get enough when he took over and used me to satisfy himself.

'You got it, Princess.'

My fingers dug into his thighs as he filled my mouth, alternating between stuffing me to bursting with cock and fucking my mouth with long strokes. I closed my eyes and focussed on the tight pull of his fingers in my hair and the way he grunted and moaned when my lips and tongue hit him just right.

'Your mouth is my fucking happy place, Esther,' he groaned, tilting his hips as his strokes grew more erratic. My moans travelled the length of his cock as I looked up at him, my lips spread tightly around his shaft. 'Look at you, such a fucking delight.'

His eyes closed as he ground against my mouth, slipping

deeper into my throat and making me cough up great strings of saliva. 'Such a good girl, aren't you? Always happy to please.'

He pulled out of my mouth and got in the tub behind me, thrusting into me with one hard stroke that took my breath away.

'Fuck, Alec!'

He grunted against my ear as he kissed and bit at my neck, my nipples grazing the edge of the tub with each hard stroke. His hand groped between my legs, angling me so that the jet hit right against my clit as I cried out.

'You... are... a... fucking... dream,' he gasped against my ear as his thrusts quickened, sending the sensations inside me into overdrive. Between the aching thrusts of his dick and the never-ceasing jet at my clit, I was tumbling quickly toward the edge again.

His hands slipped to my hips as he crushed me against his cock, his wrangled cry loud in the afternoon air. It was all I needed to send me crashing into a full-body orgasm, crushed between him, the jet and the wall as I joined him in ecstasy.

We stayed there, locked together and being blasted by bubbles until we caught our breaths, eventually settling back in the water with me in his lap, his arms tucked tight around my waist and him still lost inside of me.

'Marry me, Esther?' His voice was a whisper against my ear, and I closed my eyes as an ache gripped my heart.

'You know I can't.'

'You want to though, don't you?'

'I... I can't go down that path. I can't let myself. All it will bring is heartbreak.'

'I'll be broken-hearted either way,' he said, his fingers grazing over my hips. 'If we marry, they'll have no choice.'

He was right. I wanted to be with him. Maybe not marriage. It was too soon for that, but I wanted to see what could come from this. But I had no choice. Maeve would be next.

'One bullet and he'd make me a widow. Either that or he'd be hurting Maeve, and I just can't leave her there.'

'We can take her with us, find a new life together.'

I turned my head so that I could meet his eyes, trailing a hand over his jaw. 'We can't run forever. Harold will never let it go. You can find someone else. Have a family. You can be happy.'

'I don't want someone else.' He kissed me softly before leaning his forehead against mine and closing his eyes. 'I want you. I want to be the man you come home to, who looks after you and listens to you talk about your day. I want to be the man who kisses away your tears and makes you laugh. I want it all, Esther.

My heart was in ribbons, broken shards littering my chest. Tears gathered at the edge of my eyes as I kissed him back, both of us knowing that this thing between us had to end. Hell, we never should have started it.

'I want it too,' I whispered. 'But we know I can't.'

I was going to kill Harold with my own fucking hands if I had to.

THIRTY-TWO

ALEC

Esther's lashes lay heavy against her cheek as I watched her sleeping, her cheek pressed tightly against my chest. Her body was like a little radiator - too hot for comfortable sleeping, but neither did I want to move away from her.

The entire night had been far more sombre than I'd meant for it to be. After she refused my somewhat harried proposal, the reality of what was to come weighed heavily on us both. Food tasted like ash on my tongue despite it being cooked by excellent chefs, and the sunset had dulled to grey by the melancholy that stuck to me like tar. The moment the question had fallen from my lips, I had set the dream in stone. It was fast and foolish, but I wanted Esther to be mine.

Then she'd said no.

It should have soothed me that it wasn't because of me, but because of the situation. I'd opened myself up to rejection for the first time in a long time, and it cut deep. For the longest time I'd kept guarded, but she'd wormed her way in and left an Esther-shaped hole inside of me that I feared would never be filled. She told me I'd find someone else, but they'd never fit in her gap, no matter how hard I tried to force it to work.

She shifted against me, her lips parting slightly and her hair tickling against my shoulder. Fuck, she was beautiful. I wanted to keep her there until I memorised every freckle on her face, until I knew every curve, until the smell of her was so ingrained into my nostrils that I'd know it the second she walked into a room.

How had she done it? I'd had sex before, and it had never left me so ripped open and raw. It couldn't be that. Was it her letting me see the real her, the one behind the perfect mafia kid facade? Was it her tenacity and her fight? Whatever it was, I had fallen hard.

It wasn't fair.

Why did she have to be the one for me? When I couldn't have her?

I'd kill Harold myself, the absolute arsehole that just kept ruining people's lives.

I closed my eyes, tipping my head to breathe in the smell of Esther's hair. Was I no better than Harold? I'd ruined plenty of lives doing my job. Never for any good reason, or never any good reason of my own. I'd lived my life as a puppet, enjoying having my strings coordinated and the false sense of being needed by Logan and Malcolm.

My eyes were wet when I opened them. Painful memories bombarded me from the recesses of my mind where I'd stuffed them. The outline of my mother and father, so fucking distant and blurry with all the years that had gone by. That whisper of love that I remembered, the feeling of being wanted. Secure. Then the stacks of memories from my time after them, stuck in a system that gave little regard for me. The social workers had usually meant well, but once they'd labelled me difficult, it was my word against the foster carers. They were adults. They knew how to manipulate and lie far better than I knew how to stand up for myself. The slippery slope to where I became a man to fear, a man who didn't flinch when he removed fingers or scored threats into people with a knife. Where I'd grown so hardened that nothing mattered. The fight to have my place, something that was finally mine to keep, that no one would take away. I'd give it all up for even a whiff of a chance with Esther. To be the man she comes home to, the man who soothes her pain and brings her joy.

'Hey,' her groggy voice broke through my thoughts, her fingers wiping away the tears as I stared at the ceiling. 'It's okay. It's all going to be okay.'

'No. It isn't.'

She nuzzled against my neck. 'I know.'

'I want the chance to love you right, Esther. Not like this, in hiding and secret. But for real.'

'You love me?' Her voice shook, her eyes meeting mine as she sat up, leaning over me.

'How could I not?'

The smile that broke across her face didn't quite reach her eyes, which were as glassy and as wet as my own. 'Oh Alec, if you can't love me right, then love me wrong.'

Then she was everywhere at once, her mouth on my own, her hands lost in my hair, and her body pressed fully against me. Beams of orange light were streaking across her freckled skin as the day came to be. The day that would ruin me.

I gave as good as she did, turning us over so that I crushed her beneath me. Our tongues collided in feverish abandon, words replaced with raw emotion as our souls crashed and entwined.

Every kiss, every swipe of my tongue, every groan, it all screamed I love you. I love you. I love you.

Another roll of her body landed her above me, her guiding me inside of her with an arch of her hips that took my breath away. My fingers dug their imprints into her hips as I moved her against me, matching the harsh movements she made until she was whimpering above me.

I nipped at her lips as she moaned into my mouth, her skin hot to the touch. It was too fast, too much. I needed to slow down. In a few hours, we'd be on a plane, and I wanted to savour her.

'Slow down, baby, I'm not ready to finish, and if you keep that up, I'm going to blow as quick as a fucking virgin. You feel too good.'

She giggled as I flipped her over on the bed and knelt between her thighs, idly toying with her clit. Enough to drive her crazy, but not enough to let her come.

'Do you remember what you asked me to do before I took you home?'

The crimson that flushed her cheeks told me it hadn't been far from her mind either.

'Yes,' she said, swallowing hard as I ran my fingers down and dipped them inside of her.

'What?'

'I wanted you to fuck my ass.' She choked out the words as I rewarded her with a sweep of my fingers against her g-spot.

'Do you still want that?'

'If you want to...'

I pinched her clit, sending her hips jolting off of the bed as she yelped. 'Good girls always ask for what they want.'

Her timidness about it only made me all the harder.

'Yes,' she whispered, 'I would like you to fuck my ass. Please?'

I leant over and pulled out the lube, dripping some over her pussy as her eyes widened when the cool liquid met her hot skin. 'We're going to take it slow. Do you remember the safe word I gave you?'

'Home,' she moaned as I slipped my fingers over her clit. The word had a whole different meaning now. She was my home.

'Use it if you need to.'

I alternated between fingering her with long strokes and teasing her clit until she came hard in my hands, giving me a beautiful view of her trembling body. 'That's it. We need you nice and loose before I'm going to fill you up. Need every muscle to have been spent before you'll be ready to take me. And you will take me, won't you?'

'I will,' she panted as I didn't let up, working her up again.

'You'll be so pretty with your ass around my cock, taking every inch. I'm so fucking hard at the thought of making you my dirty girl.' I ground my cock against her ass, letting her feel for herself. Her needy whimpers were like fucking crack.

When she came a second time, I added more lube and touched my fingers to her ass, running them slowly around the puckered flesh as her muscles tightened. I kept up the slow outer tease as her mouth formed a little O, her thighs relaxing open as she moved against my touch, wanting more.

She tensed when I finally slipped a finger into her but gave in to the sensation when I used my other hand on her clit, rubbing in slow strokes. The tiny moans she gave encouraged me to add another finger, taking my time to let her adjust to the stretch, teasing her until she was relaxed and open again.

'Atta girl, you're so fucking tight, sweetie.'

When I added a third finger, she was trembling, orgasm threatening to overwhelm her. I grinned as I watched every different flash of emotion on her face. From the wince when I added a finger to the acceptance as I teased her clit, to the pure need as the sensations built.

I wanted to live right there, where I could see every part of her, forever.

THIRTY-THREE

ESTHER

My brain felt like it had melted into my spine as all my focus went to his fingers slowly moving inside me. Holy shit, it felt insane. Good, but so different from anything sexual I'd felt prior. When he slipped a fourth finger inside of me, I gripped tightly at his arm, breathing hard as the moment of fire passed.

I wanted him to be inside of me so badly, needed him close, not with the space that was between us.

'You okay? Need a break?' Alec said, pausing.

'No. I need you.'

'Just a little longer. I want to make sure you're ready.'

'Now,' I said, 'Please. I need all of you.'

'I don't want to hurt you.'

'Fuck me, Alec.'

Then he was there, lubed up and ready. I bit back a gasp as he pressed forward slowly, the head of his cock invading me. The sensation took my breath away.

'Breathe baby. Breathe and relax. If you tense up, it will hurt.'

His words soothed me, sending flutters of warmth to my

core. He teased at the tight inner ring of muscles with the head of his dick for what felt like forever, working me up from the stretching pain and fear until I was desperate to have him fully inside.

'I'm going to fuck you. Remember your safe word and use it if you want to.'

I nodded, looking up into his beautiful, ice-blue eyes as he pushed his way into my ass. My hips bucked up in his hands until he pushed them firmly downwards, holding me steady as he groaned. 'Fuck, Esther, you are amazing.'

Heat arose in my cheeks as I looked down and watched him inside me, his tattooed fingers pressing me down firmly while my legs were splayed wide. It was intoxicating.

'Do you see, baby? See how you open up for me? I knew you could do it.'

I writhed beneath his praise, warmth bubbling up in my chest as he leaned forward to kiss me, his lips hungry and demanding. The movement sunk him fully inside me, bringing a tremble to my knees as I whimpered against his tongue.

The kiss deepened, my hunger matching his as he moved within me, tilting and rocking his hips, driving me insane with lust. It was sore but in the best way. It was dirty and still so right with him. I'd do anything to see that bliss on his face the first moment he was fully seated in me, his eyes glazing and his groans sending me into a tailspin.

When he increased the speed and depths of his thrusts, I clung to his shoulders, very much being taken for a ride. I gripped my thighs around his waist and lost myself in an oblivion of sensation. His chest brushed against my nipples, leaving them hard while his stomach brushed against my clit in the most delicious way.

'Look at you taking all of me like a good girl. Letting me have something you've given no one else.'

'It feels good, I think.'

'Don't worry, baby, you are going to come so hard for me in a minute, then I'm going to fill your pretty little ass with my cum.'

'Oh, god,' I moaned as I pulled his lips back to mine, licking and sucking at him in between desperate kisses. The intimacy almost burned with the knowledge it would likely be the last time we could be together.

Then he was up on his knees, his cock moving quickly inside me as he grinned down at me, as I lost my ever-loving mind at the sensations driving me higher and higher.

I whimpered as he slid his fingers inside of me, filling me up in both holes at the same time.

'Touch your cunt, sweetie,' he growled down at me, his eyes darkening as I followed his instructions, circling my swollen clit and causing my hips to jolt. It made him thrust harder, deeper, his balls pressing against my ass with each stroke.

When he curled the fingers inside of me up against the front of my vagina, I lost it. He tipped me into an orgasm that ripped me apart, my pussy and ass gripping at him furiously as I cried out, writhing deeper into the bed. Alec rode out my waves with a punishing series of thrusts that made me see stars. He came hard, deep inside of me, his moans like an ointment to my soul. At that moment, I loved him. With every fibre of my being. I needed him, wanted him. Wanted that moment not to end.

He collapsed against me as I pushed my fingers into his hair and kissed his slick neck. I wanted to tell him, to shout it from the rooftops. *I love you. I fucking love you, Alec.*

I kept my mouth closed as I breathed him in, trying to

commit his manly scent to memory. I wanted to hold on to that perfect moment so that I could put myself back into it every time I would be forced to submit to Harold. Alec would be my safe space, the place I'd go to when I had to protect myself from my soon-to-be husband. Having him in my life wouldn't be possible, but having him locked in my heart and mind was something no one could take from me.

As his breathing became less ragged, he carried me to the bathroom and cleaned us both up, his fingers deft and strong as I let him wash me, soothe me, and bring me back to the real world.

'You were amazing, Esther. You are amazing.'

'You are pretty epic yourself there.'

He wrapped me in a towel before grazing his lips over my own, the sweetness of the gesture pricking my eyes with tears that I desperately hoped wouldn't fall.

'Hey,' he said, wrapping me up in his arms as I buried my head in his chest. 'It's okay.'

'It's not okay. It will never be okay again.' I sniffled as the tears took over.

'You are so strong, Esther, there will be an answer, a way out.'

Not if Harold broke me before I found a way to kill him.

Alec tilted my face until our eyes met, kissing my tears away. 'Are you sure you don't want to run away with me?'

'I do. I want to hide in your arms, stay hidden away with you. But I need to go back. To stop Maeve from taking my place.'

Alec sighed, his fingers tightening against my lower back as he took another kiss from me, letting me pour my angst into him, his lips like a band-aid to my breaking heart. 'If you need me, you can call me anytime.'

'I will.'

Except for the fact that I'd likely be killed when I took Harold out. You didn't take down the head of a crime syndicate with no repercussions. It would be worth it to rid the planet of Harold Thompson.

I'd take death over the misery of living with him, and without Alec and my family, any day.

'We need to get cleaned up, dressed, and packed,' Alec said against my lips, his voice cracking as he spoke.

So we did.

Darkness settled over me with each step toward the life I'd thought I could run from.

I'd make Harold regret ever messing with me.

THIRTY-FOUR
ALEC

Her silence worried me.

During the plane journey back she'd barely uttered a word, staring out of the window and tearing her paper napkin into her lap to a million pieces.

It was killing me. I'd thought hard about whether to just kidnap her. Drag her to a remote cottage somewhere and keep her in my arms until everything played out and passed at home. I wanted to protect her, to be there for her. But what could I do?

I toyed with the knife in my pocket, the metal warm beneath my fingers. It had cost me the phone I'd stolen to smuggle it through the airport. Thankfully, the young guy on the metal detectors had been open to bribery. It was one thing that had been with me for years. It had been there as part of my work, as protection, and as a threat. Usually, the touch of it by my side brought peace to me, but not anymore. What use was my knife if I couldn't protect my girl with it?

The car pulled up outside of her mansion; her father standing on the steps with a furrowed brow.

Before she got out of the car, I reached over and took her fingers in my own, squeezing them firmly as she took a shaky breath.

'You'll be okay,' I told her, trying to convince myself in the same breath.

She turned toward me, fixing those green eyes that had captured my soul. 'Thank you for everything, Alec.'

'For what? Taking you back here?'

'No. For giving me a glimpse of how good it can be. I got to have everything I've ever craved for a little while, and I'm glad it happened. That we happened.'

I choked down the torrent of emotion that threatened to send me into a tailspin. I had to be strong for her.

'You are everything I never knew I needed--'

The wrenching of the car door cut me off mid-sentence, Logan peering inside the car as I dropped her fingers and cleared my throat. 'Esther, you crazy fuck. I can't believe you ran away. Props to you. Best get your ass inside, though. Dad is livid, and Harold's on the warpath.'

He helped her out of the car as I followed a few paces behind, desperately trying to push my crumbled walls back into place around my heart. She'd obliterated them, and I needed their protection more than ever.

She'll be okay.

She has to be okay.

Would I be?

I followed behind Logan and Esther, hyperaware of her every movement. The tremble of her fingers as she reached for the door, the turn of her head, checking where I was. The way she stiffened as Logan pulled her gently across the threshold.

The need to gather her up in my arms and run with her

itched against my skin, my fingernails digging sharply into my palms as I tensed.

'Esther!' Maeve was on her within a few steps into the house, her arms wide as she threw them around her older sister. 'I've missed you so much.'

Esther's tense shoulders softened as she hugged her sister back, pulling her tight against her and breathing her in. 'Missed you, too.'

'I can't believe you're here. We were beginning to think you'd actually disappeared for good,' Maeve said as the women separated, Logan smiling at them both.

Another shot of pain to the chest. Even after everything, she still belonged. Still had people desperate to see her, to know that she's okay. I wanted to be part of her circle, her person. What awaited me on getting home? Nothing. Even my plants would be dead.

Logan came over to me and patted my back with a firm hand. 'Thanks, pal. Sorry, she gave you such a runaround.'

'She burnt down my car.'

'Didn't know she had it in her.'

Me either, I thought, watching her talk softly to her sister. There was so much I hadn't known about Esther. So much that I wish I didn't know now. How could I hand her back knowing they promised her to a man she hated? How could I watch her become his? Knowing that I want her to be mine?

'Best get this show on the road. C'mon, guys.'

Every step toward the drawing room felt tougher and tougher, like my feet were being dragged into the floor by unseen forces. It was all wrong.

Sweat glazed the back of my neck as I walked in behind them and spotted Harold leaning against the mantlepiece, looking like the cat who got the cream. I pocketed a hand, sliding my fingers over the warm metal of my knife. The muscles in my forearms tensed as I fought the urge to march over there and stab it into his neck. Sure, his men, loitering around the edge of the room, would be armed to fuck and have me riddled with bullet holes within seconds, but it would be worth it if Esther would be free.

Unfortunately, flying bullets would endanger her and her family, too.

I swallowed hard as a shit-eating grin crossed Harold's face.

'Here she is, my errant wife-to-be. I don't enjoy waiting for things that belong to me. You've been a bad girl, Esther.'

Her name on his lips was like a knife to the leg. My breath came hard through my nose as I fought the urge to pounce.

'Sorry,' she said, more meekly than I'd ever heard her.

'That's okay. You have an entire lifetime to make it up. We can start right now.'

Fury erupted inside of me as he sauntered toward her, every part of her tensing up as the space closed between them. I gripped my knife between my fingers, losing all sense of self as I got ready to cut him into fucking ribbons.

A hand gripped my arm as I went to move, Logan looking at me with a small head-shake.

'Don't do it,' he mouthed.

The delay was enough to have made it too late. Harold grabbed Esther harshly by the arms before kissing her hard, his tongue slipping against her tightly closed mouth. Revulsion roiled my stomach as Logan's fingers tightened further.

Esther stood her ground, not reciprocating but not flinching either. When Harold stepped back, there was pure hate in her green eyes.

Harold laughed. 'I like it when they fight. Don't worry, I'll fuck the fight right out of you.'

My eyes flicked to her father, who sat on the sofa, his eyes off to the left, avoiding the situation entirely. The fucker knew it was wrong, but he let it happen anyway, let the man who killed his wife and his son molest his daughter. How could he?

'We'll be married within a week,' Harold said.

'Two,' Esther countered. 'I want some time with my family first.'

Malcolm stood, finally inserting himself into the situation. 'I think two weeks is soon enough, Harold. I'll make sure she doesn't go anywhere this time.'

Harold looked from Malcolm to Esther, his jaw ticking as he mulled it over.

'Two weeks gives more time to organise a grand wedding, where you can show off the union to more of our peers. Make more impact with it.' Malcolm stroked the side of Harold that loved a spectacle.

'Fine,' he said, 'But I will put her up in an apartment with my guys watching her. I don't trust your surveillance after the last escapade.'

'I'll add some of mine too. And we need to see her.'

'I'll give access to her family members.'

That excluded me.

'And you don't touch her until you're married,' Logan countered.

Harold laughed, sending a chill down my spine. 'I've plenty cunt to use in the meantime. She's not so irresistible that I can't wait two weeks to fuck her.'

Esther's face pulled into a disgusted frown as she looked from her father to Harold.

Harold moved to leave, his men gathering behind him as

he walked up to Esther. I'd thought he would kiss her again, and tensed, ready to witness it despite every part of me wanting to run between them and rip his fucking face off.

A loud thwack resounded along with a yelp from Esther as Harold backhanded her hard across the cheek.

'What the fuck?' Malcolm said, grabbing Esther by the arm and pulling her out of his reach. Her hand cradled the spot where he slapped her, tears pricking at the edges of her eyes.

I saw red.

I was almost on him, knife drawn, when hands pulled me back from behind. I struggled against them, needing to spill his blood for hurting my girl. Needing to see his skin split and his motherfucking entrails hit the floor.

'Stand down,' Malcolm roared at me, while Logan joined the hands holding me firm.

Harold watched me, his eyes flaring with interest. 'What do you care? You were the one who brought her back. If anything, I should thank you for bringing my wife to me, but here you are acting like a lovesick puppy.'

He looked from Esther back to me, then grinned. 'Oh, I see. She's been paying you with her cunt, has she? A little slut. Just like her mother.'

I tensed against the men holding me, trying to get leverage to rip the arsehole to shreds.

'It must have been a mighty fine cunt too, to have you ready to get yourself killed. Good to know.'

He walked out without another word, followed by his men as Esther crumpled into her sister's arms. Tension thrummed around the room, hands releasing me after Harold's exit, leaving me feeling exposed.

'Dad, you need to call this off,' Esther said, her voice trembling in a way that tore me apart.

'I can't. You know we need this war to end.' Malcolm ran a hand through his greying hair, his face ashen as everyone faced him.

'He hit me.'

'You're lucky that's all he did.'

Logan interjected, 'She'd right Dad, you can't marry her off to him. He'll destroy her.'

'It is her, or all of you. I can't lose everyone,' Malcolm said, steeling his shoulders and avoiding Esther's eyes.

'Why am I worth less than them?' The pain in Esther's voice was raw.

'They are my boys. They carry on the business.'

I needed to gather her up in my arms, to soothe the aches that plagued her. To keep her safe.

'Alec, Logan, with me. Esther, go get your things packed for moving to the apartment. Maeve, go with your sister.'

We shared one last, lingering look as I followed Malcolm out of the room, my body screaming at me to stay with her. She hadn't been out of my sight, out of my reach, since we'd given into the passion between us, and it burned to be away from her. It was all wrong.

MALCOLM PACED the floor of his office as Logan and I stood rigidly in the middle of the room. A vein throbbed menacingly on his forehead, and he kept stopping to talk before deciding against it and resuming his pacing.

'I want to leave, find work somewhere else,' I said, knowing working for them and being so close, watching Esther married to Harold, it would kill me.

'I'm still deciding whether you need a bullet between

the eyes.' Malcolm fixed me with a hard stare. 'I should have your bollocks off for daring to touch my daughter.'

His threats skimmed over me, too emotional to care if he followed them through. 'You can't force me to stay here.'

'I bloody well can. You're handy with a knife, but you won't get far before my men would be in here and filling you with lead. We have spent years getting you to where you are. My boys have taken you under their wing lately, and this is how you'll thank them? Fucking their sister and then ditching them?'

His words hurt. All I'd wanted was to be one of them. To be accepted by the tight-knit family and to feel like I belonged. Even as I tried to reject them, that little boy deep inside my soul longed to grasp onto any smidgen of attention they might give me.

'It wasn't like that.'

'What was it like, Alec? Did you think she loved you? Did you think you two could waltz back in here hand in hand and that Harold would just roll over and give her up? He'll never stop trying until he has what he wants.'

Malcolm lashed out and sent an ornament flying off of his desk, the metallic object splintering a chair leg as it connected. Logan flinched and looked at his father wide-eyed. 'Do you think I want this? I love her. She's my daughter, and I don't want to see her given over to him any more than you do. But I've lost too much. She might suffer, but no more than she might have with any man she married. At least she knows going into it. She'll have all the wealth she could want, be able to travel the world, and buy anything she desires. There are worse positions to be in.'

He rounded on me, pointing a finger in my direction and jabbing it into the air. You will not fuck this up for me. You hear? What do you have to offer her? Your skills at torturing information out of people? You have nothing other than what I provide for you. Nothing!'

His words burned through me like acid, leaving sharp pains seething inside. I had nothing to offer her. My love had been enough when we were in limbo, but in the real world, what did I have? A shitty three-bed house in a rundown suburb of Glasgow. A job that paid enough to keep me fed and kept the mortgage paid. Nothing like the lifestyle she had been brought up with.

'You're right,' I sighed, sitting hard on the edge of a table and running my hand over my face. Logan rested his hand on my shoulder, squeezing lightly as Malcolm nodded.

'Good. You needed to accept that before I could keep you here. Thank you for finding her and bringing her home.'

Malcolm made for the door, his fingers gripping the handle as he turned back to fix me with a stare. 'I'm going to let it go this once, but if you even lay a hand on any of my children again, I will flay you alive.'

Logan slumped down next to me as we sat in silence, the whirlwind of events making me feel nauseated. Minutes ticked by before either of us spoke.

'I wish it was you she was marrying,' Logan said softly, looking straight ahead. 'I'd have liked for you to be my brother in a more formal way. You'd be good for Esther, you know?'

His kind words hurt almost as much as Malcolm's harsh ones. 'Thanks. I've fallen for her hard. I don't know what to do.'

'Just keep your head up. Someone's going to kill Harold one of these days. Maybe you'll both get another chance. If you can wait for her.'

Wait for her. Could I? My pulse quickened at the thought, but my brain hit me with a dose of reality. Waiting would be nothing but pain. Watching from afar as she bruised beneath his hands, as she sat beside him while he pawed at her, at her pain-filled eyes and wanting to reach out for her. To protect her. I wasn't strong enough to do it. Yet another failure.

'I can't,' I breathed, my lungs feeling like they were constricting as my chest tightened.

'It's okay. It'll all be okay.'

THIRTY-FIVE
ESTHER

The days passed by slowly as I waited in my apartment cell. It may have been far more opulent than an actual prison, but I was every bit as confined.

I stood on the small balcony, as I had done every evening for the past week, and thought earnestly about throwing myself down onto the bustling road below. The fall would likely kill me but if I timed it right so that I fell in front of a truck, I could almost guarantee my death.

I didn't want to die.

It was preferable to marrying Harold, though. There was only one week left until I had to walk down the aisle and promise myself to him. The plans were finalised, and escape was all but impossible.

My father hadn't even intervened when Harold had struck me in front of him. I'd been abandoned.

A biting wind rushed over my face as I stepped closer to the rails, closing my eyes and taking a deep breath. My stomach lurched as I gripped the railings, ready to do it this time, to throw myself over and end it all. But Maeve's sweet face flashed in my mind. Killing myself would only put her back in my shoes. Only perpetuate the situation. It would make my coming back at all utterly worthless.

I missed Alec. I needed to crawl into his lap and have him soothe my fears, have him kiss me until I forgot my name. I needed him to take over and let me escape my mind while I gave everything over to him. A choked sob caught in my throat as I pictured him smiling at me, that cocksure grin lighting up his features. He'd been ready to fight for me when no one else would, even though I'd fucked things up for him.

Tearing myself from the railing, I walked back into the open plan sitting room-come-kitchen. I flopped myself down on the large grey sofa and closing my eyes, only opening them when the front door clicked.

Maeve popped her head in, her face lighting up when I smiled at her.

'Oh good, you're still here.'

'Where else would I be?' I asked, joining her in the kitchen as she placed a pizza box on the counter. The spicy, cheese-laden aroma had my mouth watering instantly.

'Scaling the side of the building, escaping through a sewer, running off with a dashing, knife-wielding maniac. You know?'

'Ha, funny.' I glanced at the door that hid the teams of security behind it, before lowering my voice to a whisper. 'Did you get it?'

'Under the pizza,' she mouthed back.

'Ew.' I screwed up my face as she lifted the lid to the pizza box.

'You know they check my bags and pat me down every time I come in here. It was under there or up my chuff. I think that's the lesser of two evils.'

She was right, but still.

'Do you think it will still work?'

'Yeah, I wrapped it in foil first. I'm not an idiot,' Maeve said. grabbing a slice and taking a bite, revealing the sliver of silver poking out beneath.

I took it in trembling fingers and slipped it up my sleeve. I had seen no cameras in the apartment, but I didn't put it past Harold to be monitoring me.

'Bathroom?' I said.

'Bathroom.'

We locked ourselves in, flicking on the shower to add some noise over our conversation, just in case.

'Do you really think you might be pregnant?' she whispered as I opened the packet.

'I'm three days late.'

'Didn't you use protection?'

'We didn't have any, and it seemed pointless. I meant to get a pill when I came home, but I had no time. I don't want to ask Harold for some. Not until I at least know.'

'It could just be stress,' Maeve said, turning her back to me as I sat on the toilet and peed. Placing the cover over the end of the test, I turned it over and set it on the windowsill, swallowing hard.

'I hope it's just stress.' Did I, though? I certainly didn't intend to be pregnant with one man's baby while marrying another, but it would let me keep a little piece of Alec for myself. It was selfish and stupid, but my heart leapt at the thought.

'Harold will make you get rid of it,' Maeve said, sitting on the edge of the tub while I washed my hands.

'Only if he knew about it. I don't think it will take him long to--' I swallowed hard, the thought of Harold on top of me making me want to hurl. 'To consummate the marriage. And I can hide a two or three-week discrepancy.'

We waited, side by side, as Maeve reached out and held my hand. Taking a steadying breath, I reached out and held the test up. Two lines stood out against the white, as bold as you like.

'Fuck,' I whispered.

'Fuck,' Maeve agreed. 'I don't know whether to hug you, or cry for you.'

'Both,' I said as a tear fled down my cheek, a whole plethora of emotions tipping over my head. Maeve wrapped me up in her arms, and the close contact broke through me anew. Within a few weeks, my whole life had been turned upside down. I went from a single woman living with my family, having barely a care, to being engaged to a monster with another man's baby inside of me, and having felt what love could be only to have it ripped away.

'You'll be okay,' Maeve said, holding me close as I sobbed into her hair.

'I won't.' I sniffed as I reached for some toilet tissue, wiping at my snotty nose.

'Will you tell Alec?'

'No, I can't. It would kill him. All he's ever wanted is a family of his own, and he'd end up getting himself shot over it. It's not worth him dying over. He'll move on, eventually, and meet a nice girl and be able to fill her with babies.' The thought of him with someone else made my blood boil, however hypocritically. 'no one else can know. Swear you won't tell.'

Maeve's eyebrows furrowed before she nodded with a sigh. 'Alright, I won't tell him, but I still think you owe it to him to let him know.'

He deserved to know but knowing would be too painful. It was a secret I was going to have to keep from him.

For his safety and the baby's. Harold would kill them both otherwise.

'Here,' Maeve said, fishing something from her pocket before placing it in my hand. 'You ought to have Mum's necklace back.'

'Thank you,' I said, slipping it around my neck and clasping it at the back before carefully wrapping the pregnancy test back in the foil and slipping it up my sleeve. It wouldn't be able to go out the way it came in, so I'd have to find alternate means of getting rid of it. The rubbish bin definitely wasn't a safe option, with Harold's penchant for control.

Maeve stopped before we exited the bathroom, letting her hand graze my stomach as she smiled. 'I'm looking forward to being Aunty M.'

I shared her smile before removing her hand and gripping her fingers in my own.

'We still have nine months before then. First, I have to get through the wedding and survive that long.'

THIRTY-SIX

ALEC

The house was cold and darker than I remembered as I stood in the kitchen. Logan had had my payment laundered and put straight into my account, and I stared at the six-figure total on my phone screen bleakly.

I didn't want it.

I wanted Esther.

The phone landed with a clunk as I tossed it on the counter, pushing my face into my hands. What could I do? Nothing. Useless as ever.

Outside the window two kids played, running through a sprinkler and filling the air with their tinkling laughter. Their mother sat on the front step drinking from a mug while their father came up behind her. His fingers grazed her hair gently as she leant back against his thighs, and the soft, warm scene broke me. It could have been us, given the time and freedom to be with one another. Esther could have been my happily ever after, and I could have been hers. Beneath the mafia princess exterior was a passionate, warm, wonderful woman who just wanted to be appreciated. I wanted to be the person giving that to her. To at least have the chance to try.

A timid knock on the door tore my eyes from the scene across the road. I'd been so lost in my head that I hadn't even seen anyone approach the door. A glance out of the window had me sighing with relief. It was only Gladys.

My elderly neighbour stood on my doorstep clutching an ancient tin and set me with a warm smile when I opened the door.

'Welcome home, lad. Thought you might like a biscuit or two.' She entered the house without an invitation and made her way to the kitchen, ruffling around in my cupboards until she located some tea. It should have been rude, made my hackles rise, but the familiarity encased me like a cosy blanket. As if she was the granny I didn't have.

'I can do that,' I said, taking over the tea preparation and directing her to a seat.

'How were the travels?'

I'd given her a key when I'd left so she could get in if there were any emergencies, but I'd fobbed her off with it being a business meeting abroad. I hadn't expected to be away for weeks. I sat across from her, her kind eyes making my chest hollow. I wanted to talk, to spill my agonies, but I kept it in as always.

'It was alright, there were a few complications, which is why I was gone so long.'

Gladys watched me as she sipped her tea, pushing the open box of cookies toward me. 'I don't think that's the truth, Alec.'

I swallowed as I took a biscuit, taking a large bite and closing my eyes as the sweet, sugary delight hit my tongue. God, I'd missed her baking.

'I... There's a lot to know to understand.'

'I've nothing but time, as you know.'

Could I tell her? Would she hate me if she knew what I was?

'You know I grew up in care, and that when I left, I was on my own. Well, I struggled to find employment. Without an address, places wouldn't take a risk on me, and without a job, I couldn't get a place. Eventually, I was picked up by a gang, and started doing low-level jobs for them.'

'Illegal jobs?' she asked, picking out a small biscuit of her own and dipping it into her tea before taking a bite.

'Yes. Mostly. But I was good at it. I thrived. I earned enough to get a small room in a bedsit and finally had something to call my own. I dreamed of owning a nice house in a pleasant area, somewhere where I could be happy. Over the years, I advanced upward until I reached where I am now.'

'And what is it you do now?'

Pinpricks tingled up my spine as I met her eyes. I didn't see judgement there. No, she looked at me openly, neither fearful nor disgusted.

'I'm an enforcer for one of the top crime syndicates in Glasgow.'

Her eyes widened slightly before she reached out and patted my hand. 'You survived despite a terrible start. No one can begrudge you that. So tell me about this job.'

'There's a woman.'

Gladys smiled wryly, her eyes glittering at that snippet. 'Go on.'

'She's my boss's daughter. He arranged her marriage to a rival gang's leader, and the guy is a terrible man. While none of us are saints, he'd make the devil himself seem reasonable. So she ran away, and they tasked me with bringing her home.'

'To a man she despised?' The words were like a gut

punch.

'Yes. But she was more than I'd bargained for. Like a little hellcat, she made my life a misery. At first. She cut up my cash cards, threw my phone in a river, and burned my car to the ground.'

'Good,' Gladys said. 'Sound's like the lassie knows what's right.'

'Sparks flew, despite the rage, and we ended up giving in to temptation. Repeatedly. And somewhere in there, I lost more than just my bloody mind. I fell for her.'

'Oh, sweetheart.' Gladys tutted as she resumed patting my hand with her cold, papery palm.

'I thought about just staying on the road with her, disappearing with her. But when I let her know her younger sister would be next in line, she was resolute about going home.'

'Has she married him yet?'

'No. She has two days until the wedding.'

'And you are going to stop it? Yes?'

'How can I? You don't just go against this man and survive. He'd kill me, and possibly her.'

'It will kill you not to try, won't it? If you think she feels the same way about you, it has to be worth a try. You need to hold on to love, however it presents itself.'

'What about if you love her, let her go?'

'Utter hogs-wash,' Gladys said, making a sweeping motion with her hand. 'Said by an utter coward who refused to stand up for the person they loved.'

'I don't think she'd come with me. What about her sister?'

'Is she worth less than her sister? Should her life be derailed for another? No.'

My mind swirled with thoughts, regrets, and flashes of

Esther. Her sweet, bratty smile, the way she laughed with abandon when she finally let go. The way she looked when totally relaxed in my arms, her chest raising as she slept. The way I felt when I was with her. Could I really let her go? I'd been fooling myself with the belief that I could.

'If I don't die, we'd need to disappear. For good.'

'Choose somewhere warm,' Gladys said, popping the lid back on her biscuit tin.

'Why?'

'It helps with my arthritis.'

'What?'

'If you are going on an adventure, I want to come. I can't spend another ten years fading away in that old house while you are off living a grand adventure.'

'Gladys,' I said, ready to talk some sense into her.

'Don't you Gladys me. I'm old enough to decide, Sonny Jim. You are the closest person I have left, and I live for the moments when you'll come around and bring some life into my house. Plus, you'd miss my biscuits too much.'

'It would rip you away from everything.'

She let out a rich chortle. 'Away from what? Sitting in there rotting and watching life pass me by? You think you are the only one looking outside and wishing? No, I'm right there with you. We are both alone, and I'm not accepting you up and leaving me here while you run off into the sunset. I'll be right there with you.'

I gave up arguing. I had the impossibility of getting to Esther and getting us both away alive. Fuck it. If we made it, Gladys may as well join our band of runaways.

'There is it, acceptance. Now, go save your girl. If you get yourself killed, I'll be very disappointed. I'll be packed and ready to go.'

What a crazy, but wonderful, old bird she was.

THIRTY-SEVEN
ESTHER

The TV flickered to my left with pictures that I couldn't focus on and had grown numb to. The idle chittering of the contestants on the reality show nipped at my ears as I lay on the couch and stared at the ceiling. There were twenty inset lights above me. I'd counted them, as well as anything else I could count to pass the time.

The second week had inched by with barely a thing to amuse me. My phone hadn't been returned when I came home, and there were no other online accessible devices in the apartment. All I had was the TV and the chirpy people on it, with their lack of problems. I reached for the remote and flicked through the channels, groaning as nothing took my fancy, throwing the remote to the side in a huff.

The door opened, and I sat up, ready to accost Maeve to find any news from the outer world. Maybe even ask about Alec...

My eyes widened as Harold stood there, the door closing behind him and locking with a heart-skipping click.

What the hell was he doing there?

'You shouldn't be here,' I said, my pulse thrumming in my neck as he walked toward me.

'What's a few days amongst fiancés?' Harold said, his face pulling into a saccharine grin. 'It's my apartment, after all.'

He loosened his tie, his chunky fingers dragging at it until it lay limply around his neck. When he sat down heavily on the sofa next to me, I scooted to the left, making a space between us.

'You are supposed to leave me alone until the wedding.'

'Indeed. But seeing as you've been whoring yourself out to the help, I thought you weren't one for rules.'

'It wasn't like that.' My words were forced, anger burning in my chest, but I knew it wasn't safe for me to step out of line. I didn't doubt that he'd hit me again.

'I don't blame you. Your mother was just the same. It's in your blood. But look where it got her. Take it as a warning. I will not tolerate cheating. Seek your pleasure elsewhere, and you'll end up without the organs to feel pleasure. Fuck with me, and you might well end up in a shallow grave.' His words were soft, almost loving as he reached out and petted my thigh, sending waves of nausea running through me.

My body froze as he pushed his hand between my thighs, stroking upward until he cupped me, his body pressing against my side as he breathed against my ear. Repulsion made me tremble, made me want to reach out and tear his face right from his skull. 'This is mine. no one will even touch your cunt again. I'll fuck you when and how I please, and you'll thank me every time.'

A sob choked me as he added more pressure, grinding his fingers against my leggings.

'I can feel your heat, Esther. You are going to be a fine

little fuck. Ah, and look, tears too.' He leant to the side and licked his way up my cheek, catching the escaping tear and moaning in a way that turned my stomach. I needed to get away. I needed help. 'My favourite.'

'Stop,' I whispered.

'No,' he said, rubbing at me in a way that made me want to curl into a corner and cry.

'Please. I don't want it like this.' I screwed my eyes closed as he shifted his weight against me, his hard cock thrusting meekly into my thigh.

'I'm not sure how much you don't understand that I don't care what you want. I take what I want. You will give it willingly, or unwillingly. It makes no difference. If you struggle, I'll have you chained wide. If you cry, it'll only make my dick harder. if I want you to, you'll drop to your knees at a click of my fingers and swallow me down no matter who I'm in a meeting with.' His fingers pressed harder against me, making me squirm in pain. 'Even in front of your own fucking brothers. And you'll do it or face the consequences.'

How was I supposed to survive him? Everything about him made me feel sick. I was supposed to be getting him to sleep with me, so I could pretend the baby was his, but even the thought of it made me want to jump from the balcony.

'Does that feel good, Esther?' he said, continuing the painful pressure against me.

'No,' I said.

He pushed me over so that I was squashed beneath him on the sofa, his skin sticky and gross and his weight pinning me to the fabric. I squeaked as he slapped me hard across the face, my head spinning.

Then, his other hand was under my leggings, digging at me with uncut nails and pained strokes.

Writhing and bucking, I tried to free myself from him, fear causing me to lose any sense of self-preservation. I needed him off.

I screamed for help, hoping that someone on the other side of the door would burst in and save me. 'Help! Please!'

No one appeared. Another sharp crack to my cheek brought another wave of tears before he forced his fingers inside me, dragging another great sob from me. Everything hurt, but the terror was crushing, outweighing it all.

'You should count yourself lucky that I'm pleasing you. I could just fill you with my dick.' His breath was ragged as I continued to try to get him off of me. 'You should thank me.'

Another crack to my face, this time catching me at the temple, left me reeling, my eyesight blurring as pain blossomed behind my ear. It rendered me stunned back against the sofa as he tugged at my trousers, the distant sound of his belt opening and his zip undoing. *No.* I tried to move but couldn't, my limbs sluggish to respond.

He thrust my legs apart and knelt between them, reaching for me and roughly shoving his fingers inside. 'You're still dry. This will hurt.'

More tears. More fear.

The door burst open behind me before he could go any further. His son, Cameron, came into frame as I tried to cover myself.

'Come on, you're needed downstairs.'

'Five fucking minutes, Cam. It won't take me long to fill her up.'

Cam's face screwed up as he took in my tear-stained face and the heated red marks covering my cheeks.

Please take pity. Please help me.

I mouthed the *help me* to him. He quickly averted his eyes.

'The Cosgrove deal has gone tits up, we need to get over there now. They've got the rat contained, and I need to ask him some questions before our guys get to gun-happy.'

Harold grumbled as he buckled up his belt, before reaching out and grabbing my face firmly in his grip. 'Two days to wait until you get the rest of me. However, will you manage? I'll be looking forward to it.'

When he let me go, I curled up on the sofa, pulling my trousers back into place and drawing my knees up to my chest. Enough tears to drown me and great-wracking sobs that shook the couch beneath me.

Hours later, Maeve found me there, taking in my bruised cheeks and salt-stained face.

'What happened?' she said, scooping me up against her and smoothing my hair.

'Harold.'

'Oh Esther, I'm sorry.'

'You don't have to be. But he will.'

'Come on, let's get you in the shower and find you something to eat. I'll stay over with you in case he comes back.'

Next time I'd be ready. Stick him through with a knife while he was worrying about his cock.

It was the only pleasure he'd actually be able to bring me.

THIRTY-EIGHT

ALEC

The gravel crunched beneath my feet as I walked up the McGowan's driveway, the clouds overhead thick and grey and casting a headache inducing-light over the mansion.

Being known to the family, and trusted despite my recent transgression, the guys let me through with a brief nod and nothing more. I took the stairs two at a time, hoping I wouldn't run into anyone else before I found Maeve. I might lose my nerve if I did.

I rapped on her door and waited, sending up a silent prayer. Success. I heard her shuffling about before coming to the door, opening it without hesitation.

Maeve's eyebrows rose as she saw me, her arms crossing over her chest as she leant against the doorframe.

'What can I do for you?' she said.

'Can I come in?' I glanced up the long, opulent corridor, relieved to find it remained empty.

'To my room? Why?'

'I need to talk to you.'

'About Esther?'

'Yes.'

She mulled it over for a moment, taking a peek down the corridor herself. 'Fine, but make it quick.'

From her body language, I couldn't tell if she was pissed at me or not. Her brothers didn't seem to be, although Malcolm still raged on, his directions short and harsh, his eyes still avoiding mine unless absolutely necessary.

I took a seat at her desk, swivelling the chair to face her as she sat on the edge of the bed. Silence hung awkwardly as I tried to find the right words. If she went to her father or Harold, it would be bad news for me.

'How is she?' I said, eventually, the need for information on Esther outweighed everything else.

'Broken-hearted. Terrified. Lost. How else could she be?' Maeve picked up a cushion and squished it against her chest, her voice softening when talking about her sister.

'I need to get her out of there.'

'Are you fucking insane? Look where that got you both. He'd kill her without a second thought if she tried to run again.'

'That's why I have to get her out. She's not safe there. You know it, and I know it. Is that the life you want for her?'

Maeve's face darkened as she fixed me with a glare. 'Of course, it's not what I want. I want her to be happy, but what choice does she have?'

'A difficult one. Lose everything and run for the chance to be happy, or stay and spend every day knowing that she'll be hurt, tortured and abused by the man who killed two of her family members.'

'There is no choice.'

'There will be. I'll find a way.'

Maeve chewed on her lip as she watched me. 'Do you love her?'

My heart quickened at even the thought of it. 'Yes. I

know it's hasty, but I've fallen head over heels for your sister. I can't imagine going through my life without her. Having to watch someone hurt her again and again and not being able to protect her. To cherish her the way she deserves. I know it's hard as it drops you in the firing line, but I can't sit by and do nothing. She's been failed enough. I don't just want her to be happy. I need her to be happy. I can't live like everything's fine when I know she's not okay.'

Maeve's face softened as I spilled my guts, the words vomiting out of me. Words I should have told Esther while I had the chance.

'She deserves to be happy. I'm not afraid of being next in line. There's no way on earth I'd marry Harold. I'm the youngest, but my dad and siblings baby me too much. How can I go on knowing she's sacrificed herself to him for me? I've been trying to get her out, but it's impossible. Harold owns the whole building, and it's armed thoroughly by men told to shoot to kill if they see anyone not on the approved list.'

'How's she coping?'

'Badly. Harold... well, he touched her. He stopped before it went further than hands when his son interrupted and insisted there were some sort of issues he had to attend to urgently. She's hurting and scared, and I don't know how to help her.'

My muscles twitched with fury at the thought of him trying to force himself on my girl, on him feeling like he could take whatever he liked from her. My chest burned as I fought down the urge to punch something, to destroy. To lash out with the lack of control I felt.

'Will they be going to the wedding directly from where she is?'

'No. We are having a big dinner here tomorrow night with our family and theirs.'

'I wonder if I can get an invitation?'

'No chance, Dad's happy enough to keep you around, but Harold won't want you at the meal, or anywhere near him.'

'I think it's time we stopped giving a fuck what he wanted.'

'Agreed,' Maeve said, her eyes glittering. 'So what's the plan?'

'You're going to be sick, to stay out of the way for when things go south. I'm going to hide out in here until the dinner, then I'm going to get her out. Somehow.'

'It won't happen without bloodshed.'

I smirked when I met her eyes, touching the edge of my knife in my pocket. 'Good. I'm counting on it.'

THIRTY-NINE

ESTHER

The atmosphere was strained in the dining room. Even the waiters shifted uncomfortably as they waited at the side of the room between courses. The food was divine, as it always was when our chefs went all out. Course after course of delicate, intricately spiced meats and sautéed vegetables, all sat heavy in my stomach as conversation came in fits and starts about me.

Maeve wasn't even there to keep me company. And who could blame her? I'd have pulled a sickie given half of a chance, too.

Harold sat next to me, at one end of the long, mahogany table, while Dad sat at the other end. The hatred between them was palpable even as they pawned me for peace. I pulled at the collar of my dress, feeling overwhelmed by the heat in the room.

'Everything's set for tomorrow. The guests have returned their invitations, and we're looking at a full house,' Harold said, drivelling on about the wedding.

'Are you guys taking a honeymoon?' Mac asked, shovelling his food into his mouth as fast as he could to escape the meal faster.

'I thought I might whisk Esther away to my private retreat. Nothing but sun, sea, and time together. It would give us plenty of time to get to know each other with no interruptions.'

A chill shot up my spine as he fixed those watery eyes on me. There would be no one to run in and save me after the wedding. no one to hear my cries and take pity on me. I dabbed at my forehead with my napkin, the room spinning around me.

'Look at my blushing bride, all coy, before the big day.' Harold reached out and thumbed my jawline, sending a wave of nausea through me.

I couldn't do it. Fuck, I needed out.

My chair scraped loudly against the polished floor as I stood up abruptly, needing space.

'Are you okay?' Logan asked to my right, looking up at me with concern in his eyes.

'No,' I gasped, clinging to the edge of the table as my forehead broke out in a clammy sweat. 'I'm not.'

All eyes were on me. Mac, Ewen, and Logan, along with my father. Harold and his two grown children, Cam and Katie. The waiters. Thankfully, we'd had both sets of armed men from either side left outside. Their gazes burned at me as I struggled to breathe. The past weeks all came down on me at once.

Then I cracked.

I couldn't take it anymore.

'I'm pregnant,' I whispered. A collective intake of breath sounded before I dared to glance at Harold. His face turned a dreadful shade of red as my father coughed and cleared his throat.

'You fucking whore,' Harold said menacingly as he pushed his chair back, his hands slamming hard on the table, upending his plate. The remaining food slid to the floor by his feet. I inched backward as he bore down on me, his voice steely as he fixed me with a glare.

I stepped backward, nearer the wall as the waiters took the chance to scarper. Harold was on me in a second, his hand in my hair pulling me violently toward him.

'With what I'm going to do to you tomorrow, the parasite won't survive long. And if it does, I'll have you pinned down while they rip it out of you.'

I sobbed and looked at my father, who was on his feet, his face a picture of wrath.

'Enough.' The voice came from far to my right where Alec stood, his arms bathed in blood and his knife glinting in his hand.

'Alec,' I said in a strangled voice, whimpering when Harold span me around by the hair and pulled me back against his chest.

'George, Ally?' Harold shouted, but all that came from the hallway was silence.

'All dead,' Alec said, a trail of blood droplets following him as he stepped toward us.

'Stop, or I'll break her fucking neck.' Harold tightened his grip on my hair and pushed his other hand under my jaw, gripping my chin with a vice-like tightness.

Alec ignored him, meeting my eyes beneath my blurry tears. 'Is it true?'

I could see the hope beneath the fear. He wasn't upset at the pregnancy.

My voice was barely a squeak beneath Harold's grip. 'Yes.'

For a moment, delight shone in those icy blue eyes. Then all hell broke loose.

Mac hit Harold at a run, sending both him and me flying. His grip loosened on me, and Alec pulled me to him, throwing me behind his back as I inched away. Cam was on his feet, gun pulled, along with Logan and Ewen doing the same. Harold got to his feet and brushed himself off, hatred simmering in his narrowed eyes.

'Go,' Alec said to me, pushing me back toward the door.

'I can't leave them like this.'

My father stood holding his hands out, his breaths coming in quick puffs. 'Everyone, calm the fuck down. Esther sit down. We'll sort out the baby situation after the wedding. A few pills and you'll be clear. You can't be that far gone.'

He rounded on Alec and pointed toward the door. 'You can get the fuck out. I'll deal with you later.'

'He killed my fucking men.'

'We don't know that,' my dad stammered.

'I did.' Alec smiled darkly. 'They are out there in a puddle of their own fucking bowels, and I'll do it to anyone else who gets in my way. Esther is mine.'

The possessiveness should have put me off, but he was the only person who'd stood up for me, and it brought fresh tears to my eyes. The only person who loved me enough to help me.

Fuck, he loved me.

'I'm not marrying Harold,' I said, Alec's resolve making me stand up for myself.

'Yes, you are.' Harold said, moving back to where his son was, reaching out and taking the gun from his fingers. 'After I blow this upstart's brains out.'

He didn't hesitate to shoot. Alec threw me out of the

door as he ducked in the other direction, the bullet piercing a hole in the dining room wall. I cried out as another shot rang out. Alec only had his knife. He couldn't fight against a gun with that. Then I saw them, the bodies steeped in red. Harold's men. Holding back a wave of vomit, I crawled over to the eviscerated corpses and unclipped a gun from one of their belts. Sticky blood slopped at my knees, soaking up into my dress as I checked the clip, ensuring it was loaded, and pushed the safety off. The room behind had gone dangerously quiet.

Creeping back to the doorway, I saw a standoff, my brothers pointed their guns at Harold. Katie had hidden beneath the table, while Harold's gun was trained on Alec, but without a clear shot, my father being between them.

'Shoot Alec,' my dad told Logan and Ewen, and I trembled when I saw Logan waver. He never went against my father's wishes, but they knew Alec and had accepted him like a brother.

'Don't,' I said, pushing the weapon up in front of me. Harold was too swift, moving behind my dad as I tried to shoot, the gun flinching back and hitting me on the temple. A wave of red obscured one eye as I yelped.

Harold pressed the muzzle of his gun against my father's temple, and my dad's face darkened to a puce.

'Get the fuck off of me.' My father's fury emanated from him, but Harold held firm.

'Gun's down, empty them and toss them or your father's brains will be your next course.' Harold dug the gun into Dad's temple.

'Don't be stupid,' I said as they followed his instructions.

'You're the one being an idiot,' Harold said as my hands shook. 'I would have given you anything you wanted. All you had to do was follow orders and spread your legs.'

'Go,' Alec mouthed at me. 'Get out.'

I couldn't.

'She's carrying my grandchild,' my dad said, his face softening. 'Just let her go. There's got to be another way.'

'There's no other way. You cost me a woman all those years ago. You owe me one,' Harold said.

'I don't owe you shit.'

Harold looked down at my father, shocked that he'd finally spoken up against him despite the barrel of his gun digging a centimetre from his brain.

'Esther, go,' he said. 'Go with Alec, have the baby.'

Then the world slowed to a stop as Harold squeezed the trigger while Alec threw his knife. The blade lodged in Harold's shoulder, but seconds too late. All hell broke loose. My father's face went blank as blood shot from the side of his head, his body slumping. In the same moment, my dad's men poured into the room while Alec launched at me, picking me up over his shoulders and heading for the doors. Cam dragged Harold and Katie out of the window, making a run for it across the lawn.

'No!' I screamed as Alec dragged me away. 'My dad, we need to go back.'

'We can't baby, they'll be back with more men. I need to get you out of here.'

'I'll kill him. I'll fucking kill him.' But even as I screamed it, my resolve weakened as I heaved over Alec's shoulder, the past few minutes hitting me like a train wreck.

With tears and snot colliding on my face, mingling with the blood from hitting myself with the gun, Alec left the mansion with me slung over his shoulder, my sister watching quietly from the top of the stairs.

'I'm sorry,' I whispered to her.

FORTY

ALEC

Esther was catatonic, moving along with me but like an empty husk, devoid of any emotion. It had all gone wrong. I'd got Esther out, but she'd seen her father shot, and it was my fault. I slid my hand into my pocket, searching for the comforting warmth of my knife before remembering I'd last seen it embedded in Harold.

Esther sat on my sofa, staring blankly out of the window, her face still red and tear-stained. It wasn't how things were supposed to be, and I had no idea how to fix it. I couldn't have her father un-shot.

Ellis stood in the kitchen, furiously typing at his laptop. He was setting up hidden accounts so we'd have access to my money and arranging flights under our new not-so-legal names. We just waited on Wee Dave to come over to strong arm him, or beg him, into doing a rush job on some new identification for us to travel. I could only hope Maeve wouldn't let on to Harold or her brothers that we might have used him.

A knock sounded at the door, and when I pulled it open, Dave's face fell.

'No, absolutely fuckin' not,' he said, backing away.

I grabbed him by the scruff of the neck and pulled him inside, pushing him toward the kitchen. He took one look at Esther and rounded on me.

'What have you done to that, lassie?'

'I took her out of the situation she was stuck in, and now we need your help to get away.'

'Why would I help you? You left me tied to a chair with a bloody fucking finger. Cost me a fuckton of money too.'

'You can have my house. It's two-thirds paid off, and my pal Ellis there can have it put into your name within minutes.'

Dave looked around before his eyes settled on Esther. 'What will happen to her if you don't get away?'

'She tried to shoot Harold Thompson, so nothing good.' It was an understatement. When Harold regrouped with his men, he'd go all out for revenge. He detested being stood up to. I could only hope the fallout from shooting Malcolm would buy us some time.

'You need two sets of documents in what, a couple of hours? Not sure the house is worth enough to do it that fast,' Dave said.

'What if I add the house next door?' Gladys's voice came from the entryway, where she'd opened the door and was dragging a large suitcase through my hallway. 'But it'll take a third set of documents.'

I smiled at her; her face lighting up as she saw Wee Dave and Ellis, but her brow crinkled when she took in the sight of Esther. I'd cleaned myself up and done the best I could with her, but there was still blood under her nails, and a gash over her eye, and she'd refused to get out of the blood-stained dress.

'The same as this, but fully paid off?' Dave said.

'Gladys, you can't give up your house for us. You can't leave everything behind.'

'I can. And I am. I told you I will not sit here and rot while you all go off on an adventure without me. I'm coming.'

My heart swelled as she fixed me with a determined grin. Families come in lots of different forms, and maybe mine would include the sweet old lady next door after all. 'Well, alright. Who am I to tell you no?'

'Somewhere warm though, remember lad, for the arthritis.'

Dave held out his hand, and I shook it. 'Ellis, get his details and put the two houses in his name. Make it ironclad so it's good to go as soon as he's back with the IDs.'

'I'll be back in a few hours. I have a few almost complete ones ready to go at any one time for the people who really need them. Get me the names you want and a picture of each of you against a blank wall. I already have Esther's.' We both looked over to where Gladys was sitting next to her, opening a tin of biscuits and encouraging a sugary yellow square into her hand.

'You're going to have to get her looking more alive if you are getting on a plane with her. There's no way they aren't going to be suspicious if she looks like that.'

'You worry about your job. I'll worry about mine.'

GLADYS POTTERED in the kitchen making endless cups of tea as I carried Esther upstairs, stripping off her clothes and sitting her in the bathtub as I used the shower attachment to wash her down. At first, she didn't react, didn't look at me even, until I gently lathered up shampoo into her hair.

The tears fell as my fingers grazed her scalp, soon turning into great, wrenching sobs. I climbed in without undressing and gathered her up against me, letting her cry, letting her dip into the storm of emotions she'd battened down inside.

'It's okay, baby. You'll be okay.'

'I won't,' she sobbed against my chest, her half-washed hair sending suds down over my arms. 'It's my fault. He's dead, and it's my fault.'

'Look at me,' I said firmly, tipping her face upward. 'None of this is your fault. Not a single moment of it. It's all down to men with too much power, thinking they can control the world. I spoke with Logan briefly, and your dad is in a bad way, but he's not dead. He's in hospital and they are doing what they can. Do you remember the last thing he said to you?'

'To have the baby.'

'He softened because you are carrying his grandchild. He gave you his blessing.' I still couldn't believe it. My child was growing in her, and emotion rocked me at the thought. It wasn't the time to be celebrating, though, not when she needed me.

'What about Maeve? I came back to help her.'

I took a cloth and washed her face, clearing the tears, snot, and dried blood from her cut. 'Maeve doesn't want you to ruin your life for her, any more than you'd let her do it for you. She told me she isn't the family baby anymore, and she is happy to look after herself.'

'I can't let Harold take her.'

'You need to look after you and the wee one.' I spread my hand over her stomach, and she stared at it there before placing her hand on top.

'You don't think it's too soon? We haven't even started a relationship yet.'

'I love you, Esther. Despite you being the brattiest little thing, because of it maybe. You are sweet and strong and loving and for weeks now, all I've wanted is to spend the rest of my life making you smile. If you feel like it's too soon, then I'll support you in that, but for me? I want to keep you and the baby, forever. I want to marry you and call you my wife. I love you so fucking much it hurts.'

Her tears started anew as she threw her arms around my neck, covering me in shampoo and water as I grinned. 'I thought I was going crazy for falling for you as quickly as I did, but every day, all I wanted was to find a way back into your arms. I love you too.'

'I'm sorry that things went down the way they did, and I'm sorry about what happened to your dad. I don't know how I'll make it up to you, but I'll find a way.'

'It's not your action to be absolved of. It's Harold's. We both know he doesn't know the meaning of being sorry. I want to kill him. I don't know how I'll leave knowing he's going to go on unchecked.'

'You have to. For our family.'

'I know.'

'Now, sit still while I finish washing you, and then, we'll find something for you to wear. We need to get out of here as soon as Dave comes back with the documents.'

'Where will we go?'

'Anywhere you like.'

'Did you tell them where you found me?' She looked back at me over her shoulders, and I saw the first glimmer of hope in her eyes.

'Only that it was in Spain.'

'Then I want to go back to the taverna, back to Eva and Jock. We can find a little place there and I can work and pretend like I'm just a normal person. Not a fugitive.'

'If that's what you want, baby, then that's what we'll do.'

I'd have preferred somewhere new, somewhere that they didn't know to look, but for Esther, I'd do anything.

I just hoped Jock wouldn't greet me with a shotgun this time.

FORTY-ONE

ESTHER

The sun warmed my face as we walked up the hill, Alec supporting Gladys on his arm. The bus had dropped us at the foot of the road, just like when I had arrived previously, but this time I wasn't alone. Alec was there, supporting me every step of the way. Between Gladys's company and our dotting about the country from bus to bus to avoid being trailed, never mind flying into France and travelling down into Spain, we'd barely had a moment alone together.

When I'd caught him looking at me as I changed out of my sweaty top and into a summer dress, with those intense blue eyes, it made my stomach fill with butterflies. After Harold had tried to force himself on me, Alec seemed reluctant to make any sort of sexual move. With the trauma we'd both suffered at seeing my dad shot, I was wary about opening up at first too. What if Harold found us, and it ripped us apart all over again? My heart was as bruised as my face had been, and I'd needed time and distance from my world to feel free again.

I hoped it would last.

I hoped Maeve was okay.

I hoped Dad would recover.

Gladys had helped me realise that none of those things were mine to control, that I had to look forward as we didn't know what would come in and change our lives at any one moment. She'd never expected to be on the run with her neighbour and his daughter-of-the-mafia girlfriend. Seeing her delight had pulled me from my deep funk, and although there were moments where I felt it trying to drag me back under, the levity of the trip through her eyes helped. So did the quiet reassurance from Alec, the way he looked at me like I was a treasure. The way he made me feel every day, like it had been worth it. Like I was worth it. His soft praise and his never-ending patience astounded me, and made me see a whole new side of him than just the absolute sex-god I'd fallen for. He was so much more than my father's enforcer, or the man sent to drag me home, or even the man who knew how to make me come until I begged him to stop.

We were forming our own little tribe. I sincerely hoped Eva and Jock could be part of it too. I wouldn't blame them at all if they told us to get lost after I brought so much chaos to their door.

The taverna came into view as we rounded the top of the hill, sweat clinging to my brow as I panted. I hoped I'd get used to the beastly walk-up if we stayed.

Gladys let out a delighted whoop, startling some birds and making Alec laugh. Warmth encased me at the sight of them.

'Oh, Esther, it's just as lovely as you said it was. I could go a cold gin too after that walk,' Gladys said with a grin.

'Last time they saw me, they blew a hole in their wall trying to kill me. I wouldn't be counting on that gin just yet.' Alec looked nervous, his eyes scanning the taverna.

'It feels like home. Which is insane, seeing as I was

there for such a brief time, but I do feel like I'm coming home.' The taverna had been the first place I'd felt accepted without the last name I'd been birthed into or the money and respect that had always surrounded my family. The first place I could just be Esther. Well, Emily. But still.

I spotted Eva first, a smile breaking out as I waved sheepishly, hoping that she'd look just as pleased. Her eyes widened as she spotted me, her smile beaming as she made her way to me and pulled me into a crushing hug.

'You came back!' she said, her eyes tearing up as she held me at arm's length, her eyes wetting at the corners.

'I did. Is that okay?' My stomach roiled.

'More than okay. I'm thrilled to see you.'

Eva rounded on Alec, his arm still looped through Gladys's. She narrowed her eyes at him. 'I hope you've learned some lessons since your last visit.'

'So many,' he said, shifting from foot to foot under her gaze. 'I'm sorry. For last time.'

'Good. Then let's say no more of it.' Eva grasped my hands in hers. 'Will you be staying?'

'I hope so. There was an incident before we left, and I'm hoping that they didn't tie it to us?'

Eva frowned before nodding. 'He was a wicked man, and there was no one willing to fight on his behalf and bring the police into it. It's done.'

I breathed a sigh of relief, knowing that Alec wouldn't be cuffed for killing my mugger.

'We have some money and we are hoping to find somewhere for Alec, Gladys and me.' I smiled down at my stomach. 'And the baby.'

Eva clapped her hands and stroked over my not-yet-blooming tummy. 'Oh, a baby. Oh yes, you must stay. I have just the place for the two of you.'

'And Gladys?' I said, not wanting to have taken an old woman to Spain just to ditch her.

'Gladys can stay with us, if she's willing?'

'Above the taverna? It'll be the most excitement I've had in years.' Gladys smiled as she patted Alec's hand.

'Let's get you all a good feed first, and I'll go fill Jock in.' Eva led us into the taverna, the locals smiling and nodding in welcome.

'Maybe hide his shotgun...' Alec said as he pulled out a seat for Gladys.

As I sat in the taverna, the bustling of the town around us and the smell of food wafting out from the kitchen, I finally let myself relax. I reached for Alec's hand when he took the seat next to me, squeezing his fingers below the table.

'Does it feel good to be back?' he said, kissing the area behind my ear lightly in a way that made me swoon.

'It does. Thank you for agreeing to come.'

'Wherever you are is my home, baby. I'd follow you to the ends of the earth as long as you're in my arms.'

My heart thrummed in my chest as I leaned forward and grazed my lips over his, breaking the wall that had been keeping us close but separate since the dinner at my father's house. Ending the kiss, I spoke against his lips. 'There's no place I'd rather be.'

'Right, you soppy buggers,' Gladys chimed in. 'Enough of that before you make an old lady jealous. Alec, go help Eva with the drinks and make mine a double.'

She shooed him off as I giggled, watching Alec helping Eva and feeling contentment flare within me. And for the first time, hope.

FORTY-TWO
ALEC

The dinky cottage was perfect for Esther and I. Jock and I had stripped out the old moth-bitten furniture after he'd eventually stopped cussing me out every three minutes, and I'd worked tirelessly to clean, repair and paint.

Finally, it was looking ready for my girl. I'd thrown the windows open to clear the paint fumes as I moved in our new furniture, setting the house up as best as I could, but leaving plenty of room for Esther to fix it to her liking when she finished up at the taverna. Watching her was like watching a new leaf on a plant unfurl, from a tight, stiff spike into a beautiful, relaxed, and open leaf. As the first week had turned into the second, and into the third, she relaxed more every day. Her skin was sun-kissed and her shoulders were no longer tense. I'd been giving her space, letting her flourish under the fuss of Eva and Gladys, and even Jock, but being there when she needed me. Every night she would crawl into bed next to me and place her head on my chest, her warm skin soothing me.

If it was all she could give, it was enough. Knowing she was safe and happy would always be enough.

The sun dipped outside, and I stopped working, showering myself off and letting the hot water soothe my skin. A knock at the door startled me before Esther's pretty face popped around the frame. 'Can I join you?'

I tensed as she watched me showering. Despite every part of me wanting to say yes, I'd been giving her space and time to get over what Harold had done to her. I didn't want to push anything too soon and hurt her more.

'Please? Before you use up all the hot water?' She was in the room and stripping off her clothing before I found any words.

'Course you can.'

I couldn't help but skirt my eyes over her as she stripped off, her freckled skin and delicious curves making my mouth water. Tearing my eyes away, I focused on the water running in rivulets down the tiles. I didn't want to get a hard on and scare her off.

She stepped in over the side of the tub and shimmied past me to get under the spray, turning to face me and sighing.

'Good shift at work?' I asked, keeping my eyes above chest level.

'Yeah, it was pretty busy, so went really quick. My feet are aching.'

'You know you don't have to work, right? We have some money put aside.'

She smiled up at me. 'I know. I like it.'

'If that changes, let me know.'

We stood quietly as she lathered up her hair; it became more and more difficult not to watch the soapy bubbles cascading down her chest. Her hand found mine, and she pressed it against her waist, looking up at me with pleading eyes.

'Stop avoiding me, Alec.'

'I don't want to hurt you. What if you aren't ready after-'

She stemmed my words with a kiss, fighting against my resistant lips until my willpower crumbled. 'I need you to erase it. I need you, Alec. I miss you. I need all of you, not just the parts you are letting me have. Stop holding back and give me everything.'

My fingers trembled as I pulled her toward me, deepening the kiss and groaning. Fuck, I needed her too. The space I'd put between us created an awkward barrier that neither of us knew how to deal with. Her tongue slipped against mine as she pushed her fingers into my hair, her soapy tits against my chest as I reached down and cupped her ass.

She whimpered into my mouth as we discovered one another anew after our weeks apart and then chaste. Her fingers tugged at my hair as she claimed my mouth, taking no prisoners in the passionate kiss. My hands toured her body, reacquainting with every curve, even the new one that was ever so slightly rounding on her stomach. Not enough to notice, but enough that I could feel it was different.

'Fuck, I've missed you, baby girl,' I said against her throat, my teeth and tongue marking their way down her neck.

'I need you so badly,' she said breathily, as I slipped a hand between her thighs. Her body rocked as I circled her clit, her hands clinging tightly to my neck as she slid a thigh up around my waist to give me better access.

'You sure you're ready, sweetheart? You can use your safe word if it gets too much. Do you remember it?'

'Home,' she moaned against my mouth. It had a whole new meaning now. She was my home.

'Good girl,' I said, grinning as she sighed happily at the phrase.

'I need to get us out of this shower. I need better access to you.'

She didn't put up an argument as I switched off the shower and towelled us both down, taking extra time on her to minimise her getting cold. I turned her toward the mirror, leaning forward to clear away the steam. Her ass pressed back against my hard dick as we looked at each other in the reflection.

'Back where I belong,' she smiled, her voice soft. Her words were like a vice on my heart.

'We both are.'

I slipped my fingers back between her thighs, luxuriating in the feel of her as I slowly worked her into a moaning, whimpering mess.

'Look at you, baby, so beautiful. I love the way you moan so prettily when I touch your cunt.'

Her blush was visible in the mirror under her freckled cheeks. It made me all the harder.

'Do you like my fingers inside you? Stretching you?'

'Yes,' she hummed, 'but not as much as I like your dick.'

Fucking hell, what on earth could I have to have deserved her?

'Now, now, sweet girl, all in good time. Don't be greedy.'

She whimpered as I fucked her with my fingers, my thumb grazing her clit with each stroke. I used my other hand to tease her tits, pinching at each nipple until they were firm and red in the reflection.

My lips found her neck as she trembled, getting close. Not yet. I needed to taste her, needed her closer.

When I stopped touching her, she cried out, but I scooped her up in my arms and took her to our new couch, seated next to the window and overlooking the town below. I lay down and pulled her above my face, her thighs on either side of my ears.

'Sit down.'

'I might squash you.'

'Did I stutter?'

She gave up any resistance as I pulled her down over my face, my tongue deep between her folds. I found her clit and captured it between my lips as she held onto the frame, looking out of the window as I lapped at her cunt.

Barely a minute passed as I lapped at her, her hips moving jerkily as she rode my face, when her body quivered, her thighs gripping at my cheeks as she rocked and writhed.

I didn't let up. I ate like a man starved as my girl tipped over the edge and wailed her orgasm to the world.

'That's my girl,' I said into her pretty pussy.

FORTY-THREE
ESTHER

Fucking hell.

My hips slowed as the orgasm waned, and I moved to get off of Alec's face, worried he was running out of air beneath my ass.

'No,' he said, gripping my hips and pulling me down into his mouth. It was too sensitive, I couldn't go again.

'I can't, it's too much.'

'You can and you will, baby. I'm not finished.' He gripped my hips as he pressed his tongue against me, lapping me up. I wriggled against him, it feeling overwhelmingly ticklish at first.

'It's your turn,' I gasped as he nipped at my clit, sending shockwaves up into me.

'Yes, it is,' he said, giving me a moment's reprieve. 'And I want to feel you come against my tongue again. You were too quick before.'

With that, he dug in, pulling me harshly onto his mouth as I whimpered. I only hoped no one came up the road as they'd get a full view of my face and tits, and I had a feeling

Alec wouldn't care in the slightest. Fuck, he'd probably enjoy it.

The sensitivity gave way as he drove me toward another orgasm, my body craving him again already. 'God, Alec. Oh, my god.'

His fingers dug into my hips when I tried to pull up to let him breathe, dragging me firmly back into place as he ate me. I gave in, rolling and bucking my hips against his mouth, chasing the orgasm.

I closed my eyes and revelled in his touch as he wrapped his arms fully about my hips and pinned me to him right before the orgasm came crashing around me.

'Fuck,' I cried out as my body jerked and trembled, the orgasm ripping through me and leaving me quaking in its midst. Grinding myself against his face until the last wonderful tremors ebbed. My body caved, crumpling against the window as he kissed my thighs before shimmying out from beneath me.

'I'm going to fuck you now, baby. Are you ready?'

I nodded dumbly, my brain feeling a little detached from my body as he'd licked me into a stupor. Then his cock was there, nudging me open as he pushed me forward so that my arms gripped the windowsill, my head out of the window.

As he slipped fully into me, I moaned. God, how I'd missed him filling me up.

'Fuck, baby, you're too much. I'm going to blow far too soon.'

His hands trembled as he pressed his hips into my ass, my pussy adjusting to him after so long without him.

'Fill me up, please.' I moaned, sighing happily as he pulled back and thrust forward again.

'I love you, Esther,' he said into my ear as he pressed his body over mine, swallowing me up as he fucked me slowly.

'I love you too,' I groaned into the sofa as his cock worked me up all over again.

'I need to see you, baby,' he said, pulling me off of the sofa and sitting me over his thighs so I was back looking out the window but with him beneath me. He captured a nipple in his mouth as he sat me fully on his dick.

I moved against him, his hands directing me harshly down over him as he quickened his pace. 'Touch yourself, Esther. Make yourself come around my cock.'

Sliding my fingers over my still-sensitive clit, I closed my eyes as he used his hands to slide my body up and down over him.

'Eyes on me.'

I blinked them open and felt that familiar pleasure roll through me as he awarded me with a 'Good girl.'

His blue eyes were hooded with lust as I watched him, his breath ragged as he fucked me. Beautiful, he was so beautiful. He'd shown me the man he could be in the past few weeks, how much he'd risk for me, and how hard he'd work to build a life for us, and the baby, but I'd missed this side of him. When he was raw and vulnerable and heaping dirty praise upon me.

'I'm going to come. I'm going to fill you up. Are you ready?'

'Yes,' I moaned, quickening my fingers to meet him. His grunts and moans as he pumped into me, filling me up with rope after rope of hot cum, sent me over the edge. I pulled his mouth to mine and swallowed his moans while giving him my own.

At some point I melted against him, my body limp as he

slid out of me and got a cloth to avoid any cum related spills on the new sofa.

'We're going to need that plastic wrap on all of our furniture,' I sighed, happily.

'At least a washable cover,' he said with a grin, pulling me into his arms as he spooned me on the sofa. 'Ruined furniture or not, I can't wait to spend forever with you.'

I squirmed happily in his arms.

'I can't wait either.'

'Will you marry me yet?'

I stilled before turning in his arms to face him. 'Do you think you're ready?'

'Fuck, sweetheart, I've been ready since the first time I asked you, before then, even. Are you ready?'

Showering him with kisses, I laughed. 'Yes, I'm ready.'

'So, is that a yes?'

'Yes!'

He planted a kiss at the edge of my mouth before stroking my hair away from my eyes and smiling his dimpled smile at me. A smile I'd not seen shining as brightly for a while.

'Good girl.'

EPILOGUE
ALEC

Dark tresses whispered in the wind as I watched her, Jane balanced on her hip as she put the finishing touches to the table in the taverna. Esther fussed to get everything just right because Maeve was finally coming to visit. The past almost two years had been hard on Esther even as she flourished in Spain, surrounded by people who loved her.

It had only been the second time we'd seen Maeve having to wait until Harold had finally lost his grip on their family.

I loved watching Esther, seeing her sunny smile as she talked to our daughter, or the simple grace she had when moving between the tightly packed tables. Her freckles had deepened with time as her skin had turned a darker hue with the sunny days. My heart still skipped a beat when she set those emerald green eyes on me, calling me to her with a tilt of the head.

'Stop staring at me and help,' she said with a laugh, handing our daughter to me. I almost couldn't believe her first birthday had arrived already. She smiled up at me through her toothy little grin as I held her, melting me every time I looked at her.

The luckiest man in the god-damned world.

'I can't help staring at you,' I said, pulling Esther to me by the waist and kissing her neck. 'I still can't believe you're mine.'

She flashed her wedding band at me and winked. 'All yours, promise.'

Jane, named after Esther's mother, whom I'd never had the pleasure of meeting, pushed a chubby little hand between us and tried to pull my face to hers, forever wanting to steal all of our kisses for herself.

'You wee scamp,' I said, planting kisses on her cheeks to a high-pitched giggle that stopped me in my tracks every time. I didn't think it was possible to be happy, truly happy, but we'd found our blissful corner of the world and relished in it. We'd spoken about moving back once the coast was clear but found that the taverna with Eva, Jock, and Gladys had become home for us both. Not the family we might have imagined when we were both younger, but the one which made our souls content.

Esther still worked at the taverna, taking on more of the cooking and cleaning as it grew more difficult for Eva and Jock, while I worked as a handyman for whoever needed me around the town. The money wasn't as hefty as my job as an enforcer, but I was greeted daily with smiles and thanks rather than hatred and fear. It was worth the change, plus we didn't need too much in the way of material things. Esther hadn't been lying when she'd said she didn't care about all of that.

I left Esther to her fussing over every little detail of the party prep and took Jane to the tables outside where Gladys was soaking up the sun, decked out in the most colourful dress I'd ever seen.

'Oh, give that baby over,' she said, putting down her gin to reach out for Jane. Dutifully, I passed her over. 'My wee Jane, och, you're a star, aren't you?'

I leaned against the wall of the building and tilted my face to the sun, basking in its warmth.

'She's the best,' I said, smiling at the two of them. Gladys had become like a surrogate grandmother to Esther and I, regularly bursting into our home to fuss over the baby and to bundle her into the pram for a walk about the town, or to bring us mountains of biscuits, hell we were overrun by them while Esther was breastfeeding, Gladys insisting they'd help bring the milk in.

Glancing through the window, I saw Eva slip her arm around Esther's shoulder, calming her with her casual affection and kissing the side of her head. A godsend. They'd all been a godsend.

'I'm so glad you went back for her,' Gladys said, playing peekaboo behind her napkin, to Jane's delight.

'Me too. Best decision I ever made.'

Jane's giggles sounded out as multiple faces turned toward us with smiles.

'I don't miss sitting in that house rotting away in the rain one bit.'

'Me either,' I said, thinking back to the families I always envied out of the window, and now I had one of my very own. People who cared if I wasn't there, and who wanted me to be around. People who smiled and welcomed me with open arms. My girls, with their dark hair and green eyes, brought peace to my soul. Parenthood had hit us like a tonne of bricks, as it did most people, but together we'd found our way to happiness. Having three people who adored our baby helped too.

'Maeve!' Came a scream to my left as Esther flew out of the door and practically ripped her sister off of her feet. Tears sprung from her eyes as they gripped onto one another, the past giving way to a happier future. 'I've missed you so much.'

'Where's that husband of yours?' I asked, picking up Jane and walking over to meet them.

'Urgh, delayed by a work thing, so he'll be here tomorrow, but I absolutely wasn't missing my niece's birthday for work nonsense.' Maeve handed her case to Esther and reached out to Jane. I hesitated, not knowing if she'd be weird with the practical stranger, but the video calls had clearly done their thing, and Jane happily went to her aunt, pulling at her hair and giggling.

'We could have picked you up,' I said as we made our way inside.

'I'm perfectly able to get a cab,' Maeve said, nudging me with an elbow.

'It's not that I don't think you're able--' I started before the two women burst into laughter.

'I'm just messing with you. Guys, this place is bloody adorable.' Maeve's eyes widened as we went inside. 'No wonder you abandoned me for Spain.'

Later, when we'd eaten the cake, and Jane had torn all her presents open and played with them, and then crashed out in the cradle upstairs, we sat beneath a star filled sky enjoying a glass of wine. Jock and Eva had begged to keep Jane for the night, and we'd put up little fight. Maeve and Gladys were bedded in their rooms upstairs, and Eva and Jock had turned in for the night.

'I didn't think I could ever be so happy,' Esther said, her legs in my lap on the bench we sat on.

'Let's get you home, and I'll show you just how happy I can make you,' I said into her ear, grazing my teeth over her throat.

'Mmmm, baby-free nights shouldn't be wasted,' she said, tipping her head to give me better access to her neck.

'I love you so much it hurts sometimes.' It did too, a deep ache that left me forever needing more of her.

'I can kiss it better,' she whispered, running her hand up the side of my face. 'Where does it hurt?'

'Here?' she asked, running a thumb over my lips.

'Yes.' She tasted like wine as she kissed me, her lips opening to kiss me harder as I groaned into her mouth.

'Here?' Her fingers grazed my collarbone as she leant down to nip at me before kissing the tender spot as I nodded.

'Or maybe here?' she said, dragging her fingers over my crotch and eliciting a growl. Even after almost two years, I could never get enough of her.

Her laughter rang out as I threw her over my shoulder and stalked away from the taverna, heading for our cottage.

'Be a good girl and stop wriggling,' I said, slapping her ass as she writhed. She wriggled all the more.

'Oh, the brat's come to play tonight, has she? Good, I'm just in the mood to tan your ass before I fuck it.'

Her whimpers had me hard before I could take another few steps.

'Will you let me ride your face first?' she said, in a voice dripping with innocence.

'Always, baby. Always.'

THE MCGOWAN SERIES

Book 1 - Dark Escapes - Alec and Esther
She's on the run, he's bringing her home. She's not going down without a fight

Book 2 - Dark Enemies - Cam and Maeve
Forced to wed, determined to burn his world down.

Book 3 - Dark Obsessions - Mac and Katie
He's going to save her from her awful relationship, even if it means becoming her masked stalker.

Book 4 - Dark Desires - Logan and Valentina
He's engaged to her cousin, but she knows he's the man for her. She won't stop until he knows it too.

Book 5 - Dark Corruptions - Ewen and Anna

A NOTE FROM THE AUTHOR

Thank you so much for reading my debut novel, Dark Escapes. I know it can be a big thing to take a chance on a new author, and I really appreciate the time you've put into reading this book. You're a star!

I've been a long time reader (ahem, devourer) of romance, especially any that step over the line into darker territories. Delving into Alec and Esther was a fun few months as I worked on building their story, as well as that of the McGowans as a whole. I actually wrote the second book first as enemies to lovers is my absolute favourite. I've included a wee snippet for you over the page if you want to have a look at what Maeve gets up to once Esther rides off into the sunset.

A huge thank you goes to my wonderful husband, the man who encourages me to write, and brings me endless coffee when my butt's stuck to the chair and my fingers are furiously tapping away. He's one in a million and I couldn't have written this book without his support.

A thank you also goes to my children, who are angels at

least ninety percent of the time, and pretty understanding when Mummy is beavering away at the computer. I just hope you never actually read this.

This is the first in five books that I have planned for the McGowan siblings, all with different stories to tell. I hope you'll join me for the others. You can read on for a preview of Dark Enemies.

If you liked Dark Escapes, I would love a review on Amazon. You'd make my day.

Much love, Effie

If you'd like to keep up with my books and me, you can find me on TikTok (@effiecampbellauthor), Facebook (effiecampbellauthor), Instagram (effiecampbellauthor) and Amazon.

Subscribe to my mailing list for new releases and news.

PREVIEW OF DARK ENEMIES
MAEVE

The monitors bleeped calmly, just a steady chirping which belied the turmoil that roiled inside my head.

I sat across from my dad, who looked like he was sleeping peacefully. Over the weeks, his face had healed where they'd patched it back together, but his brain remained static, broken. He'd never really looked peaceful before the coma. It was awkward visiting him, but we did it out of obligation. It was expected. I just didn't really know what to do with myself once I was there. We weren't very close as I grew up. He was very much the figurehead who directed our lives, a strict headmaster, more than a dad.

Anger still scraped at the back of my mind every time I looked at him. If he hadn't promised Esther to Harold, none of us would be in the mess we were. He must have believed it to be the best course of action, because why would he make a deal with a man he detested so thoroughly?

I sighed and scooted my chair closer to the bed. The room was plush in the private hospital, and there were always at least two of Dad's men stationed outside. The hospital had security too. It was exactly the sort of place people with money and a need for protection used.

'Dad,' I said, lowering my voice in case Ewen came back from grabbing us some coffee, 'I'm getting married today. This afternoon to Cameron Thompson. Please wake up and stop it. He has Mac and I'm just so scared. Marrying him brings Mac back, but then I'm stuck with them. What should I do?'

The only response was that same rhythmic chirping.

'I know I need to be strong, and I'm putting a brave face on for Logan and Ewen so they don't feel too guilty, but it's so hard.'

I slipped my hand beneath his, needing some sort of human contact for comfort. The warmth of his fingers caught me off guard, not realising how much I needed the tender touch.

'I'm going to tear them down though, Dad. For Mum, for Malcolm, for Esther, for Mac, and even for you. I'm going to drag their very worst skeletons from their closets and use them to burn the family to the ground.'

A twinge of guilt bit at me. Katie had seemed like a nice person. It could all have been a ploy to fuck with me though, and I couldn't afford to be soft. Take no prisoners.

'I wish Esther was here.'

Dad's skin wrinkled as I smoothed my thumb over the back of his hand.

'Me too,' Ewen said, opening the door with his shoulder as he balanced two paper takeaway cups of coffee. I swiftly removed my hand from Dad's and sat up straight. 'Come on, kid, we need to go get you ready for today.'

'I'm never going to be ready for today.'

'I know, but Logan says the make-up artist is losing her shit about timings, so we'd better get a move on.' He passed a cup to me and nodded at our dad. 'We'll tell you about it later, Dad. You'll not be sad to miss it, I'm sure.'

I took one last look at Dad before closing the door. As much as we'd been distant, I'd never imagined him not there to walk me down the aisle. The level of sting which attacked me surprised me as I swallowed down a sob.

Get it together, Maeve. Dad not being there is the least of your worries.

My reflection was utterly misleading.

I gazed at myself in the large mirror in my parent's bedroom where I'd just got fastened into my dress. Credit where it was due. The seamstress had done an impeccable job of fitting it to me like a glove at such short notice. The embroidery that went from my neck to my feet was exquisitely positioned to both be extremely revealing, but keeping the important pieces covered. It had the effect of making me want to peer around the embroidery to see what hid beneath. Taunting and teasing and utterly perfect. The dress was backless down to near the base of my spine and tightly fitted to my knees where it flared out dramatically. I looked like something from the runway, with the precise glossy waves of brown about my shoulders and the intricate makeup. It had taken the make-up artist a surprising amount of time to paint my face, but I had to admit the look was flawless. I might have to put her on Harold's payroll to make me look fantastic every day.

A veil finished the look to bridal perfection. I'd tried to argue against it in the shop, but Katie had been right. The sheer length of material added a little more mystery to the back of the dress while still revealing enough to see how low the back of it dipped. It was never the dress I'd have chosen for my wedding. I preferred light florals and flouncier fabrics, and definitely wouldn't have braved the sheer spots at the front, but the effect had been exactly what I had been seeking. Powerful. Confident. Defiant. Devastating.

I would go in and out fighting if I had to do this. I'd go in as I'd go out. All guns blazing.

I'd spent the previous night packing up some clothing, chargers, books, and toiletries. Nothing sentimental would leave my home, as I fully intended to be back as soon as I could. I glanced at the two cases that sat near the door, the only things joining me on my mission in enemy territory.

A light tap on the door pulled me away from the mirror as the hair stylist popped her head in. 'Are you ready for your brothers to come in?'

'As ready as I'll ever be.'

Logan and Ewan walked into the room, and the door shut softly behind them.

'Fuck Maeve. You look incredible.' Ewen grinned before dabbing at the corner of his eye with the back of his hand.

'Christ, it's revealing.' Logan's eyes widened as he took in my dress. 'It's like drizzling yourself in gravy before offering yourself up to the wolf.'

'I was going for impact.'

'Well, no doubt it has that. Just be careful, Maeve. Don't antagonise them. Just do your best to hold tight until we can get you back.' He softened as he walked toward me and gave me a hug about the shoulders. 'You look cracking though, going to knock 'em dead.'

I swallowed hard in my brother's arms, relishing in them. God, I was going to miss them. I doubted Harold and Cameron would encourage regular visits with them.

'Thanks guys.'

'We have something for you.' Ewen took out a square navy box and handed it to me.

'A gift? I didn't think you guys had it in you to be that organis--' My words cut off as I opened the box. Its velvet interior held a ring and a bracelet that I recognised instantly. Tears sprung to my eyes as I gently touched my mum's engagement ring and the diamond bracelet. There had only been three little discs on it the last time I'd seen in, but now a fourth, shiny metal disc joined the others at the clasp. The tiny initials read MM and joined with the three initials of the women in my family who had worn it on their wedding days, and to many events thereafter. My mother had worn it often, and I still remembered late nights at parties when I was curled in her lap and toying with the bracelet as her arm wrapped around me.

My voice caught as I tried to talk. 'Shouldn't... shouldn't it have gone to Esther?'

'She wanted you to have it. She wished she could have been here for you, wished she could have come back and taken you from it.' Logan took the box from my hands.

A sob fell from my mouth as Logan lifted the bracelet and fixed it around my wrist. My hands shook so badly that it took me a moment to get the engagement ring onto my finger.

They wrapped me in their arms and we stood there together until the make-up artist found us and went into a flap about the state of my face.

Katie found me as I stood outside of the ceremony room in the foyer of a grand castle and squeezed my hand. Logan directed a foul look at her, which she studiously ignored.

'You're a knockout, Maeve,' she said with a smile. 'Keep your head up and you'll be through it in no time.'

She let herself into the ceremony room, allowing me the briefest of glimpses beyond the doors. There wasn't a spare seat to be seen, people packed in like sardines.. Harold must have invited every god damned criminal in Scotland.

Logan put his hand on the arm I'd linked through his as I trembled. He was so tense at my side that I could feel the angst radiating off of him.

'It's not too late to run, Maeve. I wouldn't blame you if you did.'

'Mac is in there. We can't let him down.' I steadied my shoulders and used my other hand to smooth down my hair before a lady passed me my bouquet. 'We can do this.'

'We can do this.' He repeated my words, and I wasn't sure they particularly comforted either of us.

The doors opened, and I saw my intended at the end of the aisle. Cameron Thompson, the ice king himself. His suit was tailored to perfection, skimming his muscled torso just so. I hated him all the more. If he was as ugly as his rotten father, at least there would be some justice in the world.

Muttered voices and gasps followed as we entered the room. I focused on keeping my head high and my posture in check. I wouldn't let them see my despair. My resolve wobbled slightly as I saw Mac seated near the front, his face full of utter fury. He mouthed what I read as don't do it. It's okay, I mouthed back, spying the gun held firmly to his side as one of their men sat close to him.

Taking a deep breath, I approached the front of the room, where the celebrant dismissed Logan, leaving me alone with my soon to be husband.

His eyes met mine only as I took up the space next to

him, with a brief glance at my dress. Without even a flinch of reaction or greeting, he turned back to the humanist.

Two could play at that game.

CAMERON

The doors to the room opened, and the buzz from the congregation amplified. I resisted the urge to turn and look at my forced bride, staring straight forward as soft music from a string quartet rose to a crescendo.

It wasn't until the air beside me moved, and the bottom of her dress skimmed my ankles, that I turned toward her.

Fuck.

I expected her to be coming to the altar a bag of nerves and hate, but she came throwing punches. I only allowed myself the briefest of glances down her dress and back up to her face before I turned my focus forward.

She looked incredible. She had no right to. I expected her to be in some princess number or something so simple as to not attract attention. I hadn't expected her to show up in a dress that made me want to rip it off of her.

There was zero chance of that. The thought of touching a McGowan with anything other than fists was incomprehensible. My dick didn't seem to get the memo, though.

'Get on with it,' I said to the humanist as he stared at Maeve's chest.

'Yes. Yes. of course.' He cleared his throat before launching into his spiel. I'd ensured it was as brief as possible, focusing primarily on the legal obligations. I had insisted on no frills. No hand fasting, no rings, no drinking from a quaich. We were hardly there to celebrate the joining of two people. It was for everyone except us.

'Face one another,' the man said and reluctantly, we complied.

It was surprising how little you needed to say to get married, really. Only one line each to bind ourselves together, as far as the government was concerned. I'd refused the oaths of love, and forsaking others and honour and all that shit. I was largely a man of my word, and I had no intention of living by any of those oaths.

Maeve met my eyes with her chin high and a steely determination about her face.

'Repeat after me, dear.' The man instructed us to follow his words.

Maeve's voice was clear and light as she repeated his phrasing word for word.

'I, Maeve McGowan, solemnly and sincerely declare that I know of no legal impediment to accepting you Cameron Thompson as my lawful wedded husband.' Only at the husband did her voice falter, belying her nerves.

'Now you, Cameron.' The man hurried along after my father glanced at his watch.

My neck was clammy beneath my collar as I watched Maeve. Hoping she'd chicken out and head running for the door. Anything that would get me out of the wedding without it being my fault. But she didn't. She just kept staring at me like she was cut from stone.

I sighed and gave in. There was no getting out of it.

'I, Cameron Thompson, solemnly and sincerely declare that I know of no legal impediment to accepting you Maeve McGowan as my lawful wedded wife.' The word was sour on my tongue. I didn't want a wife. Marriage was just another vulnerability I hadn't intended on exposing myself to.

'The couple have chosen to forego rings, so that leaves me delighted to say that you are now husband and wife. You may kiss your bride.'

Pockets of applause broke out amongst the crowd while Maeve and I about mutually died up on the small stage. There was no way I was kissing her. I didn't kiss.

Maeve glanced at her brothers and then at my father before inching closer and stepping to her toes so her mouth was level with mine. My heart may well have stopped as I debated whether to let her kiss me, to appease them, or to push her away from me.

Maeve deflected at the last moment, looking to all the world like she was placing a chaste kiss on the edge of my lips. Instead, she whispered to me below her breath.

'I am going to destroy everything you hold dear.'

She stepped back to a rapturous cheer from all but our own families.

I struggled to decide whether to be impressed or annoyed.

Either way, it was done.

Husband and wife.

Until my father tore us asunder, naturally.

Find DARK ENEMIES ON AMAZON

Printed in Great Britain
by Amazon